THE WORKHOUSE DOCTOR

THE WORKHOUSE DOCTOR

Sara Fraser

This first world edition published in Great Britain 2001 by
SEVERN HOUSE PUBLISHERS LTD of
9-15 High Street, Sutton, Surrey SM1 1DF.
This first world edition published in the USA 2002 by
SEVERN HOUSE PUBLISHERS INC of
595 Madison Avenue, New York, N.Y. 10022.

British Library Cataloguing in Publication Data

Fraser, Sara, 1937–
   The workhouse doctor
   1. Workhouses – Great Britain – History – 19th century – Fiction
   2. Historical fiction
   I. Title
   823. 9'14 [F]

   ISBN 0-7278-5762-2

Typeset by Hewer Text Ltd.,
Edinburgh, Scotland.
Printed and bound in Great Britain by
MPG Books Ltd., Bodmin, Cornwall.

The story so far . . .

In the month of January 1841, twenty-year-old James Kerr leaves his widower father's small country estate in Leicestershire and comes to the house of his maternal uncle, Septimus Nairn, in the hamlet of Tardebigge, Worcestershire.

Septimus Nairn is a widely admired and respected surgeon, and it has been James Kerr's lifelong dream to become a surgeon himself. This ambition is strongly opposed by his father, which has resulted in their estrangement.

Septimus Nairn, a taciturn, middle-aged bachelor, has few close friends and is inwardly very lonely. He agrees to take James as his apprentice, and a strong bond of affection is quickly forged between them. Under the tutelage of his uncle, and his uncle's assistant, the Irishman, Sean Fitzgerald, James makes rapid progress in the study and practice of the arduous profession he has chosen. In the time of pre-anaesthesia this necessitates the surgeon to possess nerves of steel, and both physical and mental strength.

James's work brings him into contact with the sinister Enoch Cull, a bodysnatcher and proprietor of freak shows, and with Henry and Amelia Melen, the Master and Matron of the Bromsgrove Workhouse, who have their own dark secrets to conceal.

During the first year of his apprenticeship, James also meets Lydia – Liddy – Landser, the eighteen-year-old daughter of George Landser, owner of a salt works in the neighbouring village of Stoke. James is greatly attracted to this spirited, intelligent, pretty girl, and she is also drawn towards him.

But because of her familial situation she is forced to discourage the young man's desire for any close relationship, other than friendship. Her mother, Beatrice, is a mentally unbalanced, at times violent, invalid whom Liddy cares for unaided, as well as keeping house for the family. George Landser is beset by business problems which are driving him to financial ruin and alcoholism, and her only brother, Robert, is a selfish, feckless spendthrift.

Feeling rejected and hurt by Liddy, James meets and becomes infatuated with a much older woman, the wealthy widow, Mercedes Wybergh, an attractive, sensual Andalucian, and they embark upon a passionate sexual relationship. Yet in James's deepest heart there still remains the image of Liddy Landser.

His affair with Mercedes Wybergh brings with it the enmity of a rival for her affections, Edward Harcourt, Esq., who wants Mercedes for her money.

Harcourt – banker, magistrate, local politician – is a wealthy, powerful and evil man, who ruthlessly furthers his own ambitions, while hiding behind a mask of benevolence. He possesses an insatiable appetite for money and for women, and is prepared to use any methods to satisfy these appetites. Harcourt's sexual desires centre upon Liddy Landser, and he becomes obsessed by his ambition to possess her, body and soul.

Harcourt secretly ensures the ruin of George Landser. He then tries to overcome Liddy's instinctive dislike towards himself by offering help to her family. He accommodates George and Beatrice Landser in a small cottage, and finds Robert work as a clerk in London. He also finances Liddy's training as a schoolteacher, and she is deceived into thinking that she has sadly misjudged him, and that in reality he is truly a good, decent man, who is doing his utmost to help her become self-supporting.

During Liddy's period of training in London, her brother Robert steals money from his employers and when this is discovered he loses his position. Liddy breaks the strict rules of the teacher training establishment in her efforts to help her brother, but can do little. Robert's plight becomes so desperate that he is forced to enlist as a common soldier. Unaware of his enlistment, Liddy is torn by anxiety over his disappearance, and to add to her troubles her rule-breaking is reported to the establishment authorities: consequently Liddy is expelled before completing the full period of training and she apprehensively returns to Bromsgrove.

Edward Harcourt takes advantage of her predicament to strengthen his hold over her. He offers no recriminations, but instead, in his capacity as Chairman of the Board of Parish Guardians, he obtains her an appointment as schoolmistress to the pauper children in the Bromsgrove Workhouse. By doing this he succeeds in gaining her full trust, and now is confident that he will also soon succeed in his primary aim: to possess her.

As the story continues, it is the month of January 1843, and Liddy is entering the workhouse to take up her new position.

One

Bromsgrove, Worcestershire
January 1843

T he great gates of the Bromsgrove Workhouse were standing ajar and Liddy Landser crossed to the front door of the building, her boots crunching on the gravelled forecourt.

A pauper woman opened the door at the jangling of the bell and frowned suspiciously. Before Liddy could speak she told her, 'You'm not supposed to come to the front. If you wants shelter you must go round to the side gate. Go back out the gate theer and go round to your right.'

Good Lord! Liddy thought ruefully. Am I that shabby-looking that she takes me for a tramper?

'I'm Miss Lydia Landser,' she told the woman. 'I'm to be schoolmistress here. Now I'd like to speak with the Master, if you please.'

'He's not here.' The pauper appeared totally unimpressed with the information she had just been given.

Although irritated by the woman's surly attitude, Liddy requested quietly, 'Then is there anyone else here who has authority to receive me?'

'I suppose I could go and ask the Missus if she'll spake to you,' the pauper offered grudgingly, and closed the door, leaving Liddy staring at the black-painted panels.

Minutes passed slowly and Liddy put down the battered carpet bag containing her scant belongings, pulling her thread-bare cloak tighter around her against the chilled air. Her new-found confidence dissipated and she was depressed by this reception.

Through the open gates Liddy could see the row of tenements which stood opposite the workhouse. She watched a man enter a doorway from which noisy children spilled excitedly to greet him. A sense of acute loneliness struck her, depressing her spirits even further.

Behind her the door opened. 'You'm to come and see the Missus.'

Liddy followed the woman's clumping clogs along the corridor.

'Go in there.' The pauper pointed to a door.

The warmth of the room enveloped Liddy.

'What is your name, young woman?' Amelia Melen was sitting in an armchair to one side of a roaring fire.

'Lydia Landser.' Liddy was surprised at how handsome and well dressed her questioner was.

The rosy features frowned. 'You will address me as ma'am, young woman. Do you have a letter of introduction?'

'I do, ma'am. Here it is.' Liddy brought out the folded sealed paper from her gown pocket, then hesitated.

Amelia Melen frowned interrogatively at Liddy's hesitation.

'I was instructed to present the letter directly to the Master of the House, ma'am,' Liddy explained.

'My husband is a very busy man, and I am empowered to deal in all matters respecting the staff of this house. Give me the letter.'

Amelia Melen held out a beringed hand and Liddy gave her the letter, which she opened and swiftly read.

'According to this you are not well qualified, Miss Landser. Three months' training only. However, Mr Harcourt recommends you highly, so I suppose you will do well enough to teach our brats here.'

She put the letter aside and stared hard at Liddy.

'I am Mrs Amelia Melen, the Matron. My husband, Mr Henry Melen is the Master. The boys' schoolmaster is Mr John Pursell, but you will have little enough to do with him since we keep our paupers strictly segregated. You will take your orders from Mr Melen and myself. There is one thing above all else which I must impress strongly upon you. Whatever takes place in this house is not to be talked of outside. It is hard enough as it is to keep the paupers disciplined and tractable without having busybodies from outside trying to interfere with our regime here. If it comes to my attention that you have been discussing workhouse affairs with anyone other than myself or Mr Melen, then you will be subject to instant dismissal. Do you understand, Miss Landser?'

Liddy was beginning to think that she had made a grave error in coming here, but knew that she had no other choice but to accept.

'Yes, ma'am.'

'Very well. I shall allocate a servant to you, but a word of advice, Miss Landser. Do not allow any familiarities either from her or any other of the inmates. Remember at all times that the able-bodied paupers are here because they are worthless good-for-nothings.'

She rose from the chair and went to a chest of drawers to extract several sheets of printed paper which she gave to Liddy.

'These are the rules of this establishment. Learn them well, and adhere to them at all times, and ensure that the inmates adhere to them as well. Any infringements of the rules that you observe any of the paupers committing are to be instantly reported to either myself or to Mr Melen.'

She lifted a handbell from the table and rang it loudly, and within seconds the sullen pauper woman came through the door.

'Show Miss Landser to her room, Blackford.'

She turned again to Liddy. 'Blackford will supply you with a candle, Miss Landser. Your servant will be a woman named Duggins. She will come to you at the rising bell tomorrow morning. You will take all meals in your room, Duggins will bring them up from the kitchen for you. She will also show you where the necessaries are. You may commence your teaching

3

duties at eight o'clock tomorrow morning. I will talk further with you at that time. Good day.'

'Good day, ma'am.'

Once more Liddy followed the clumping clogs along echoing corridors and up flights of stairs. She was surprised by the silence in this huge building. She knew that there must be hundreds of people within its grim walls, yet it seemed deserted, no sounds of voices carrying on its dank chilled air.

She shivered involuntarily. It's like a great tomb, she thought.

Her room was cold and cheerless, the small rusty firegrate empty. The dark green walls were stained with damp, the bed narrow with a horsehair mattress and musty-smelling sheets and blankets.

Blackford pulled a stub of candle from her pocket and placed it upon the small dresser.

'Duggins 'ull bring you a fresh candle tomorrow, miss. You'll have to light this 'un in the passage there when the lamp is lit.'

'Can I have a fire?' Liddy requested.

'Not today. Duggins 'ull bring the coals tomorrow,' the woman told her and left.

Liddy sank down upon the mattress, suddenly light-headed and nauseous with hunger and bodily weariness.

'Dear God, what have I come to,' she muttered despondently, and could have wept with loneliness.

'Come on, wake up now. The bell's rung long since. Come on now.' Bony fingers dug deep into Liddy's shoulder. 'Wake up, miss. Wake up now.'

Half-dazed, Liddy roused herself and sat up in bed.

'I'm Duggins, miss.' The lined features of the grey-haired, scrawny-bodied woman were kindly. 'I'm going to be seeing to you.'

The dawn's cheerless light did not make the room appear any more appealing than the day before and the damp coldness caused Liddy to shiver.

'Your breakfast's on the dresser there.'

Duggins indicated a tray on which was a mug filled with black coffee, a small crock bowl half-filled with rice gruel and a chunk of brown bread.

Liddy was now fully awake. 'Where can I wash?'

'I'll bring you a washbowl and water, but I should get your breakfast afore it goes cold.'

A good night's sleep had done wonders for Liddy's morale, and to her own surprise she felt buoyant and cheerful. Her hunger even made the unappetising food and the gritty un-sweetened coffee seem palatable.

Duggins returned with a large chipped washbowl and jug of water.

'I've scrounged a drop of hot water from the kitchen for you, miss. I knows that young ladies like yourself aren't used to roughing it like we am.'

'Thank you very much.' Liddy was grateful and warmed by the friendly attitude of the woman. 'That's very kind of you. By the way, my name is Lydia Landser, I'm to be schoolmistress here. What's your name?'

'Duggins, miss.'

'If we are to be friends, and I hope that we shall become so, then I can't keep calling you Duggins, can I? What's your Christian name?'

The lined face became doubtful. 'It's best you just call me Duggins, miss. The Master and Missus am very strict about names.'

Liddy recalled Amelia Melen's warning about familiarity with the paupers. But her own nature was outgoing and friendly and she experienced a stirring of rebellion against the stricture.

'Surely when there are just you and me together here we don't need to bother about that?'

'Oh, but we does, miss,' Duggins stated flatly. 'The walls has got ears in this place.'

Liddy reluctantly conceded. 'Very well then, I shall call you Duggins, if I must.'

5

'The Missus says that you'm to be allowed a fire tonight, miss. I'll bring some coals up later. And the Missus told me to tell you that you'm to go to the schoolroom as quick as you can. It's downstairs and along the corridor to your right-hand side.'

'Very well, thank you, Duggins.' Liddy smiled.

The classroom was fairly large but contained only three long backless wooden benches. There was no blackboarding, no raised platform, teacher's desk or stool. In a doorless cupboard Liddy found several old writing slates and a few stubs of slate pencils. The only books were three tattered copies of the Bible. There were several windows set high up in the walls and two doors, one opening on to the passageway Liddy had come along and another smaller door set into the opposite wall. It was through this door that a man entered.

'You are the new schoolmistress, I take it. Allow me to introduce myself. John Pursell, schoolmaster of this establishment.'

He was middle-aged, stoop-shouldered, pot-bellied, with the mottled-veined complexion of the heavy drinker. His eyes were bloodshot and he breathed an aroma of gin and cloves. His black frock coat was shabby and threadbare, his linen yellowed with age. His thinning grey hair hung down to his shoulders in greasy locks, putting Liddy in mind of a dilapidated poet.

She bowed slightly. 'Miss Lydia Landser, Mr Pursell. I expected Mrs Melen to be here.'

He winked roguishly and chuckled.

'I beg you, Miss Landser, do not mention that exalted name in my hearing at this ungodly hour of the morning. I have not yet had sufficient time to gird my loins for the fray.'

'The fray, Mr Pursell?' Liddy queried.

'Fray indeed, my dear young lady.' His gapped, tobacco-stained teeth bared in a broad grin. 'For Mrs Melen I am the Amalekite whom she smites both hip and thigh.'

Despite his debauched appearance Pursell radiated a certain

mischievous charm and Liddy found herself quite taken with him.

Clogged feet clattered upon the stone flags of the passage.

'Here come your delightful scholars, Miss Landser. I shall make my escape before our redoubtable Matron appears.'

Pursell disappeared back through the door and a moment later children trooped into the room followed by Amelia Melen.

'Take your ranks,' the matron ordered sharply, and the children formed into lines.

Liddy examined her new charges with interest. There were nearly fifty of them at quick count. The front ranks were mixed boys and girls aged, she judged, from two or three to six or seven years of age. The rear ranks were solely girls, the eldest looking about fifteen years, the youngest seven or eight. All of the children, boys included, were wearing the female pauper rig of brown dress, grey apron and mob cap. Facially the majority were sallow-complexioned, with lustreless hair and wary, watchful eyes. The stale smell of their unwashed bodies hung heavy on the air.

Poor little souls, Liddy thought, her heart full of pity for the smaller children. What sort of life can it be for them imprisoned in this place?

Then she remembered the ragged, half-starved guttersnipes that swarmed in the streets of the borough: these children were at least fed, clothed and sheltered.

'You will teach them until dinner at one o'clock, Miss Landser,' Amelia Melen instructed. 'They are to have lessons in reading, writing, arithmetic and religious instruction, paying particular attention to the Catechism.'

She glowered warningly at the children. 'If any of these misbehave you may strap them, Miss Landser. And after strapping them you will report their names to me, and I shall give them further punishment.'

She nodded at Liddy and began to walk out of the room.

'Ma'am?' Liddy stepped forward to stop the matron leaving.

The handsome features frowned at her.

'Ma'am, if I am to teach I need chalks, blackboarding, slates

7

and slate pencils, and reading books. And for the elder girls, pens, ink and writing paper.'

'Oh, indeed!' Amelia Melen exclaimed, and demanded aggressively, 'And where am I to obtain the money for such luxuries?'

Liddy experienced a tremor of nervousness at her employer's heated reaction but her own stubborn courage steeled itself, and she replied firmly, 'These are necessities, not luxuries, ma'am.'

Amelia Melen's light-coloured eyes were hard and challenging. 'Necessities?'

Liddy deliberately kept her tone low and unaggressive. 'With all respect, ma'am, yes, these are necessities for any school. Even the Ragged Schools make provision for them.'

'This is a workhouse, Miss Landser,' Amelia Melen hissed venomously. 'We shelter, clothe and feed the inmates. The doctor gives them medical assistance when they are ill. The parson gives them the Word of God while they live, and buries them when they die. These are the only recognised necessities.'

'But how can I successfully teach these children if I have not the tools with which to do so?' Liddy protested.

'If you cannot teach these brats, Miss Landser, then I shall recommend to the Board that they employ some other woman who can do so,' Amelia Melen threatened, then paused a moment, before adding warningly, 'You're making a very bad beginning here, Miss Landser. If you continue on this present course I can assure you that you will not remain here for very much longer.'

Her eyes challenged Liddy, whose own fiery temper rose to accept that challenge, but before she could voice any retort a pauper rushed into the room, shouting, 'Missus! Missus! Come quick, Dorcas Wright's just collapsed. Come quick, come quick, Missus!'

Amelia Melen turned and went with the woman, and despite her anger Liddy could not help but feel a sense of relief that this intervention had occurred to end the confrontation.

I can't afford to lose this position, she accepted reluctantly, so I'll just have to swallow my words until my fortunes improve for the better.

She faced the rows of curious faces and then noticed a small red-haired girl standing at the end of the front rank. The child's pretty face looked strangely familiar, and for a moment Liddy wondered when or where she had seen her before. She also wondered why the long sleeves of the child's dress were tied in a loose bow on her chest. Then with a shock she realised that the girl was armless.

'What's your name, child?'

'Katie Kennedy, miss.'

'She's got no arms, miss,' an older girl informed unnecessarily. 'She was born like it.'

'But she can do all sorts o'things with her toes, miss,' another girl said, and then other voices chimed in with proprietorial pride.

'Yes, miss, she can even scribe her name.'

'And she can dress herself, miss.'

'And feed herself.'

'And thread a needle.'

Liddy smilingly held up her hands. 'Don't all speak together. Be quiet now.'

The voices stilled.

Liddy was greatly intrigued by the recital of the armless girl's attainments.

She fetched a slate and a stub of slate pencil from the cupboard and beckoned Katie Kennedy to her.

'Will you show me how you write your name, Katie?'

'Yes, miss.'

The child slipped her feet from the clogs and sat down on the floor. She then lifted the slate pencil between her toes and scrawled 'Katie' in wavering letters across the slate.

'That's very good. Very good indeed,' Liddy said admiringly and the child smiled in gratification.

'Go back to your place now, Katie.' Liddy had decided on a course of action. 'I want you smaller children to sit on the floor and you older ones to sit on the benches.'

9

When they had settled themselves she went on, 'My name is Miss Landser, and I'm to be your teacher. This morning I want to come to know you better, so there will be no lessons. Instead I shall ask you in turn to tell me your names, your ages, and also whether you can read, write or do sums.'

She took the three Bibles from the cupboad and the rest of the slates and slate pencils. Then she pointed at the snub-nosed older girl sitting on the end of the rear bench.

'What's your name?'

'Maria Peat, miss. I can read and write a bit, miss, so long as they'm only little words. And I can do my tables up to the fives and I can count on me fingers.'

'Let me hear you do the fives times table.'

'One five is five, two fives is ten, three fives is fifteen . . .'

Nearly three hours passed before Liddy had heard from all the children.

Those that claimed to be able to read or write she brought out and had them demonstrate their skills by reading from the Bible or writing on the slates. She tested the claims of numeracy by setting simple sums, or getting them to recite the tables.

She found that the majority of the children were completely illiterate. A few of the older girls had had some basic schooling and displayed varying degrees of ability. One girl only, the wan-featured, troubled-eyed, frail-bodied Hannah Kearns, possessed any real proficiency in reading, writing and arithmetic.

'Where did you learn your lessons, Hannah?'

'Please, miss, I went to the Dame's school in Tardebigge, and after that my dad used to teach me.'

'Where is your father now?'

The girl's thin face twisted in grief and tears filled her eyes. 'Dead, miss, and my mam and sisters. They was all took by the fever a year since.'

'I'm so sorry.' Liddy was genuinely sympathetic. 'Go back to your seat, my dear.'

She pondered briefly, then told the children, 'I've been teaching in a big school in London. We used the Lancastrian system there. That is when some of the children who already know how to read, write and do sums help the teacher to teach the other children. They are called monitors. We shall be using that system here from now on.

'Hannah Kearns and Maria Peat, I have selected you to be my monitors. I want you to come here after dinner and I shall begin your instruction as monitors then.'

'We can't come, miss,' the snub-nosed Maria Peat stated.

'Why not?'

'We has to work, miss. All of us.'

'Doing what?'

'The little 'uns mostly picks oakum. Us big 'uns does all manner o' things. It depends on what the Missus has found for us to do. Like now, in the wintertime, we goes stone-picking in the fields a lot. And sometimes we does jobs at the Guardians' houses. And sometimes we does rag-sorting and dust-riddling. We does all manner o' things, miss.'

'I see.' Liddy nodded thoughtfully.

Maria Peat grinned cheekily. 'Well, we am in the Work'us, aren't we, miss? So we has to work, don't we?'

The great bell began to chime the dinner signal, and Liddy told them, 'Go and get your dinner. I'll see you tomorrow morning. Don't make any noise now, and walk, don't run.'

Left alone in the classroom, she seated herself on a bench to take stock of the situation.

All her life Liddy had harboured resentment of the subservient position of women in society and that women were generally regarded as chattels expected to obey the dictates of men. During her time at the School for Women she had come to believe fervently that only through education could women achieve any degree of independence, any hope of liberation from their dependence upon men. Above all other classes she believed that the women of the poor had the greatest need to be educated, made literate, because she had witnessed at first hand how all too many women of the poor were treated like beasts of burden by their menfolk, fit only to be used and abused in any manner that those menfolk chose.

11

Surely, she thought, I can bring Amelia Melen to see that if she allows me what I need I can educate these pitiful little souls here sufficiently for them to be able to find decent work – to set them free from the workhouse when they are old enough to make their own way in the world.

Two

Manchester
February 1843

T he wagons and caravans of the travelling show were parked on a patch of muddy wasteland overshadowed by the soot-covered towering walls of cotton mills.

A great marquee had been erected, fronted by a black-painted castellated wooden facade and platform. Bright flaring naphtha lamps illuminated the platform on which the black-cloaked, black-masked barker was pacing up and down, haranguing the crowd of grimy mill workers who had just left their factories in the murky drizzle of the evening.

'My lords, ladies and gentlemen, do you want to feast your eyes on the most unique collection of living monsters in the entire world? Monsters that will turn your blood cold! Monsters that will make you shiver! Monsters that will fill you with horror! And all of them alive!' Jonas Hardkin lowered his voice to a hoarse growl. 'Is there any one of you brave enough to come inside my Phantasmagoria of Horror?'

'Iffen I can stand looking at thee, then I reckon I'm brave enough to look at your bloody monsters,' a youth shouted, and his sally was greeted with jeering laughter from his workmates.

'Brave enough you may be, my bucko,' Hardkin retorted, 'but looking at you I don't believe you've got the fourpence needed to enter my Phantasmagoria.'

'That's bloody dear for a freak show,' another man accused. 'Bellamy only charges a penny entrance.'

'Quite right, sir. Bellamy does only charge a penny entrance,'

13

Hardkin readily agreed. 'And he only charges a penny because half of his exhibits are dead, and the other half false. But this show is not the usual type of freak show, ladies and gentlemen. This aren't one of them freak shows where everything is false, and half the exhibits are dead. Every exhibit is the real thing, the real genuine article. True monsters, one and all, and every one of them living and breathing. And unlike Bellamy and false rogues like him, we don't keep you distant from our monsters. You can touch them. You can feel them with your own hands and be certain that they're the genuine article.

'I'll not hold anything back from you. I'll tell you true, that this show will give you nightmares. So if there's any among you who're subject to the vapours, or hysterics, or of a nervous disposition, then don't enter this Chamber of Horrors. Because I'll not be responsible for the awful consequences which might follow.'

Enoch Cull was standing to one side of the platform, watching his barker work the crowd. A burly, black-cloaked and masked man came from the marquee and told him, 'Everything's ready, Mr Cull. Croco is being saucy again, though.'

Cull's pallid grey features scowled. 'Is he? Then I'll give him his lesson before we let the crowd in.'

Inside the great tent were several large wooden cubicles, their interiors individually lit by overhanging oil lamps. Cull paused briefly at each cubicle, his cold eyes examining the hideously deformed or disfigured creature it contained: a small hydrocephalic child, a half-naked woman with hugely hypertrophied breasts, another almost naked woman covered with thick coarse hair, a skeletal young girl, a man with elephantisis of the face, another man whose spine was bent double so that his head hung lower than his knees, two cretinous dwarfs, an immensely fat man, so obese that he could not stand unaided, and several unfortunates with terribly disfigured features, some with faces half eaten away by bloody, pus-oozing ulcers.

In the end cubicle was a young negro man dressed only in a scanty loincloth. His sullen face was handsome, but the body

14

beneath was so thickly covered with evil-smelling black-green scales that it resembled a crocodile's hide.

Cull frowned at the negro. 'I'm told that you're being saucy, Croco. You know what that'll earn you, don't you?'

'I'm not being saucy, Master.' The young man's English was fluent, his accent thick. 'But I'm not feeling good at all. I feel very bad. I feel too bad to work tonight.'

'All you have to do is to stand up and turn round to let the people look at you. That's not hard work, is it?' Cull pointed out in a reasonable tone.

'But they don't just look at me, do they,' Croco argued. 'Some of them poke me and pinch me and slap me. And when they're drunk they try to do other things to me. Bad things.' He shook his tight-curled head. 'I can't work tonight. I'm feeling like I'm dying.'

Cull walked some yards away, and returned with a piece of rope and a short wooden rod in his hands.

The negro's eyes widened in fear. He had suffered the rope tournequet being mercilessly tightened around his skull many times before.

'I'm not being saucy, Master. I'm feeling like I'm dying.'

'You'll be feeling a lot worse than that when I've done with you, you black bastard.' Cull still spoke in that reasonable tone. 'You'll be wishing that you're dead.'

He knotted the ends of the rope together, then asked quietly, 'Well, Croco? What's it to be?'

The negro gnawed his thick lower lip, then nodded. 'I'll work, Master.'

Cull walked away.

There were now three burly men, masked and cloaked, waiting inside the marquee entrance.

'If that black bastard gives you any more trouble, then kick his lights out,' Cull instructed. 'Now let's open up.'

Outside on the platform Jonas Hardkin announced, 'The time has come, ladies and gentlemen. Pay your money now, and enter and feast your eyes on the horrors within.'

There was an eager surge towards the pay-booth entrance.

The marquee became a hubbub of noise and the tragic exhibits once more endured the purgatory of bestial insults and torments inflicted upon them by a crowd who regarded them only as inhuman monsters.

Hardkin and Cull left the other three men to overlook the show and took the takings to a caravan.

When the amount had been totalled Cull frowned. 'We're not earning as much as last month, Jonas.'

'Times are hard all over, Mr Cull.' Hardkin's plump red face was thoughtful. 'Do you reckon we need a fresh attraction? Something a bit more unusual to draw them in?'

Cull nodded. 'You could be right, Jonas. And I think that I've got just the thing. How does a pretty monster sound to you? A monster who can do tricks. Is that unusual enough for you?'

The plump red face showed puzzlement. 'A pretty monster? How can you have a pretty monster?'

'I know where there's one for sale, Jonas,' Cull told him. 'A pretty little monster named Katie. I shall send word that I'm ready to make a bargain for it.'

Three

I n the workhouse laundry room the air was so thickly clouded with steam that the clothing of the toiling women was saturated with moisture. Meggie Kennedy stood leaning over a great copper of boiling water pummelling the mass of bedding with a heavy wooden dolly. Sweat streamed down her face, her arms and shoulders ached, her eyes were inflamed and sore with the stinging of acidic carbolic fumes, and her bodily discomfort was matched by her mental turmoil.

Since her visit to George Landser she had received only one brief message and a few shillings from him, brought to her secretly by a wagoner who had delivered some blocks of salt to the workhouse. And that message had been only that she must be patient. But with each passing day she was becoming increasingly desperate to escape the workhouse.

Patient! She spat now in disgust. I've been fuckin' patient, haven't I? And I'm still trapped in this fuckin' rotten hole. Patient! I'll give that lying bastard, patient! He's gammoned me. He's got no intention of helping me, has he? The rotten lying bastard!

The ringing of the great bell signalled the paupers' dinner-time. With a sigh of relief Meggie laid aside the dolly and joined her fellow toilers to file from the laundry to the hall where they took their meals.

She picked up a small tin bowl and a spoon from the pile set just inside the door and stood in the long queue in front of the table where the food was served out.

17

'I 'ope it's not roast pheasant again today. I'm bloody well sick of it,' a woman in front of her quipped sardonically, and jeers of laughter sounded.

'Be silent.' Amelia Melen scowled from her post at the rear of the table, and the laughter muted to isolated resentful mutterings.

The pauper servers handed each woman and girl a five-ounce chunk of coarse brown bread, an ounce of hard cheese, and slapped a small ladleful of boiled cabbage from an iron cauldron into the tin bowls. As each received their portions they went to sit on the benches flanking the long rows of planked tabling which stretched the length of the hall.

Breakfast, served six hours previously, had consisted of four ounces of bread and a pint and a half of watery rice gruel, and during that six hours interval Meggie had toiled in the laundry for five hours. Her ravenous hunger exacerbated her foul mood and when the small portion of cabbage was slapped into her tin bowl she didn't move on, but stood scowling at the soggy vegetable.

'What's the matter?' the female pauper overseer superintending the serving demanded.

'This is the fuckin' matter. This fuckin' muck!' Meggie snarled, and pitched the bowl across the table. It struck the cauldron and bounced on to the floor spilling the cabbage.

'Missus!' the server shouted in alarm. 'Her's gone mad, Missus!'

Amelia Melen instantly recognised the opportunity she had been seeking ever since she had received Enoch Cull's letter the previous month.

'Pick up your bowl, Kennedy, and scrape that cabbage back into it,' she ordered calmly.

Meggie was already regretting her outburst, knowing that it could lead to grave consequences for herself and her child.

'Do as I say, Kennedy, and you might be forgiven.' Amelia Melen spoke coaxingly.

Meggie went down on her hands and knees and crawled under the table to retrieve the bowl. Amelia Melen moved to stand above her, and shouted as she did so, 'Come along, you others, and take your rations.'

The line moved forwards once more as the serving recommenced.

Amelia Melen glanced down at Meggie who was now scraping the spilled cabbage into a small heap with her hands. On her knees she was hidden from the view of the other paupers and Amelia Melen seized her chance and suddenly stamped down hard upon Meggie's fingers.

'Agghhh! You fuckin' bitch!' Meggie howled with pain, and in blind fury she jumped up and swung her fists at the Matron's face.

Anticipating the attack, Amelia Melen easily evaded the wild swings and shouted to the overseers, 'Get hold of her!'

Shrieking and struggling, Meggie was smashed down by weight of numbers and pinned to the floor. She twisted her head trying to sink her teeth into the hands holding her but Amelia Melen took a big wooden serving spoon and forced its bowl into Meggie's mouth. She then used her handkerchief to tie it in place so that Meggie was gagged and helpless to bite, or even to talk.

'What shall we do with her, Missus?' an overseer wanted to know.

'Bring her along to the refractory ward.'

Lifted by her arms and legs, still kicking and screaming, Meggie was carried bodily from the hall and down to the labyrinth of cellars beneath the house.

The refractory ward was a small dank gloomy cellar with only a tiny grating to admit light and air. Wrist and ankle shackles were set into its walls and it was only the work of seconds for Meggie to be chained and locked so that she could barely move.

'Shall I take the spoon out of her gob, Missus?' an overseer asked.

'No. Leave it in. Bitches who bite have to be muzzled until they learn their lesson.'

Amelia Melen grabbed Meggie's hair and forced her head

19

back so that she could look directly into her eyes. 'You'll be brought before the Board for this, Kennedy. And if I have my way, you'll be brought before the magistrates as well.'

Hatred glared from Meggie's eyes, and guttural growls of rage sounded from deep in her throat.

Back in the hall there was a noisy hubbub of talk going on. For many of the paupers such exciting events as this one were pleasurable enliveners of their dull, tedious, constricted lives.

There was little sympathy being expressed for Meggie Kennedy among the elder women, however. The majority of them knew from past experience that any act of rebellion against authority by an individual pauper only served to make that authority even more repressive towards the inhabitants of the workhouse as a whole.

'She oughter . . . get a . . . bloody good . . . whipping,' a toothless old crone declared fiercely, between noisy sucks of her chunk of bread.

'She didn't ought to get any bloody whipping.' Maria Peat hotly defended the culprit. 'She was only saying what all the rest of us am thinking. Only we aren't got the guts to speak out.'

'What does you know about anything, Maria Peat? You'm only a bit of a kid,' another woman accused scathingly.

'I knows that we'em bloody well half-starved in this fuckin' hole,' the girl countered.

'Some of us am half-starved, you means,' the woman sneered. 'Them of us as don't get extra grub, like what you does.'

Maria Peat flushed scarlet, but refused to be cowed. 'What does you mean by that?'

Now other women came into the attack.

'She means that we don't earn extra grub by opening our legs for Daniel White.'

'There's some of us who won't play the whore.'

Before Maria could make any reply, Amelia Melen reappeared in the hall followed by the overseers.

The matron walked between the rows of tables and demanded, 'Is there anyone else who wants to complain about the food?'

Her eyes went from face to face, challenging for reply.

But none came.

Amelia Melen nodded curtly. 'Very well. Now get it eaten and get back to your work.'

As she walked towards the serving table she caught one pair of eyes fixed upon her. She slowed and warned, 'If you don't stop glaring at me like that, Maria Peat, I'll be giving you another taste of my cane.'

Maria Peat instantly dropped her head, and mumbled, 'I'm sorry, Missus. I wasn't meaning nothing by looking at you.'

'Weren't you now, Maria Peat.' The matron scowled. 'Well, I mean what I say, so take care. Take great care because I'll be watching you closely.'

She stalked on, and the young girl silently promised herself, I'll have you one day, Melen. I'll settle the score with you, just see if I don't.

James Kerr stood in the doorway of the workhouse infirmary looking down the long narrow room which was partitioned by a wooden screen. On one side, a row of beds held women and female children, on the other side men and male children.

'THE HEAVENS DECLARE THE GLORY OF GOD; AND THE FIRMAMENT SHEWETH HIS HANDI-WORK.'

James Kerr read the biblical quotation printed in huge black letters along the limewashed walls of each section and grimaced wryly as he looked at pauper faces ravaged by suffering.

'If this is indeed his handiwork, then God is a cruel crafts-man.'

He sniffed the air, and acknowledged that it was as free of stench as could be expected where so many sick were crowded together in a confined space with windows tightly shut. He noted also that the sheets and coverlets and the white mob caps and nightshifts worn by all the patients appeared to be clean.

Footsteps sounded in the corridor behind him and he turned to see Amelia Melen, and the stocky Nurse Kings approaching.

'Forgive me for not being able to come sooner to meet you,

Mr Kerr, only the paupers were at their dinner. How are you today?' Amelia Melen smiled rosily.

'I'm very well, thank you, ma'am. And yourself?' He returned her smile, appreciating the sight of a handsome woman in her full bloom.

'I'm very well also, I thank you. I sent for you to come, because there's a woman who looks to be seriously ill. That's her there.'

James went to the side of the cot.

The woman's face was livid and her breathing laboured. James took her chin in his hand and pulled it down to peer into her mouth. Her tongue was dry and yellow-coated, her breath hot and offensive.

'Have you moved your bowels today?' he questioned.

She made no reply, appearing half fainting, moaning brokenly, 'Me head hurts. Me head hurts.'

'She used the po,' Nurse Kings, standing on the opposite side of the bed, told him.

James bent and pulled the utensil out from beneath the bed, noting the paleness of the urine. He dipped his forefinger into the urine and tasted it, testing for sweetness, but found none. Mentally he was listing symptoms, shuffling through the files of his memory. Finally he found what he wanted.

He stared for several seconds into the sick woman's inflamed eyes, then pulled the bedclothes back and lifted her nightshift so that he could see her body.

A dull mottled rash of spots covered the rivelled skin of stomach and breasts, and he pressed the tip of his forefinger upon several of the spots in turn. Satisfaction filled him as the spots failed to disappear under the pressure.

He let the shift fall and covered the woman with the bedclothes.

'What ails her?' Amelia Melen asked.

'She has the typhus, Mrs Melen.'

The matron's rosy face frowned with concern. 'She most likely caught it in the jail then. We took her in last week after she was released from the Worcester Bridewell.'

She looked at the other beds occupied by women and girls, and questioned worriedly, 'Just how how contagious is the typhus?'

James shrugged. 'Opinions vary. Some medical men consider it to be so, others do not. For myself I am inclined to think that it is most probably contagious. I believe it would be better if we isolate this woman.'

'There's no other room available.'

'Is there a shed or outhouse that can be utilised?'

'There's the death shed, where we put the corpses.'

'I trust it's not occupied at the moment.' James grinned.

Amelia Melen smiled grimly, and nodded towards an old woman lying comatose in one of the beds. 'Not at present, but Bridie Harper might well be going there in a day or so.'

James looked down at the typhus case and muttered, 'I fear there's not much hope for this one, Mrs Melen. I believe that she has the malignant typhus. That being the case I don't expect her to outlive Bridie Harper.'

'Is there no treatment you can give her?' the matron asked.

Once more James racked his book-memory. 'Antimony is recommended where there is much excitement and furious delirium, but the relative quantities of opium and tartar emetic must be suited to the particular case. Chloral and digitalis can also be efficacious. But in this case I propose to commence a course of bleeding and cold sponging in the first instance. I'll prescribe any necessary medication when I see how the disease is progressing. Anyway, let us have the woman removed into isolation now, if you please, Mrs Melen.'

A few minutes later, Nurse Kings and Daniel White were both breathing hard as they carried the stretcher bearing the sick woman into the death shed. A makeshift bed of trestles and planks had been set up and with the help of Amelia Melen they settled the woman on it.

James felt uneasy as he examined the chill, grimy interior with its bare brick walls and earth floor.

'This isn't a very suitable place, Mrs Melen.'

'I can have a brazier brought in to warm it up, Mr Kerr.'

'Thank you, ma'am, but no. I don't want it to be overheated; she must be kept cool.'

He opened his medical chest and extracted the items he needed to draw blood from the sick woman. He bled twelve ounces from her arm and while binding up the cut vein told Nurse Kings, 'Fetch some towels, and water as cold as can be drawn. I want you to wet the towels, wring them out and cover her with them from head to toe, leaving them in place until they begin to become warmer. Repeat this eight times, and then every four hours carry out the same procedure.'

'All through the night?' the woman demanded incredulously. 'What about me sleep?'

James raised his eyebrows in silent query at Amelia Melen, who was quick to tell him, 'I shall make sure that it is done, Mr Kerr.'

'Thank you. Now I want to go back to the ward and check the women who were on each side of this one.'

Back in the infirmary Amelia Melen stood watching anxiously as James examined these other women, but to his relief he found no signs of typhus.

As they walked back along the rows of beds, he commented, 'In a way it's fortunate that these patients are mostly merely infirm with age. It saves me a deal of work.'

'That's so, Mr Kerr. There's precious little any doctor can do for them. We just try to ease their passing as much as we can.'

James briefly studied two old men lying side by side in the nearest bed. One had his eyes closed, but the other was holding a mumbled conversation with an imaginary friend.

'Is it normal practice to keep the lunatics here, ma'am?'

'Indeed it is, Mr Kerr. Just so long as they're harmless. But those who are a danger we have to send to the lunatic asylum at Powick.' Even as she spoke an idea came into Amelia Melen's mind, and she questioned, 'Do you have any experience of dealing with lunatics, Mr Kerr?'

He shook his head. 'No. I've seen lunatics, of course, but have yet to treat one.'

24

'Perhaps you could come and have a look at one now. It's a young woman who we've been forced to put into our refractory ward. She attacked me this dinnertime.'

James acquiesced readily and Amelia Melen took him down into the cellars, and unlocked a door.

As they entered the ward James stared with interest at Meggie Kennedy.

Chained upright against the wall, her hair a tangled mass, eyes wide and wild, in the gloom she did indeed look to be insane, an impression she confirmed in his mind by heaving against her fetters and shrieking loudly. What he couldn't know was that she was screaming for his help.

'I had to tie that spoon in her mouth to stop her biting the other paupers,' the matron explained. 'And she'll have to stay locked up until this present fit passes. Otherwise there's no telling what harm she may do to herself and others.'

The matron's handsome face showed pity. 'I'm afraid that she'll have to be removed to Powick. I can't risk the safety of the other paupers.'

This statement provoked even more violent struggling and shrieking from Meggie Kennedy.

'Do you see, Mr Kerr, what a danger she is?' Amelia Melen sighed regretfully. 'Perhaps it might be best if you report this case to Dr Nairn and ask him from me to attend upon us as quickly as possible. He'll need to examine her and sign the committal papers.'

Meggie Kennedy was frantic with worry and consumed with rage against the matron. Her shrieks became despairing wails and as the young man turned to leave, and in her desperation she rammed her head backwards against the wall. The impact thudded audibly and James looked back with concern.

Half-stunned, Meggie Kennedy sagged down, her head fell forwards and as James stepped up to her he saw blood glistening in the tangle of matted hair on the back of her head.

Amelia Melen was filled with a savage satisfaction. It was all working out even better than she had hoped.

James gently parted the bloodied hair, trying to ascertain the extent of the wound, but the light was too bad to see clearly, and he told the matron, 'She'll have to be moved, ma'am, so that I may examine her properly.'

'Of course, Mr Kerr,' Amelia Melen assented. 'But we'll need more hands to hold her. You and I alone will not have sufficient strength.'

'Then will you please fetch help, ma'am? I'll stay here with her.'

Amelia Melen had no intention of leaving James Kerr alone with Meggie Kennedy.

'You'll need your bag, won't you?' she questioned, and he nodded.

'You go and collect your bag and then go to the room at the left of the infirmary, Mr Kerr. I'll have her carried there.'

'Very well, ma'am.'

He hurried to fetch his bag from the entrance hall of the house, and then went to the room next to the infirmary.

Nurse Kings and Daniel White, together with two pauper women, carried Meggie Kennedy into the room, which contained a large table.

'Lay her face-downwards,' James instructed.

They obeyed and then released their grip on her arms and legs and Meggie Kennedy instantly tried to loosen the handkerchief which held the spoon in her mouth.

'Hold her,' Amelia Melen barked, and a violent struggle erupted as Meggie fought desperately to get free, knowing that her only chance of avoiding committal to the asylum was to convince this young man she was sane.

Henry Melen came into the room and his practised eyes instantly evaluated the situation.

'With your permission, Mr Kerr, I'll make her quiet.'

His hands clamped on Meggie Kennedy's throat and his broad thumbs pressed hard upon the carotid arteries, cutting off the blood supply to her brain.

Within seconds she was unconscious.

James felt embarrassed that he had not thought to do this.

'Where did you learn that trick, Mr Melen?'

'In the army, Mr Kerr.' Melen grinned smugly. 'It came in useful whenever a man was mad drunk and we needed to get him into the cells.'

He twice repeated the action when Meggie showed signs of returning to consciousness while James cut away the matted blood-soaked hair and sutured the torn flesh. Then he fashioned a thick turban from lengths of towelling and sewed it securely in place around Meggie Kennedy's head.

'That should give her some protection if she tries to break her skull again.'

Meggie recovered consciousness again as she was being carried down to the cellars, and once more struggled fiercely but was unable to break free.

James accepted the Melens' invitation to have a drink in their private quarters, and after he had taken several glasses of hot whisky toddy and was feeling extremely mellow and relaxed, Amelia Melen suggested casually, 'I wonder if it's absolutely necessary to give Dr Nairn the trouble of coming here to examine the Kennedy woman. After all, you've seen what her mental condition is, haven't you, Mr Kerr? I'm sure that Dr Nairn will have complete confidence in your diagnosis. If you wish I can send the porter with you to bring back the committal notice. If it were up to me I would be more than happy to have you draw up the committal, Mr Kerr. You've impressed me greatly today with your skills. I don't know what we could have done if you had not been here. You were quite wonderful in the way you handled such a dangerous lunatic.'

'You speak truly, my dear,' Henry Melen said, adding his plaudits. 'I think that we have been most fortunate to have obtained the services of our young friend here. I can't think of any other medical man in this parish who would have behaved so coolly when treating a dangerous lunatic. With the exception of Dr Nairn, perhaps.'

The flattery from this good-looking couple pleased the by now half-drunk James inordinately, and he basked in the warmth of their admiration.

For the next hour they continued to bolster his self-esteem, and he began to feel that he was truly destined for greatness in his chosen profession.

When it was time for his departure he was sorry to leave the company of these new-found admirers.

'Shall I send the porter with you then, Mr Kerr, to bring back the notice of committal?' Amelia Melen asked.

James suddenly remembered that Septimus Nairn had gone to Birmingham that morning on business and was not returning for several days.

When he informed the matron of this, she frowned worriedly.

'It causes me much unease to think that we shall have to keep the Kennedy woman chained up below for so much longer. It would be far more merciful to have her sent to Powick where she can be properly cared for by those who are more experienced in treating the mad than we are.'

Henry Melen smiled. 'I'm sure that the Board will be more than happy to accept Mr Kerr's recommendation on this matter, my dear. Particularly when Mr Harcourt hears from us about the professional expertise he has demonstrated today.'

James experienced the most tremendous gratification and pride as he wrote out the notice of committal and signed it with a flourish.

He rode home to Tardebigge in a haze of drunken well-being, feeling every inch the professional medical man.

Four

I t was the last Saturday of March, and Liddy had no classes. But her free time could not be spent as she wished. Under the terms of her employment she was only free to leave the workhouse on Sunday afternoons. At all other times she must be available to the Master and Matron and obtain their permission to leave the premises. This afternoon she sat in her bleak room, staring out at the falling rain, feeling depressed and lonely. During the weeks she had spent in the workhouse Liddy had learned the bitter lesson that to the Melens she was an unwelcome appendage who had been forced upon them, and they considered her to be of no more importance or value than the pauper inmates.

Faced with this attitude, and sadly conscious of her own powerlessness to change matters, Liddy had ceased from trying to establish any sort of friendly relationship with the couple, and behaved with a cold courtesy whenever there occurred the unavoidable necessity to speak to either of them. Her requests for schoolbooks, slates, pens and so on had been met with scathing rejection, but this only served to make her more stubbornly determined that she would do her utmost to teach the pauper children all that she could. She had spent what little money she had left on slates, pencils and chalks, and improvised a blackboard from some old planking which she scavenged.

However, no matter how determined she might be to teach, Liddy was slowly being forced to recognise the unpalatable fact that undernourished, harshly disciplined children who were both physically and emotionally deprived were, with rare exception, simply not capable of easily absorbing educational knowledge. At times she felt close to despair when after hours of instruction in the simplest basics of reading, numeracy or spelling, the majority of the children could still not answer a single question correctly. But there were three girls who did readily assimilate her teachings. Tough, sturdy Maria Peat, wan-featured, troubled-eyed Hannah Kearns, and the tragically handicapped Katie Kennedy, all displayed a high intelligence.

Liddy pitied Katie Kennedy from the bottom of her heart, and that pity was coupled with a fondness for the child. She had found out that Katie's mother had been committed to the Powick Lunatic Asylum, but knew only that bare fact. Any attempt to discover the details of the committal from the inmates was met with averted faces and silence, or protestations of ignorance.

Liddy did not press hard for a fuller answer; she was unhappily well aware that fear ruled the workhouse: fear of the Melens, the absolute monarchs of this enclosed and secretive realm.

She had heard nothing from her brother, which was of great concern to her, but had visited her parents' cottage and done what she could for them in the limited time available to her.

Duggins came into the room to tell her, 'The Missus wants you, miss. She's in her parlour. I should go down there quick, because she aren't in the best of moods.'

Liddy sighed wearily. She expected that Amelia Melen had some complaint to make to her. This was invariably the case when she was summoned to the woman's presence.

'Mr Harcourt has sent this for you.' Amelia Melen handed the folded sheet of notepaper to Liddy.

Liddy saw that the seal had been broken and questioned, 'How did this seal come to be broken, Mrs Melen? I would hope that you haven't read this?'

The woman smiled provocatively, making no reply, and

Liddy felt her temper rising. But she knew that any confrontation would end only to her own disadvantage.

She quickly scanned the short message. Edward Harcourt was advising her to go to see her parents as soon as possible. Concern struck her. Something must be very wrong for him to advise her so.

'Can I have leave of absence this afternoon, Mrs Melen? Mr Harcourt advises me to visit my parents without delay. I fear that they may be in some difficulty.'

The matron frowned. 'Your parents' difficulties are none of my concern, Miss Landser. And since tomorrow you will have the afternoon free, I do not see any necessity for you to absent yourself from your place of duty today.'

Liddy kept her temper in check. 'I'm sure that Mr Harcourt would not have written to me unless it was a matter of urgency that I should go to see my parents, ma'am.'

'And I am equally sure that the urgency you speak of is not particularly urgent,' the matron retorted sourly.

'But I'm doing nothing of any use here. I'm only sitting in my room.' Liddy was struggling to keep her voice calm. 'And I shouldn't be gone more than two or three hours.'

'Make sure that you're not.' The matron frowned.

Liddy was taken aback by this abrupt volte-face, and made no answer.

Amelia Melen jerked her head in dismissal. 'Go now, before I begin to regret my generosity.'

With mingled emotions Liddy returned to her own room to fetch her shawl and bonnet.

I suppose I should be feeling grateful that she's allowed me to go, she thought. But damn it! I don't! Why does the miserable cow always have to act so awkward!

Half an hour later Liddy felt increasingly apprehensive as she walked up the lane towards her parents' cottage. There was no smoke rising from the chimney even though the day was bitterly cold.

She knocked on the warped panels of the door, her trepidation increasing every moment that her knock stayed unanswered. She rapped again, this time harder, louder, longer.

'Who's there?'

Liddy gusted a sigh of relief as she heard her father's voice and called, 'It's me, Pa. Open the door.'

Iron bolts scraped, the door opened and her father's blanket-swathed figure appeared.

'Oh my God!' Liddy exclaimed in angry disgust as she saw that he was drunk, and wearing only a filthy pair of drawers. 'Couldn't you at least have put some clothes on, Pa?'

He regarded her blearily, and announced bluntly, 'You've come too late, Liddy. Your mamma died hours since.'

Stunned by the shock, she could only stand motionless, until her father swayed, lost his balance and fell down into a sitting position.

Liddy helped him to a chair, then went into the other room.

Beatrice Landser was lying on her back, arms spread wide, eyes open and glazed, jaw fallen.

Liddy stood looking at the woman who had birthed her, and felt nothing. It was as if she were looking at a stranger. All she could think was how ugly her mother was in death.

Am I wicked, because I feel no grief or even any modicum of distress, she wondered uneasily. Am I unnatural to be so callous? She was my mother, after all. I ought to feel something.

Why should you have to feel something? a voice asked in her mind. This woman never showed you any love or affection. She wouldn't have wept any tears if you had died. You're well rid of her. Now look to the living. Your father needs your help.

Liddy could not bring herself to touch the corpse. She merely took her handkerchief and laid it over her mother's face.

In the other room her father was slumped over the table, head on arms, snoring loudly. Liddy couldn't rouse him, and was forced to let him stay there.

I'll have to get some help to deal with this, she thought. But who will help me? She was faced with the painful realisation that in this hour of need she had no relatives or friends whom she could call on. She felt an irrational flare of anger against her brother: You should be here to help me, Rob, instead of disappearing like you have done. You should be here with me now.

A desolate sensation of utter loneliness assailed her. Then the image of Edward Harcourt rose up in her mind, and she gratefully recalled his previous kindness to her.

I'll go to him, she decided with relief.

As Liddy walked, rain began to fall and she bent her bonneted head against the gusting wind-blown drops and drew her shawl tighter around her shoulders. By the time she had reached the long High Street of Bromsgrove her clothing was sodden.

Edward Harcourt himself opened the door to her.

'Miss Lydia, this is an unexpected pleasure. Do come in.'

He led her to an opulently furnished room where a large fire blazed in the ornately tiled grate.

'You're soaking wet. Please take off your shawl and bonnet and sit yourself close to the fire. You must have something to warm you. What shall it be? Tea, or coffee, or perhaps a glass of wine?'

She was grateful for his consideration for her. 'Tea would be very welcome. I thank you.'

He tugged a hanging silken cord to summon his housekeeper.

'Tea, Mrs Simons, and some cake also. And will you take this young lady's shawl and bonnet and dry them.'

He smiled at Liddy and with an avuncular air asked her, 'You have been to visit your parents?'

'I have, sir. My mother has died some hours since, and my father is senseless with drink.' It was now that the shock of her discovery hit her, and she burst into tears.

Harcourt's eyes locked on to the sight of her full high breasts heaving with her sobs and he experienced a sexual arousal.

I've got to have you, he thought. I've got to have you, no matter what it costs.

His housekeeper brought in a tray laden with tea and cakes, and her eyes widened at the sight of the weeping girl.

'Not now,' Harcourt told her. 'Come with me.'

He took the woman into the passage and issued a rapid series of instructions before coming back into the room.

He sat on the arm of Liddy's chair and put his arm around her shoulders. 'I shall help you in this sad time, my dear,' he assured her. 'I shall care for you.'

For several minutes he remained in that position as Liddy's weeping gradually eased, and when finally she was able to wipe her eyes and blow her nose, he smiled at her and squeezed her shoulder, then resumed his own seat.

'Now, Lydia, do you feel able to talk about your parents?' he asked gently.

'Yes, Mr Harcourt.'

'I've sent my manservant to fetch the undertaker to the cottage to perform the necessary offices for your poor mother. My man will remain there and care for your father, so you may be easy in your mind about his welfare. I shall arrange for the funeral and meet all expenses.'

'I can't let you do that, Mr Harcourt,' Liddy protested. 'I'm very grateful for your kind offer, but it must be my responsibility.'

He shook his finger in negation. 'No, I must insist. I shall not accept any refusal from you, Lydia.'

'But I can't let you do this for me. I'm not a relative, indeed you know me only as my father's daughter.'

'I trust that we now know each other as friends. And I am doing this as your friend, Lydia. So please do not deny me.'

After some further argument, she surrendered to his wish, but only on the condition that the expenses should be treated as a personal loan which she would repay.

The housekeeper brought in another tray of tea and Harcourt insisted that Liddy should try to eat and drink.

To her own surprise Liddy found that she relished the dainty pastries and delicately scented tea which were in stark contrast with the meagre, low-quality workhouse diet.

The delicacies, the warmth and comfort of the room, the avuncular attentiveness of Harcourt soothed her tormented thoughts and she began to feel relaxed and at ease. Once more she experienced a sense of guilt that she had previously so misjudged this man.

When she had finished eating, Harcourt asked, 'May I speak frankly?'

She nodded. 'Of course you may.'

'I have to say that I cannot help but think that your father would be better off if he were in an establishment, where he could be properly cared for.'

Liddy was appreciative of the delicate way he had phrased this, but was ready to speak more bluntly herself. 'He should be somewhere where he can't obtain drink. That is what you mean, isn't it?'

He sighed regretfully, and nodded. 'Yes, my dear. There are private establishments where drink mania can be treated and cured. At Henley in Arden there are several such.'

'These private establishments where the drink mania is treated are private lunatic asylums, are they not, Mr Harcourt?'

'Yes, they're private asylums, Lydia. But they treat all manner of mental afflictions there, and I fear that if your father does not obtain such treatment very soon, then you might well lose him also.'

'I agree that he needs treatment, but such establishments charge high fees, and my salary is not sufficient to cover the costs.'

Harcourt feigned a hesitancy that he was far from feeling. 'Lydia, I'm going to suggest something which I would like you to give careful thought to. We are both in agreement that your father cannot continue as he is now situated. You will recall that I told you how I feel somehow responsible for his present plight . . .'

'I do not hold you to be responsible in any degree,' Liddy interrupted, but he brushed her words aside.

'Nevertheless I do. Therefore I am ready to meet the expense of having your father properly treated. This of course will be an arrangement that will be known only to you and me. It will be our secret.'

'Oh no. I couldn't accept such an arrangement. It isn't your responsibility,' Liddy protested.

'Lydia, I beg you to think on this very carefully. Your father most definitely cannot be allowed to remain in his present situation. It is sheer cruelty towards him to allow him to remain so. If the drink doesn't kill him quickly, then his drink mania will before too long affect him so badly that he will inevitably end up being incarcerated in the public lunatic asylum at Powick. And I can tell you that the poor unfortunates imprisoned there do not always receive kindly treatment or proper care. He should be placed in a private establishment, where he will receive the best of care and treatment. It is his future well-being which must be paramount, Lydia, and not your reluctance to accept what you may perceive as charity.'

Liddy could find no immediate answer. She knew that everything the man had said was true. But it was not a reluctance to accept charity which kept her from accepting his offer. It was rather the reluctance to become even more obligated towards him than she already was.

Harcourt was wise enough not to press her further at this juncture. He was confident that before too long she would accept his offer. And then she would be so deeply obligated towards him that when the time came for the repayment he envisaged she would not be able to refuse him.

Now he told her, 'Please, think on this matter.'

'Very well,' she agreed, and then the chiming of the clock caused her to tell him, 'It's getting late. I'd better return to the workhouse.'

He rang for the housekeeper. 'Are this young lady's shawl and bonnet dried? She has to leave now.'

He walked to the front door with Liddy, and shook her hand as they parted, telling her, 'Now you leave everything to me, Lydia. I shall come and see you tomorrow. And please do think on the offer I've made for your father. I truly believe it is in his best interests for you to accept it.'

'I will think on it, Mr Harcourt,' she told him sincerely. 'And

36

I thank you very much for your kindness. I truly am very deeply grateful for it.'

He watched her walk away, his mind visualising the firm lissom body hidden beneath her clothing: Just wait until I have you naked beneath me, little Liddy. I'll make you squeal then.

Liddy's mind was troubled with guilt that she still felt no grief for her mother, and was only concerned for her father and brother. But she took comfort from the thought that in Edward Harcourt, she had found a true friend.

Five

T he muffled thudding of iron-shod hooves upon the layers
    of shredded tan'bark reverberated up to the high cob-
webbed ceiling arches of the long riding school. The rays of the
morning sun lanced through the high-set, dirty windows,
shimmering the floating dust motes. On the manège the troop
of ten mounted men cantered round and round with arms
crossed and without stirrups. In the centre of the ring Rough
Rider Sergeant Joseph Blackstone stood brandishing a long
coach whip, watching the circling men with contemptuous eyes
and continually venting his scorn upon them.

'I've shit better riders than you lot. You'll never make Light
Dragoons. You should have joined the fuckin' foot sloggers. I
reckon when you lot was born your mothers chucked away the
babbies and kept the fuckin' afterbirths. But why you had to be
sent to me is a fuckin' mystery. I reckon the Good Lord is trying
to punish me, sending you lot to me. Useless shitheaps that you
are!'

A figure appeared in the great open doorway of the school,
and Blackstone lifted his whip in greeting.

Sergeant Henry Keating grinned and returned the salute,
then stood watching, his expression gloatingly expectant.

Blackstone selected one of the cantering horses and suddenly
flicked his whip sending the long lash writhing out to cut
painfully into its hide. The horse snickered and jumped sideways and its rider lost his balance and toppled to thud face-first
on to the ground.

'Get up, you bastard! I didn't give you the order to dismount!' The riding instructor's face purpled with rage and he rushed to the sprawling man and kicked him hard in the ribs. 'Get up, you useless bastard. Get up! Get up!'

Rob Landser's breath wheezed and his nose poured blood as he painfully levered himself up on to his hands and knees.

The circling troop glanced at the crouching figure as they passed and their faces displayed differing reactions. Some grinned with enjoyment, some snarled with contempt at the fallen man, and some displayed anger and resentment on his behalf.

Rob stood, adjusted his pillbox forage cap to the correct jaunty angle and came stiffly to attention.

Blackstone glared at the fresh tan stains upon the front of the other man's blue shell jacket and overalls.

'Look at the state of you, you filthy animal!' he bawled. 'You look like a bloody tramp.'

Rob stared woodenly to his front, showing no emotion.

'Remount!' Blackstone ordered.

Rob was forced to run in pursuit of his horse which was still circling with the troop. He caught the beast, mounted and resumed his place in the formation.

During the next half hour Blackstone's whip snaked out again and again to send horses jumping and rearing and their hapless riders crashing to the ground. But the most frequent target was Rob Landser, and by the time the period of instruction was finished Rob was a mass of bruises, blood and filth.

Blackstone formed the troop into line then stood at attention in front of them and ordered, 'Prepare to dismount.'

The riders' hands moved to the horses' withers.

'Dismount.'

The riders vaulted to the ground then stood to attention at the near sides of their mounts, reins in their left hands.

'Stand to your horses.'

A corporal hurried into the building and the troop was turned over to his charge. As the men filed out leading their horses, Henry Keating moved aside to give them passage and his eyes locked upon Rob Landser. He smiled tauntingly, but remained silent, and Rob did not look at him as he passed.

When the troop reached the stables Sean Shea, one of the Irishmen who had enlisted with Rob, came to speak with him, his youthful features hot with anger.

'Those bastards won't be happy until they have you dead, Rob. They hates your guts, don't they? Why are they so much against you?'

Rob picked up a handful of straw and wiped the blood still trickling from his nose. He grimaced as he touched the swollen flesh. Then he shrugged. 'It is a fact of life, Sean, that every man will at times encounter other individuals, who hate him for no apparent reason. But in this present case they hate me because I am a gentleman.'

The young Irishman grinned and teased, 'Oh, you are that, all right, Robbie. It's easy to see that you've been used to the better things in life. I don't know how you can stand to be living with all us roughs and scruffs.'

The orderly sergeant wearing full regimentals and plumed shako came bellowing into the stable block. 'Come on, you lot, get these horses seen to.'

Sean Shea went to his allotted stall, leaving Rob alone. As he stripped the saddlery from his horse he thought wryly, They hate me because they think I'm a gentleman from a wealthy family . . . Jesus Christ! If they only knew the truth of it!

'That bugger, Landser is a tough nut to crack, Henry.' Joseph Blackstone spoke with grudging admiration. 'I'd expected him to break well before now. Most would have done a runner long since.'

Keating chuckled grimly. 'Oh, he'll break, Joe. They all does eventually. I swore to meself the day that I 'listed the saucy bastard that I'd break him.'

'You might have to move a bit careful though,' Blackstone said thoughtfully. 'You don't want any of the officers to start thinking that you're being too hard on the bugger.'

Keating shrugged uncaringly. 'It makes no difference what they thinks, does it. It ain't the bleedin' officers who runs the regiment, is it? It's us.'

Steam swirled in hot damp clouds from the big copper resting on the fire at one end of the barrackroom and dampened Gabey Patterson's face and hair as she used both hands to lift the copper and set it on the floor.

'Hand me the bowls, Dorcas.'

Gabey ladled portions of meat, gristle, bone and potatoes into the crock bowls which the other woman passed to her. She tried to even out each portion so that no one should have an undue proportion of bone and gristle, but it proved to be unavoidable. The food smelled sour because both the meat and potatoes were of the worst quality and tainted.

The women carried the bowls and laid them out on the two trestle tables between the rows of beds, and as they did so the men came clattering into the room, bringing with them the stench of sweaty unwashed bodies and stable muck.

Thomas Patterson, a sandy-haired, pleasant-featured young man, smiled at his wife.

'What's it today then? Pheasants and port wine again?'

'It's a feast that the Royal Family wouldn't turn their noses up at,' she joked.

'Their arses, you mean,' he rejoined.

'Let's get the grog sorted, Tommy. Me bleedin' belly thinks me throat's been cut,' a man urged.

'Did you get me the beer?' Private Donal Murphy, grizzle-haired, squat and powerfully built, demanded of his wife.

'Where the fuckin' hell am I to get the rhino to buy it?' Dorcas Murphy demanded in her turn.

'Don't take that tone wi' me, you cow.' He lifted his clenched fist threateningly and the woman instantly snatched a scab-barded sabre from its hanging hook and unsheathed the shining blade.

'Just try it, Murphy, and I'll ram this up your fuckin' arse.' She spat at him, then waved the blade under his nose and

41

challenged, 'Come on, just try it. Come on, let's see how brave you are, you fuckin' arsehole.'

'Give over, the both of you,' Thomas Patterson ordered, and told Murphy, 'Do the calling, Donal.'

The Irishman went to the far end of the room and stood with his face turned to the wall.

Patterson pointed at one of the steaming bowls and asked, 'Who shall have this?'

'Anderson,' Murphy answered, and the designated man took the bowl, produced a battered spoon and began to eat voraciously.

The process continued, the corporal selecting bowls at random and the unseeing Murphy calling out names until every man had been allotted his ration.

Although some of the bowls contained disproportionate amounts of bone and gristle instead of meat, there was little or no grumbling. Each mealtime was a lottery, and over the course of time everyone received about the same number of good and bad portions.

'My Christ, milord, you're a mess.' Gabey Patterson grimaced at Rob Landser's filthy uniform and blood-stained face.

'Will you wash it for him this afternoon, Gabey?' her husband asked, and told Rob, 'You can wear fatigues for sword drill, milord. I'm taking it so Keating won't be around to see you.'

'Thank you very much.' Rob was grateful for this unasked-for kindness.

When he had first joined the troop, most of the men had been fiercely hostile to him because of his gentlemanly accent and manners. But his stoical silent endurance of Sergeant Keating's constant harrassment had turned that initial hostility into a grudging admiration for his unyielding spirit, and more now liked him than disliked him.

'You know, you ought to give in to him,' Patterson advised. 'Go and crawl to him and beg him to leave off you. Because he'll be having you on the triangle next.'

42

Rob grimaced and shrugged. 'What's to be, will be. Keating is determined to break me, and I'm determined that he shan't do so. I'll not crawl to the bastard.' He paused as if considering something, and then went on, 'Yet strangely enough I can't help but feel that Keating has his own twisted sense of fair play. I don't believe that he will ever manufacture a false charge against me to get me flogged.'

The corporal frowned doubtfully. 'I wouldn't like to bet me life on that, milord.'

'A touch of the cat won't kill you anyway,' a heavily muscled, bullet-headed man put in. 'You're not a real soldier until you've tasted the cat. Mind you, the way you're shaping up, Landser, I don't reckon you'll ever make a real soldier. You're a bit too much of a nancy-boy.'

Private Judah Hayes was one of the men who disliked Rob, and lost no opportunity to denigrate him.

'How many times have you had the cat?' Rob asked him.

'I stopped counting long since,' Judah Hayes boasted. 'The bastards can flog me till the cows comes home for all I cares. It never feels more than a tickle to me.'

'It just goes to show, that where there's no sense, there's no feeling,' Rob said, sneering.

Judah Hayes glowered as laughter erupted, and growled, 'I can prove that there's no truth in that when I breaks your fuckin' face, milord. You'll be squealing like a stuck pig then.'

'I'm not afraid of you, Hayes,' Rob told him, and hurled himself at the other man.

The two grappled and crashed backwards, bringing the bench and its other occupants down with them. The rest of the men carried on eating. Brawls were such a commonplace in the barrackroom that little notice was taken of them unless weapons were used, or a man seemed near to death.

Sean Shea grinned happily as he reached across for Judah Hayes' bowl and tipped the contents into his own, and another two men squabbled over who was to take the remains of Rob's ration.

Thomas Patterson chuckled and shouted to Dorcas Murphy

who was smoking a clay pipe with Gabey behind the corner blanket.

'Now's your chance, Dorcas. Bring that sabre and get stuck in.'

Then the trumpet shrilled the parade call, and the corporal and others forced the combatants to separate and prepare for the afternoon's drill.

'By Jasus, Robbie, that was great the way you got stuck in there,' Sean Shea congratulated. 'You showed the bastard that you're not feared of him like a lot of these scuts are.'

Rob fingered the cut lip he had now acquired to keep company with his other injuries.

Judah Hayes glowered threateningly from across the room.

'You'll need to watch yourself when that bastard's around though, Robbie. He's an evil bleeder, so he is. He'd shove a blade in your back given the chance,' the young Irishman warned.

'I'll watch him, Sean.' Rob nodded. 'And it might be him who gets the blade in his back first if he doesn't leave me alone.'

The brutal barrack life had roused in Rob Landser a gutter-devil that he had never known he possessed, a quality of savagery that drove out all fear of consequence. The spoiled, soft-living, petulant youth had gone, and in his place was a tough and reckless man, whose innate selfishness had hardened to a self-serving callousness.

While the men clattered out of the room Rob quickly stripped off his soiled uniform and put on the canvas fatigue suit.

Gabey Patterson came to take the discarded clothes from him. She smiled invitingly and leaned close to whisper, 'I like the way you took on Judah Hayes, milord. I've always liked blokes who can handle themselves in a fight.'

There was a sensual gleam in her eyes as she suggestively fondled his discarded clothing. 'I'll be thinking of you while I'm washing these.'

The celibate life he had been leading in the barracks had filled Rob with sexual frustration, and he frequently envisaged what it would be like to make love to this pretty gamine. She, on her part, had often given him reason to think that she would not be adverse to any sexual advances he might make towards her. But to pursue another soldier's wife, especially the wife of an NCO, was to risk grave trouble. And to pursue his own troop corporal's wife would be to invite disastrous consequences.

The old Rob Landser would never have dared to take that risk. And the fact that Corporal Patterson had treated him well might also have given him cause to hesitate. But the old Rob Landser had gone.

Rob returned her smile, and whispered back, 'I'm always thinking about you, Gabey. Especially when I'm in my bed of nights. I'm always wishing you were sharing it with me.'

Her small pink tongue moved suggestively between her lips. 'I might just be wishing the same thing, milord.'

Outside from the parade ground the trumpet sounded again.

'Jasus, come on, Robbie, the parade's forming,' Sean Shea urged, and Rob caressingly touched Gabey Patterson's cheek as he left her smiling after him.

As they hurried towards the parade ground Sean Shea demanded, 'Haven't you got enough bastards after your blood, Robbie, without looking for more?'

'I don't know what you mean.' Rob grinned.

'Well, if Patterson finds out that you're meaning to shag his missus he'll have your blood.'

'He's not going to find out, is he? Because I shan't be telling him, and I'm sure Gabey won't.'

'And I'm sure I won't neither.' The Irishman grinned. 'But there's plenty who will. And you should know by now, that nothing stays hidden for long in barracks.'

'Well then, I'll just have to make the most of it while it still stays hidden, won't I?' Rob returned the grin.

Six

A melia Melen was sitting by her parlour fire digesting her ample breakfast of poached eggs and toasted muffins when her visitor was announced by the pauper servant.

'Why, Mr Harcourt, this is an unexpected pleasure.' Amelia Melen rose from her chair by the parlour fire and smiled rosily at her visitor. 'Will you take some refreshment, sir?'

'Perhaps a glass of wine, ma'am.'

'At once, sir. But can I take your cloak and hat? Please do sit down and be comfortable, I beg you.'

While Harcourt removed his cloak and top hat and handed it to her, Amelia Melen chattered on. 'I'm so pleased that you've come. There was a matter I wished to ask your advice on.'

Harcourt always enjoyed being fussed over by this attractive woman, who behaved towards him with such deference, and who hastened to implement his every suggestion concerning the administration of the workhouse.

'It's Madeira, sir. I hope it's to your taste?'

He sipped the wine appreciatively. 'Indeed it is, ma'am.'

'Can I ask what brings you here at this early hour, sir?'

'I need to speak with your little schoolmistress concerning the arrangement I've made for her father to receive treatment for his affliction.'

'She's a fortunate young woman to have such a friend as you, sir. The way you organised her mother's funeral was a real act of Christian charity.'

'Well, as you know, I'm an old friend of her family, and so I take an interest in her welfare,' Harcourt went on smoothly. 'The poor girl has had a great deal of tribulation over these last years and I feel it is my duty to try and help her as much as I can. Particularly in her present time of trial.'

Amelia Melen was a woman with much worldly experience and had long since made her own judgement of Harcourt's sexual propensities. She was cynically certain that his interest in this young woman was anything but altruistic. She also recognised that there now existed a possibility that Lydia Landser might soon come to exercise a great deal of influence over Harcourt. She knew how older men could become infatuated with pretty young girls, and how foolishly those men could behave when a cunning girl took advantage of that infatuation. With that in mind, she decided that, for the present at least, it might be advantageous if she became more friendly with Lydia Landser.

With an expression of benevolent concern, she said, 'I do hope that Miss Landser is not finding her position here a trial, sir, or that she has any cause for complaint. Mr Melen and myself treat her with kindness, I assure you.'

'I'm sure of that, ma'am.' He smiled conspiratorially. 'And you know me well enough to be sure that if any complaint were to be made about this establishment I should disregard it. I have complete confidence in yourself and Mr Melen as regards the humane and efficient way you discharge your duties here.'

'With you overlooking and guiding us, sir, there is no other way in which those duties could be discharged.' She flattered outrageously, knowing that his vanity was such that he accepted even the most fulsome praise as being nothing more than his due.

'I shall need to take Miss Landser with me this morning, ma'am. She may be absent until tomorrow. I trust that will be convenient.'

'Of course, sir. She may remain with you as long as you consider it to be necessary.'

He drained his glass and she hastened to refill it. 'Could I ask your advice on the matter I mentioned, sir?'

He nodded.

'It concerns the armless monster, sir. The little Kennedy girl.'

'What of her?'

'A lady has approached me who wishes to take into her care an orphan from this house, with a view to eventual adoption.'

'Do I know this lady?' Harcourt asked disinterestedly.

'I think not, sir. She is a maiden lady, a Miss Farquar who lives in Manchester. She is comfortably situated with a private income.'

At the mention of money Harcourt showed more interest. 'But if she lives in Manchester, how is it she should approach you here?' He grinned, and demanded jocularly, 'Are there not an ample supply of orphans there? I'm told the poor die like flies in that city.'

'What a quiz you are, sir.' Amelia Melen laughed dutifully at his sally. 'Miss Farquar is an old acquaintance of mine, and a very devout Christian. She has a most tender heart and wishes to help an orphan who is sadly afflicted, but who has intelligence and the capacity to improve in manners and become a lifetime companion to her.

'Miss Farquar is presently visiting old friends in Birmingham. She took this opportunity of approaching me because she trusts my judgement in such matters. The Kennedy girl, being afflicted, would be ideal for her purpose. Although a monster she has intelligence and a sweet nature.

'But, I am not so wise in these matters as yourself. What should I do, sir? Shall I recommend Miss Farquar to apply to the Board for guardianship of the girl?'

Harcourt steepled his hands in front of his chest. 'If I remember correctly, the monster's mother was committed to Powick Asylum, was she not?'

The matron sighed regretfully. 'She was. And I gather has become even more violent and deranged since her committal.'

'Does Miss Farquar know that there is insanity in the monster's family?'

'Oh yes, sir. I've informed her fully. But it makes her even more determined to take the monster. As I said, she is a most devout Christian. She believes that by helping the most unfortunate on this earth she is following in the footsteps of our Saviour.'

Into Harcourt's eyes there came a sly gleam. 'And you yourself, ma'am, what are your true thoughts on this matter? Are we following in our Saviour's footsteps if we let Miss Farquar take the monster?'

Amelia Melen smiled knowingly. She and this man understood each other so very, very well.

'Well, sir, I'm not qualified to know if we are or not . . . But I am qualified to know that if we let Miss Farquar take the monster, we shall be saving the parish the expense of maintaining a useless pauper for God knows how many more years to come.'

He nodded judiciously. 'That is a very strong argument for this adoption, ma'am. You may ask Miss Farquar to attend upon the Board at her convenience. I don't anticipate any objections being raised to her application.'

'Thank you, sir. I will.' Amelia Melen beamed.

'And now, perhaps you'll be so kind as to send for the schoolmistress?'

'I'll go directly myself and fetch her.'

'. . . three times three are nine, four times three are twelve, five times three are fifteen, six times three are eighteen . . .' the children's voices chanted in shrill unison, then raggedly lost the tempo and fell silent as Amelia Melen came into the room, shouting for quiet.

Liddy sighed in exasperation. 'I didn't think that they were being unduly noisy, ma'am.'

'I could hear them from my own quarters,' the matron lied. 'Anyway, dismiss them. Mr Harcourt has come to see you, concerning your father.'

She saw the pleased reaction in Liddy's expression, and thought sourly, I'm right, aren't I. The little bitch thinks she has her claws into the old fool.

When the children had been dismissed and the two women were alone she feigned sympathy. 'I'm sorry for your present troubles, Miss Landser. I know that the situation is difficult for you, so you may take whatever time off is necessary before resuming your duties here.'

'Thank you very much, ma'am.' Liddy was greatly surprised by the other woman's sudden change of attitude towards her.

Eager though she was to know exactly what Harcourt proposed to do with Lydia Landser during the next hours, the matron judged that her own interests would best be served by playing a waiting game.

'I've no wish to intrude upon your personal affairs, Miss Landser. Mr Harcourt is waiting in my parlour. You may speak to him in privacy there. You'd best go to him immediately, and as I said, you need not resume your duties until your present problems have been resolved.'

'Very well, ma'am, and thank you again.' As Liddy hurried away she couldn't help wondering if she had misjudged Amelia Melen's character as badly as she had misjudged Edward Harcourt's.

Amelia Melen reflected briefly, and was satisfied that she had manipulated the situation with Lydia Landser and Edward Harcourt to her advantage. And best of all, the way was now clear to sell little Katie Kennedy to Enoch Cull. She hummed happily to herself as she set off on her rounds.

'I've a confession to make,' Edward Harcourt told Liddy apologetically. 'I've visited Dr Burman at Henley in Arden, and discussed your father's mental and physical condition with him. The doctor has agreed to take your father as a patient immediately. That is assuming that you consent to it.'

'I take it that Dr Burman's establishment is a lunatic asylum?'

'Yes, but a very exclusive asylum, and very well regarded.'

'But my father's not mad!' Liddy objected.

'And he will not be treated as such, my dear.' Harcourt's manner was avuncular. 'Your father will enter there as a guest-patient. He will not be subjected to any restraints or be under the same regime as the lunatics. Dr Burman has had much success in treating alcoholics and those who are addicted to opium. I'm sure that he will be able to help your father, and restore him to full heath and vigour.'

Liddy was still doubtful. 'I don't believe that my father will agree to this, Mr Harcourt.'

'Do you want him cured of his drink mania?'

'Of course I do.'

'Then you must persuade him that this is what he must agree to.'

When she made no reply, Harcourt added stick to carrot.

'I will speak frankly, Lydia. The Board is no longer prepared to allow your father to continue receiving the Parish Outdoor Relief. Despite all my arguing to the contrary, they are insisting that if he remains on the Parish, then he must be taken into the workhouse. They say that he is abusing their charity by wasting the Parish Relief money on drink.' He shrugged as if in resignation. 'I am outvoted on this matter, my dear. There is nothing I can do to change their minds.'

Liddy reluctantly accepted defeat. 'Very well, Mr Harcourt. I shall do my best to make my father agree.'

'It is for the best.'

'This asylum, is it a comfortable place for the patients?' she asked. 'I could not be easy in my mind unless I was sure that my father will be made comfortable.'

'You shall be made easy in your mind.' He smiled reassuringly. 'You shall travel to Henley with me today, and meet Dr Burman yourself, and if you are not happy with what you see of him, then we shall try to make other arrangements.'

His kindness made Liddy feel near to tears. 'I don't know what I would do without your kind help, Mr Harcourt. I don't know how I will ever be able to repay you for it.'

Through Edward Harcourt's mind there passed a series of vivid mental images of several ways in which she would be repaying his kindness. And sooner rather than later, if all went as he planned.

Seven

The private asylum was a large red-brick Georgian house secluded behind high walls on the outskirts of the village of Henley in Arden.

Its proprietor, Dr Aloysius Burman, was glossy from his bald pink scalp, round pink face, protuberant satin-waistcoated belly, to his gleaming polished boots. He received Liddy and Harcourt in a large study, three of its walls filled with books, the fourth wall covered with shelving on which stood lines of human skulls.

Liddy stared at the macabre spectacle with a queasy fascination, and Burman laughed heartily.

'I pray don't be alarmed, Miss Landser. None of these belong to my patients. They are solely aids to knowledge.'

'I'm relieved to hear that, sir,' she murmured.

'I am a disciple of Gall and Spurzheim, Miss Landser, and for several years studied under Mr George Combe of Edinburgh.'

The names meant nothing to Liddy, and she could only look blank.

Burman laughed even more heartily and said to Harcourt, 'I see, sir, that this young lady knows nothing of the renowned masters of phrenology.' He turned back to Liddy and explained. 'Phrenology is the study of the organs of the brain, Miss Landser. It is an invaluable aid in diagnosing the types of mental disorders that afflict my patients.'

She was instantly interested. 'And when you have made that diagnosis, then is it possible to effect a cure?'

'In certain cases, yes. In other cases I am able to treat them so that they show improvement. Sadly, other cases are hopeless, and only God can restore their minds.'

'How does this phrenology enable you to make your diagnosis, sir?'

'Allow me to give you a very brief explanation.' Burman led her to a side table on which was placed a large porcelain bust of a hairless human head. The cranium area was marked out in numbered sections of varying sizes and shapes.

'This can be termed the map of the brain.' Burman's voice became fervent, as if he were preaching a doctrine of religious faith. 'Each of these numbered sections corresponds to a portion of the brain, and each portion is the seat of one of the brains' faculties, such as amativeness, combativeness, constructiveness, destructiveness, et cetera, et cetera.

'The size and development of each region enables the phrenologist to judge its effect on the personality of the subject and its constituent element in the character of the subject. You see, the correspondence between the outer surface of the skull, and the contour of the brain-surface beneath is sufficiently close to enable me to recognise and evaluate the relative sizes of the organic regions by my examination of the outer surface of the subject's head.

'I can recognise any abnormality in any particular region's development. This recognition in turn enables me to make an accurate diagnosis, and empowers me to prescribe a course of treatment to restore my patient to full health and sanity.'

He spoke with such throbbing conviction that Liddy found hope suddenly stirring within her.

'Then it is entirely possible that you can restore my father to full health, sir?'

'Of course, Miss Landser. I would not accept him as my patient otherwise.'

'What would the treatment consist of?' she pressed eagerly.

'It would depend on the individual being treated. I have to make my diagnosis before I can prescribe the treatment. It varies greatly for the different conditions and degrees of mania: Generally, however, I treat the entire body as well as the mind. I commence with a course of bleedings to weaken the bodily fibres and loosen the grip of the mania. I follow this with a vigorous series of attacks upon the mania by means of purging, blistering and vomiting. All through the treatment I also administer various medicines of my own composition which have proven to be uncommonly efficacious. So much so that I am constantly being pestered by other members of the medical profession for the composition of my potions.'

His smile held a hint of smugness. 'Needless to say, I do not oblige my pesterers. It has taken me many years of long and arduous practice and study to perfect my treatments, and I do not see why I should give my rivals the benefit of my own hard-won expertise.'

He radiated such an air of confidence, of certainty, of professional competence that Liddy was wholly won over, and felt convinced that if anyone could cure her father, this was the man to do it.

'And now, you must allow me to show you the rooms your father will be living in.'

The hallway and staircase smelled of lavender, the woodwork gleamed with polishing, the wallpapering was an expensive flock, the furnishings and pictures would have graced the home of a magnate.

Liddy was greatly impressed, and could not help but wonder anxiously just how expensive it was going to prove, and how much in debt she would be to Edward Harcourt, before it was all over.

Her father's bedroom and sitting room adjoined each other on the first floor, and were both equally well and comfortably furnished.

'We practise absolute privacy and discretion here, Miss Landser. Your father's identity will be known only to myself, and my staff can be relied upon not to pry. Here he will be assured of the peace and tranquillity that I believe is essential for the well-being of the mentally afflicted.'

Liddy had already noticed how quiet everything was, and the absence of any human presence or sounds. Apart from the manservant who had answered the door to them, she had seen or heard no other person apart from Aloysius Burman.

'Visitors, sir? How often are the patients allowed to have visitors?' she asked. 'I shall want to visit my father regularly, you see.'

Burman's eyes flicked momentarily towards Edward Harcourt, and from behind Liddy, Harcourt frowned warningly and shook his head.

Burman beamed at Liddy. 'That depends on the progress the patient is making, Miss Landser. I have found that during the initial stages of treatment, receiving visitors has a most deleterious effect upon the patients. It greatly disturbs the equilibrium of their minds.'

'How so?' Liddy wanted a more detailed explanation.

Burman didn't falter. He was an expert at dealing with worried relatives.

'I shall speak bluntly, Miss Landser,' he told her gravely. 'The majority of my patients are here because of the stresses they have endured in their domestic lives. Visitors only serve to rekindle unhappy memories of those same stresses, to re-open the wounds. Therefore I do not permit any visitors until my patients are recovered sufficiently to suffer no ill effects from the rekindling of those unhappy memories.'

'But I have not given my father any cause to have unhappy memories of me,' Liddy argued. 'I'm sure that it could only benefit him for me to visit. We have always been very close.'

Burman reacted smoothly.

'I am going to make an exception to my general rule, Miss Landser. I am going to take you to see two of my patients. But I must press upon you the necessity for your absolute discretion. I must have your word that you will never speak of what I am going to show you to anyone else. And you also, Mr Harcourt.'

'You have my word, sir,' Liddy readily assented, as did Harcourt.

Burman took them up another flight of stairs to a board landing and tapped on one of the doors leading off from it, calling softly, 'May I enter, Mr Hoyle?'

55

A voice sounded from within, and Burman smiled at his guests, and whispered, 'Follow me.'

Liddy stared interestedly at the gentle-faced, white-haired old man wearing a tasselled skullcap and a voluminous dressing gown who was sitting by the window in a capacious armchair.

'How are you feeling today, Mr Hoyle?'

'I'm very well, I thank you, sir,' the old man replied and bowed his head courteously towards Liddy and Harcourt.

Burman made the introductions, and for a few minutes the four of them exchanged polite small-talk before Burman led Liddy and Harcourt out of the room once more.

'That old gentleman came to me almost a year past. He appeared to be a hopeless case, his mind dreadfully deranged. Now he is shortly going home once again. Cured!' Burman announced impressively, then crooked his forefinger. 'Now, let me show you another case. Don't be alarmed at what you will see, Miss Landser.'

He led them further along the landing to another door, and called out, 'It's me, Mr Garner,' and led the way into the room.

The moment she entered Liddy could detect the same peculiar feral smell that she had found emanating from her mother. There were two men in this room. A burly man dressed in a rusty-black frock coat and trousers stood watching the other man. This second man was lying on a bed, trussed in a strait-jacket, his eyes rolling in his head, threads of spittle trailing from his mouth, muttering incoherently.

Liddy gasped in horrified shock, and Burman quickly took her arm and led her out from the room.

'That patient came to me from another establishment three days ago,' Burman informed her sombrely. 'His family begged me to take him because they have discovered that no other doctor is able to cure him.

'The old gentleman, Mr Hoyle, was in worse condition than that poor unfortunate when he was brought to me, and you have seen for yourself the result I have accomplished with him.'

His manner became stern. 'I will tell you bluntly, Miss Landser, that I brook no interference from relatives or friends of my patients in the manner of my treatments. I permit visitors only when I am convinced that it will not retard my patient's cures. If you are not agreeable with that, then I deeply regret that I am not prepared to accept your father within my establishment.'

Liddy was dismayed, and looked at Harcourt with mute appeal.

Edward Harcourt clucked his tongue sympathetically, but shook his head. 'I'm afraid that I can offer no advice to you on this matter, Lydia. It must be your decision. But Dr Burman is the expert in this field, and has a well-merited reputation for success. Personally, I bow to his wisdom.'

In her heart Liddy knew that she had no choice, and that there were no other options which she could take. After a few moments she nodded.

'I will be happy for you to treat my father, Dr Burman, and will accept whatever advice you give me concerning visits.'

'You have chosen wisely, Miss Landser,' Burman said gravely. 'I shall have the necessary preparations made to receive your father. As for arranging his transport here, I will send my own people to collect him tomorrow. I find that to avoid distress it is always preferable that relatives are absent at this time, but you need not concern yourself, Miss Landser. All will be done with tact and gentleness.'

'I'll meet your people at the cottage, Dr Burman,' Harcourt said. 'That way, Miss Landser can have confidence that all will go well.'

'But surely I should be there myself?' Liddy said.

'No, Miss Landser.' Burman seemed adamant. 'Believe me, my experience has shown that it is better that you are not present.'

Liddy experienced a sense of guilty shame at her own relief that she would not have to witness her father being removed from the cottage.

'And I am confident that when we next meet, Miss Landser, it will be in happier circumstances.'

Burman accompanied the couple to the front door and

exchanged a sly wink with Harcourt above Liddy's head. After waving them off he went upstairs.

Hoyle grinned toothlessly when Burman came into the room. 'How was I, Doctor?'

'Convincing as always, Johnny!' Burman smiled. 'Now go and give Garner a hand to shift that loony bugger. He's stinking the place out.'

Edward Harcourt turned the horse's head towards Henley village, and engrossed in her own thoughts Liddy did not at first realise that they were heading away from the route they had come.

When they entered the village she asked in puzzlement, 'Why arc we coming this way?'

'It's getting late, Lydia. It will be dark long before we can reach Bromsgrove, and I've no fancy for travelling by night. It's not safe these days with so many tramps and roughs wandering about looking to see who they can rob. There's a very decent inn. I shall engage rooms for us, and we'll return to Bromsgrove in the morning.'

'But is that proper?' she questioned.

He saw her doubtful frown, and chuckled.

'Don't worry, my dear. You can trust me. Your reputation will not be compromised. The inn has the highest repute for probity. The landlord is also the local church warden. He insists upon young maiden ladies being lodged separately from the gentlemen.'

She felt embarrassed, and in her confusion apologised hastily. 'I'm sorry, Mr Harcourt, I didn't mean to imply that I mistrusted you in any way. It's just that . . .'

'Enough, I beg you, Lydia.' He was smiling broadly. 'There is no need for apologies between friends.' He looked keenly at her, and asked more seriously, 'And we are friends now, are we not? Good friends, I hope?'

She smile wryly at her initial stupid reaction to the prospect of staying at an inn, and told him warmly, 'Yes, Mr Harcourt. We are good friends.'

'In that case, let me make a request to you, as a good friend.' He was casual, relaxed. 'When we are alone together, as we are now, will you please address me as Edward. It would please me so much to know that you felt easy enough in my company to use that familiarity.'

Liddy was glad to be able to please him. She owed him so much.

'Of course I will, Mr Harcourt.'

'Who?' He mock-scowled.

'Edward,' she amended, smiling.

The evening they spent at the inn proved to be one of the pleasantest occasions Liddy had known for a long time. They dined, and took some wine, and talked. Edward Harcourt could exert a great deal of charm, and was a knowledgeable man who was able to converse interestingly on many varied topics. After a while, Liddy, made slightly tipsy by the wine, was able to forget her many worries and problems, and enjoy herself. Despite the difference in their ages, she thought Harcourt a physically attractive man, and at last she could not resist asking him, 'Why have you remained a bachelor, Edward? I would think that many ladies have set their caps at you?'

Harcourt was an experienced seducer and could sense that he was making good progress towards his goal. He seized this opportunity to appeal to her sentimentality.

He assumed an air of sadness. 'Some years ago I met a young lady and fell deeply in love with her, and she returned my feelings. We were going to be married.' He sighed heavily. 'It was not fated to be.'

Liddy was totally intrigued. 'But why? What happened?'

He looked down and shielded his eyes with his hand. 'Forgive me, my dear. But I find it too painful to talk about.'

Sympathy whelmed up in Liddy. 'Oh, Edward, I'm so sorry. It was very wrong of me to ask you.'

He feigned a brave smile. 'Not at all, my dear. I've never spoken of it to anyone before, you see, so it is hard for me to do so now. Someday I will tell you. It makes me very happy to know that I have a friend whom I can tell.'

He reached across to take her hand, and for some moments their fingers interlocked and gently squeezed.

Inwardly Harcourt was congratulating himself: Soon. I'll have her soon.

He released Liddy's hand, and shook his head ruefully.

'I'm becoming maudlin, I fear, and spoiling your pleasure.'

'No, you're not!' she contradicted forcefully. 'I've enjoyed tonight more than I can say. I'm very grateful to you, Edward.'

'We must dine together again, and very soon, my dear.' He became brisk. 'And now we must get to our beds. We have to start out at an early hour tomorrow.'

As they parted he pressed a quick fatherly kiss upon her forehead. 'Sleep well, my dear.'

'And you also, Edward,' she wished happily.

In her bedroom she undressed to her shift, her mind full with the day's happenings. In bed she found herself thinking fondly of Edward Harcourt.

I'm so lucky that he's become my friend, she told herself gratefully, and, still thinking of him, drifted into sleep.

In his bed Edward Harcourt was fondling his erect penis, visualising the smooth soft nakedness of Lydia Landser. His bladder suddenly felt uncomfortably full, disturbing his lustful imaginings. Cursing, he got out of the bed and pulled the chamberpot from beneath it. As he started to urinate a sharp pain lanced through his penis and he swore savagely.

'Damn and blast this fuckin' clap. Will I never get free of it!'

Eight

It was early afternoon when James Kerr looked down from his bedroom window at the carriage and pair which had just come to a halt before the front door, and wondered if this was the mysterious patient who his uncle had said might be staying at the house for several weeks. The closed carriage bore no escutcheon on its doors, and the windows were covered with leather curtains so its interior was hidden from view. The pair of horses were of fine quality, and the coachman and footman on the driving seat were uniformly neat in cockaded top hats and multi-caped overcoats.

As James watched, the footman jumped down and came to ring the doorbell.

Within moments Septimus Nairn was standing at the side of the carriage talking to whomever was concealed within. Then the carriage door opened and a tall man, whose head and features were completely hidden by a voluminous black hood, got out and followed Nairn into the house, while the carriage drove away.

Mrs Biddle came hurrying upstairs and knocked on the bedroom door. 'Jamie, your uncle wants you in the study straightaway.'

In the study the hooded visitor was standing staring out of the window when James entered.

Septimus Nairn smiled at his nephew, and winked meaningfully. Then told the hooded man, 'My lord, allow me to present my assistant, Mr James Kerr. You may of course rely on his absolute discretion. If you will permit, we will now carry out our examination.'

The man threw back the hood and turned to face into the room. He wore a thick veil across the lower half of his face so that only the eyes and the broad brow were visible beneath the thick shock of iron-grey hair.

'If you will be seated, my lord.' Nairn indicated a chair placed to face the window. 'And remove the veil, please.'

James felt a momentary shock of horror as he saw the deformity the veil had concealed. The man had no nose; instead an ulcerated, red raw-fleshed hole made his face hideous to look upon.

James's initial reaction quickly metamorphosed into an intense interest as he and his uncle bent close to examine the gaping wound which oozed a watery bloody pus.

The man breathed stertorously from his mouth, and his eyes were closed.

Nairn frowned, and asked, 'Does it pain you greatly, my lord? And what form does the pain take? Is it a throbbing, or a dull aching?'

'The pain is bearable. But it throbs constantly.' The man's voice was distorted, the words malformed. 'Can you help me?'

Nairn nodded confidently. 'Oh yes. But I must again warn you that it will be a long and tedious process, during which you must remain here in my house, and you will have to undergo considerable suffering.'

The man's eyes opened. 'I am prepared for that.'

'When do you wish for the procedure to be carried out?' Nairn asked.

'Immediately,' the man stated firmly.

'Very well, my lord. I shall have my housekeeper make ready your rooms. Now if you will wait here, I must leave you for a short time while I prepare for the operation. Come, Mr Kerr.'

Nairn went to the kitchen and gave instructions to Mrs Biddle, then led the way to the laboratory-outhouse. James followed, burning with curiosity.

As soon as they entered the outhouse he questioned eagerly,

'What are you going to do, Uncle? And who is he, and how did he come by such a dreadful disfigurement?'

'He is Humphrey Chamberson, the Earl of Allesley, and he's disfigured by syphilis, fine upstanding nobleman that he is,' Nairn stated bluntly. 'And I am going to create a new nose for him.'

'Have you done this operation many times? You've never spoken of it to me before. How did you learn rhinoplastics?' James never ceased to wonder at his uncle's expertise.

Nairn smiled grimly. 'I read Carpue's account of his experiments. I've performed it twice. And both times the damn things exfoliated and sloughed. I made the grievous error of allowing the patients to return to their own homes, so I was not able to keep a constant watch upon the progress of the granulation. However, I learned much from those failures, and I'm confident that this time I shall succeed.'

'But if you should fail, will it not harm your reputation? The earl must be a man of influence, with powerful friends. Might he not cause you damage if you fail?' James queried with concern.

'I shan't fail,' Nairn stated with absolute certainty. 'But even if I did it wouldn't matter a damn. He will not condemn me, because I hold his reputation as an upright, God-fearing Christian in my hands. The world believes he has lost his nose because of mercurial poisoning, but we know differently. However, you must never breathe a word of it to anyone. It wouldn't do for the world to find out that the county's most politically powerful man is riddled with syphilis.'

He handed a length of narrow silver tube to James.

'Take this and cut two pieces from it of two inches each. Then file their ends smooth, and round them.'

While James sawed and filed, Nairn sketched on to a sheet of paper a heart-shaped design with two elongated protrusions at top and bottom, which he then used as a template to cut out a piece of soft leather of the same shape and size.

'It's a relatively simple procedure,' Nairn explained. 'I shall firstly pare down the remnants of the destroyed nose to obtain a fresh surface. Then this leather template is laid upon the patient's forehead so . . .' Nairn demonstrated. 'The outline is traced upon the skin, and then the flap of integument and cellular tissue dissected and brought down and fixed in apposition to the base by points of suture to form the new nose. The blood supply for the flap is ensured by cutting a trifle deeper at the lower end; the twist will not impair the flow. The nostril openings will be primarily formed by some tubes of oiled lint, and they will also give support to the flap.'

James listened intently, excitement churning his stomach. He thought it wonderful that he was going to assist in such a dramatic restoration of a deformed face. And for the hundredth time he blessed the good fortune that had brought him such a mentor.

'Afterwards we merely have to keep the nose covered with lint moistened with warm water and shielded by oiled silk. We'll use stimulating lotion to expedite the cicatrisation of the wound, and when granulation commences the silver tubes will be placed in situ in the nostrils.'

'Will that be the finish of it, Uncle?'

'Good Lord, no. Merely the first part. Once the main body of the nose has become consolidated and healed I shall then restore the columna, utilising a section dissected from the upper lip for that purpose. But I will explain that procedure in detail when the time comes. The only aspect which causes me some concern is that there is presently some infection of the tissues. But I should be able to cut those parts out.'

'Sean will be sorely disappointed he's missed seeing you perform this operation,' James remarked.

Fitzgerald had gone to Ireland to visit relatives and would not be back for some weeks.

'It's perhaps for the best that Sean is not here.' Nairn smiled. 'In his cups he at times becomes less than discreet, and as I told you, the cause for this deformity must remain our secret.'

He sorted out the necessary implements for the operation and then told James, 'Go and fetch our patient, Nephew.'

*   *   *

The solidly constructed wooden armchair with its unusually high backrest was directly beneath the fanlight and Nairn invited Chamberson to seat himself in it.

When he saw the leather straps in Nairn's hands, Chamberson protested. 'I do not need to be trussed, Nairn.'

'My lord, it is for your own benefit. The pain will be intense, and if you should move while I am cutting close to vital nerves then it might cause irreparable harm to yourself.'

'I shan't flinch,' Chamberson stated positively.

'But, my lord—' Nairn began, and was cut short.

'I shall not flinch, Nairn. If I should, then I will take full responsibility for any consequence.'

Seeing that the man was adamant, Nairn reluctantly surrendered.

'Very well, my lord. But at least take a draught of laudanum to deaden the pain somewhat.'

'Do you have brandy?'

'I do.'

'Then give me a glass of it, and be damned to the laudanum.'

Chamberson drained the glass in a single gulp, then seated himself and nodded. 'I'm ready.' He pressed his head back against the high rest, and gripped the wooden arms.

Nairn placed the leather against Chamberson's forehead and traced its outline with pen and ink, then laid it aside and took up his scalpel.

James stood at his uncle's side ready to use the dry sponge to mop up the blood, waiting expectantly for Chamberson's screams of pain, confident now that they would not disconcert him as they once did.

The scalpel sliced into the raw flesh of the gaping hole. Chamberson's eyes bulged and he emitted a strangled moan. His hands squeezed so tightly upon the wooden arms that they whitened, but he made no movement.

James marvelled at his courage, and simultaneously marvelled at his uncle's dexterity as the scalpel delicately sliced minute slivers of flesh which Nairn took between finger and thumb and tossed aside.

The hole prepared, it took only scant minutes to dissect the flap from the forehead and place it in position. Blood ran freely creating a scarlet mask of Chamberson's features.

'Clear the blood and suture there and there.' Nairn indicated the lowest section of the dissected area.

James quickly obeyed, aware only of the necessity for mechanical expertise. He was completely unconscious now of the continuous keening moaning, and bulging, agony-filled eyes of the patient.

'Good.' Nairn grunted in satisfaction. 'Now apply damp lint to the forehead, and cover it with oiled silk. I'll suture the nose when the bleeding stops. Watch carefully now, Nephew, for the edges of the wound to assume a glazed appearance. That always precedes the beginning of secretion, and that is the time to suture the nose, because that is the most likely time for successful union to occur.'

A little later he sutured the new nose in position and adjusted the tubes of oiled lint in the nostrils.

'We'll replace these with the silver tubes in three or four days.'

Then he straightened and regarded his handiwork with a satisfied air.

'That will do splendidly.'

James stared at the bloodied lump of flesh, and was forced to admit to himself that it bore little or no resemblance to a nose.

Nairn grinned perceptively. 'Believe me, Nephew, in a month or so, after I've fashioned the columna, that will indeed be a new nose. Now, apply the dressing over it and use tape to keep it in position: dampened lint and oiled silk, the same as for the forehead.'

Chamberson's moaning ceased, and Nairn told him, 'You have borne it extremely well, my lord. Allow me to express my admiration for your fortitude.'

With the dressings in place, Chamberson's bloodshot eyes peered through a slit. Only his mouth and chin were fully visible, his lips torn and bloody from where his teeth had gnawed in his anguish. He expelled breath in a series of loud gasps, and then choked out distortedly, 'Give me brandy.'

His hands shook so violently as he took the glass that its contents were spilled before he could raise it to his lips.

James took the glass from him, refilled it, and with one hand resting on the back of Chamberson's head, lifted the glass to the torn lips. Chamberson gagged and coughed and the liquor ran down his chin, but he begged, 'More. I need more.'

James had refilled the glass three times before Chamberson signalled enough, and slumped down in the chair, panting wheezily. James looked down at the bent head and inwardly applauded the man's courage.

Nairn waited a while, then suggested, 'We shall take you to your bed now, my lord, if you feel able to move. You will be more comfortable there.'

They half led, half carried the tottering man up to his bedroom and made him as comfortable as they could.

Back downstairs in the study Nairn poured two glasses of brandy and handed one to James.

'This has been well-earned, Nephew. Though I say it myself, I've made a fine job of it today.'

'Indeed you have, Uncle,' James agreed enthusiastically. 'I was surprised at Chamberson's courage.'

Nairn nodded. 'Yes, I have to give him full credit for his fortitude.'

He sipped from his glass and eyed James speculatively.

'There's something I've been meaning to talk with you about. Rather a delicate matter.'

'What's that, Uncle?'

James felt a stirring of misgiving, which escalated uncomfortably as Nairn said, 'It's about the Widow Wybergh. Rumour has it that you are seeing a great deal of her lately. What displeases me is that rumour also has it that you have been spending nights at her house?'

James could feel the flush spreading up from his throat, and at first made no reply.

'Well?' Nairn pressed. 'Do you deny the rumour?'

James drew a deep breath. He had been dreading that this confrontation might eventually occur. Now it had, he steeled himself to be truthful.

'Rumour has it correctly, Uncle. Mrs Wybergh and I are lovers.'

Nairn scowled. 'Lovers? And her husband not yet cold in his grave?'

'He's been dead more than a year,' James protested.

'She is still in full mourning,' Nairn countered. 'It is disgusting that you both should behave so. It is an insult to her husband.'

James shook his head and replied defensively, 'I do not feel it is disgusting, Uncle. Julius Wybergh is dead and gone. How can he be insulted?'

'You are offending the proprieties of polite society. You are behaving like ignorant labourers instead of gentlefolk.'

'Offending the proprieties of polite society?' James's temper flared suddenly. 'And who are these polite society? These gentlefolk? Men such as Edward Harcourt, who has brought many trusting fools to ruination? Or the Bromsgrove nail-masters and Redditch needle-masters who grind their opera-tives to premature deaths by underpaying and exploiting them so unmercifully? You shock me, Uncle, by holding up our local polite society as examples of virtue, when you have always been so critical of them yourself. I have to tell you that it smacks of hypocrisy.'

The harsh truth of the words struck home and forced Septimus Nairn to question whether or not he was justified in castigating his nephew for what was after all no real sin.

For several minutes he stood ruminating silently.

Faced with this silence James's temper subsided as quickly as it had flared, and he felt ashamed at how harshly he had spoken to this man who had shown him nothing but kindness.

'Uncle, I had no right to speak to you in such a tone. It was unpardonable. I'm ashamed of my words and apologise most sincerely for them.'

Nairn shook his head. 'There is no need for any apology, Nephew. You spoke only the truth.' He paused reflectively, then went on. 'But while I accept the truth of your words, you must also accept that we are dependent for our daily bread upon this same society. Without their patronage we should be reduced to poverty.'

'I would be reduced to poverty, Uncle. But not you. You are too skilled a surgeon for that. They need you more than you need them,' James asserted forcefully, and believed utterly in that assertion.

Nairn grimaced wryly. 'It's a sad fact of life, Nephew, that we doctors kill more than we cure. Our patients would many times be better served by doing without our treatments.'

'No, Uncle. I cannot accept that.' James refused to believe this statement.

'You will learn,' Nairn said quietly. 'However, let us return to the matter in hand, namely your relationship with Mrs Wybergh. What do you intend to do about it? Take the time to think very carefully on it before you give me your answer.'

'Very well, Uncle,' James agreed.

Now Nairn's manner changed and he became brusque and businesslike.

'I have to go on my rounds now. I want you to remain with our patient. Dampen the dressings every three hours. The second time of dampening apply a stimulating lotion to the wounds. If he is able to take food or drink, then give him some port wine or beef tea, but not overmuch of either. Mix a draught of laudanum with whatever he takes. When he sleeps you will need to remain wakeful and ensure that he does not interfere with the dressings or handle the wounds in any manner.

'I shall relieve you at midnight and you will take over the watch again at six o'clock tomorrow morning. We'll continue to watch over him turn and turn about for the next forty-eight hours. By then he will have recovered sufficiently to be left by himself.'

69

James nodded, and still driven by feelings of shame offered, 'I can continue the watch through the night.'

'No. You must have some sleep.' Nairn added, 'And I trust that before too long you will be able to give me your answer concerning Mrs Wybergh. Much depends upon it.'

Nine

C hamberson gave James no cause for concern. He drank the port wine with its admixture of laudanum and slept throughout the evening, moaning and muttering, but hardly moving.

The hours passed very slowly for James and his mind was greatly troubled. He sat staring at the fluttering candle flames, examining his feelings towards Mercedes Wybergh. Their affair had now lasted for several months, and he was becoming increasingly aware that the heat of the passion he had felt for her was cooling. Her demands that he should tell her of his love for her now irritated him. Her constant questionings of how he spent the time away from her had started to feel like a domineering intrusion into his personal privacy.

Previously he had taken pleasure in the aftermath of love-making, savouring the way that she clung to him, murmuring endearments, nuzzling his body with her lips, running her fingers through his hair. Lately, however, he was finding that after making love he wanted to be lying alone, free from her embrace.

He was also realising that the age gap between them mattered more and more to him as time passed. He could not help but compare his own body's smooth tautness with her slack belly, drooping breasts and heavily dimpled thighs. He had begun to find himself looking at the young girls he encountered and judging their freshness of skin and body against the ageing skin and body of Mercedes, to her detriment.

During the previous weeks Mercedes had begun to talk frequently of marriage, and James had experienced a rapidly escalating disquiet as he realised that she was becoming determined that he should someday marry her. The situation had culminated during their last assignation when she had said openly that he must marry her when her period of mourning was over, and when he had refused to commit himself they had parted in an atmosphere of tension.

Even before his uncle had brought the matter up, James, knowing that he didn't want to marry Mercedes, had already toyed with the idea of breaking off their relationship. But he was a kind-hearted young man, and guilt racked him when he thought of how he might hurt her by doing so. He was also honest enough to admit to himself that he still enjoyed their physical relationship, and was flattered by the fact that she was so obviously besotted with him. But at the same time this also troubled him, and he wondered uncomfortably if he was behaving with a selfish cruelty by wanting her more for sex, than for loving companionship.

Am I just using her, as I would use a whore? he asked himself over and over again during the long hours. I like her well enough as a person, and I treat her kindly. Yet do I do this solely because I still want to bed her at times? Am I one of those men who enjoys wielding power over women for its own sake? Am I in all truth a cruel and heartless man?

James was finding out the hard way that he was a creature of conscience.

At midnight Septimus Nairn came to the sickroom. He briefly studied the sleeping patient and nodded.

'He looks well enough. Go and get some sleep, Nephew.'

James knew that sleep would not come easily to him, troubled as he was by thoughts of Mercedes Wybergh.

'Can we talk, Uncle?'

'If you wish.'

'It's about Mrs Wybergh.'

Nairn's eyes were kindly as he saw the drawn look in the younger man's face, but his voice was deliberately devoid of any inflection.

'I am of the opinion that if you wish to build a successful practice here, then you would do well to end your relationship with her, Nephew. People expect their doctor to lead a moral life'. He shrugged. 'Of course, if it is your intention to marry her, and live off her money, then it will not matter how successful or unsuccessful your practice might be. She is a very wealthy woman and can keep you in luxury.'

'I've no wish to marry her. It has never been any part of my ambitions to have a woman keep me.' James was both hurt and indignant that his uncle should think this of him, and now he voiced this. 'I'm sorry that you should hold me in such low regard as to even think such a thing. I had hoped you knew me better than that.'

Nairn frowned and said sternly, 'Don't take that tone with me. I stand here as your employer and your mentor, and perhaps even as your surrogate parent. By indulging yourself with this affair, you risk bringing my name into disrepute as well as your own. Because it will be said that *he* knew of it, and winked at it. You also risk bringing Mrs Wybergh into disrepute, and with her, her son. No matter how hypocritical polite society may appear, we still must live by its proclaimed mores. And as physicians we ourselves, above all others, must be seen to follow the code of a gentleman: to behave with honour and rectitude. That is why our patients trust us with their innermost secrets, and place their lives in our hands. If a physician takes advantage of any person's weakness to gratify his own base instincts, then he is a disgrace to our profession. And that is what you have done, Nephew. You have taken advantage of a woman's weakness. And what is worse, you did so when she was at her most vulnerable.'

He paused, waiting to see if James would make any protest.

James stayed silent as guilt and shame whelmed over him.

'Don't stand silent, Nephew,' Nairn goaded. 'Say your piece.'

James was experiencing heartfelt remorse, and he could find no words.

Nairn sensed that he had struck hard and deep, and was glad that this young man, whom he cared so much for, was now

73

conscious of having behaved wrongly. Again he goaded, 'Acting surly will not serve you, Nephew.'

James forced himself to admit quietly, 'It is not surliness which keeps me silent, Uncle. It is shame.'

'I'm glad to hear it,' Nairn snapped curtly. 'And now tell me, how do you intend to put matters right?'

James shook his head in helpless bafflement. 'Indeed, I don't know what I can do. If I tell Mrs Wybergh that all is over between us, then I fear that she will be heartbroken. On the other hand, if I were to marry her, then I would be acting dishonourably, because I do not have sufficient love for her to want her for my wife. I fear that in time she would come to know this, and eventually we would begin to hate each other because of the falseness of our union.'

Nairn smiled in grim amusement.

'Your tender heart does you credit, Nephew. But I don't think that you need worry too much about Widow Wybergh's broken heart. Women's hearts are made of resilient material. They mend very quickly. Her pride will be hurt more than her heart. But she is an attractive and very wealthy woman. There are a great many men hereabouts who will be more than happy to pay court to her, and assuage her hurt pride.'

James couldn't repress a feeling of mortification that his uncle could so cavalierly discount the intensity and depth of Mercedes' love for him.

'As for the question of marriage, I am very glad to hear that you would never consider marrying for mercenary motives. I also believe that such unions eventually lead to mutual hatred between man and wife . . . So then, what's to be done, Nephew?'

James could only shake his head helplessly. 'I truly don't know. Can't you tell me what I should do?'

'You must end the relationship immediately, before these rumours become established facts,' Nairn stated bluntly.

'But how shall I tell her?' James was woefully aware of his own lack of worldly experience when it came to the love of women. 'How can I avoid causing her pain and distress?'

Again the smile of grim amusement hovered on Nairn's lips.

'I shouldn't overestimate the potential pain and distress you may cause her, Nephew. She is more likely to react with fury. I advise you to speak frankly and honestly to her. Tell her that you have no wish to marry, and that because of these rumours you feel it best that you should cease from being lovers, and prevent her reputation from being irredeemably tarnished.'

James considered what he had been told, then nodded unhappily. 'Very well, Uncle. I shall go to see Mrs Wybergh tomorrow.'

Nairn patted the younger man's shoulder with commiseration.

'Don't feel too guilty, Nephew. You haven't ruined the life of some young innocent girl. All you have done is to allow your sexual hungers to rule you. But let this be a lesson that you fully absorb. Pleasures must be paid for, and the price is all too often a painful one to pay.'

'I think I have learned that already, Uncle,' James agreed miserably.

Ten

Mercedes Wybergh stared anxiously into the mirror as her fingertips traced the faint line on her forehead which she was convinced had not been there the previous day. She tilted her head back to tighten the skin of her throat and firm the puffiness of her jawline. Then bared her teeth, drawing her lips up to examine whether her gums were receding.

Long in the tooth, she told herself with despair. I'm becoming long in the tooth. A sense of desperation burgeoned. I'm becoming old and ugly, she thought.

This is why he is cooling towards me. She felt near to tears as she dwelt on the dark shadows beneath her eyes, which in her depression she exaggerated to deep pits.

For some time Mercedes had feared that her hold over James Kerr was slipping, and that fear was becoming a torture for her. The affair that she had entered upon as a purely physical satisfaction of her flesh had escalated beyond her emotional control, and she was now utterly besotted with her young lover. He dominated all her thoughts, all her emotions, all her desires, and she was terrified that some day she might lose him.

She heard the beating of horses' hooves, and went to the window to see who was approaching the house. Her heart pounded as she saw James Kerr riding up the driveway. She wondered what was the reason for this totally unexpected daytime visit, and hope and dread simultaneously battled for mastery. Has he come to tell me he wants to marry me? she asked herself Or is there some other reason?

She refused to surrender to the impulse to rush downstairs and welcome him. Mercedes Wybergh possessed a strong personal pride, and a character moulded by years of strict chaperonage and self-discipline. No matter how wantonly she might abandon herself to her young lover in the privacy of her bedchamber, in public Mercedes Wybergh always conducted herself as a gentlewoman was expected to.

Her maid came to announce that James Kerr wished to speak with her.

'Tell the gentleman I shall be down presently.'

Mercedes waited for some minutes with hands tight-clasped, fervently praying: Dear God, please make him ask me to marry him. Please make him want to marry me.

But even as she prayed a cold voice whispered in her mind, He doesn't. He won't.

Tense-bodied, stomach nervously twisting, upbraiding himself for his own cowardice, James Kerr was dreading what was to come. He feared that if Mercedes reacted with any hysterical display of emotion to what he was going to tell her, he would not be able to cope with it, and would take to his heels like a coward.

'James?' She came towards him, her face pale, a forced smile upon her lips, her eyes fearful. 'This is an unexpected pleasure. I was not thinking to see you today.'

They were alone in the room and Mercedes went to kiss him.

In involuntary reflex, his hands went up and held her back, and the instant instinctive realisation that this signalled the end of their relationship made Mercedes feel faint and nauseated.

James fumbled for words. 'Mercedes, I have something to tell you, which I fear may cause you some distress. It has never been my wish to hurt you . . .'

She drew upon depths of pride and strength which she had never known she possessed.

'Please, there is no need for explanation. Just go.'

He stared in shocked surprise, and she met his gaze with steady eyes, and repeated firmly, 'Go now, James. Please. Go now.'

Relief coursed through him, and he opened his mouth to tell

77

her how sorry he was, how he hoped that they might continue to be friends. But before he could voice a single word she ordered sharply, 'Go! I don't wish to hear anything you might say. Go!'

He surrendered to his own overwhelming desire to escape, and bowed, then turned and almost ran from the room.

Outside on the forecourt he mounted and kicked the horse into a fast canter down the long driveway. His spirits soared; he was giddy with relief, saying to himself, It was just as Uncle told me. She really didn't give a damn, did she? What a fool I've been to have been worrying so about her, to have been feeling so guilty. She really didn't give a damn, just as Uncle said she didn't. Thank God it's all over. Never again! I'll never get myself into such a pickle with a woman ever again.

Back in the drawing room, Mercedes Wybergh was on her knees, body racked with harsh heaving cries of grief, while in the hall her maid listened avidly, ear pressed to the closed door.

Eleven

T he sounds of retching carried clearly to Liddy as she walked past the row of outdoor privies at the side of the workhouse early on Sunday morning. She would have walked on if the retching had not ceased and a voice she recognised as Hannah Kearn's wailed, 'I wish I was dead. I wish I was dead and gone out of this.'

Liddy halted and listened intently.

'Now don't say such things. It might be you've just got a sick stomach.'

The second voice was Maria Peat's. Both girls were in one of the privies.

Liddy waited, uncertain of what to do. If Hannah Kearns was ill then the workhouse regulations stated that that fact must be reported to the matron immediately. But Liddy knew only too well that the inmates were reluctant to report sick because the invariable reaction from Amelia Melen was to accuse them of malingering in an effort to avoid work.

There came the sounds of more retching, and then after a little time the door of the privy opened and the two girls came out. Hannah Kearn's thin face was white and clammy-sweated, and Maria Peat looked worried, but the instant they saw Liddy both girls' expressions became sullen and guarded.

Liddy was concerned at how ill Hannah looked, and told her, 'Hannah, you must report to the matron that you're ill.'

The girl wouldn't meet Liddy's eyes, but stood mutely staring

79

at the ground. Liddy turned to Maria Peat. 'How long has she been like this, Maria?'

The pug features were belligerent. 'Not long, miss. She's just got a sick stomach, that's all. She'll be all right.'

'Are you in pain, Hannah?' Liddy questioned, and when the girl still refused to meet her eyes, sharpened her tone. 'Hannah, will you answer me, please. Do you have any pain?'

'No, miss,' the girl muttered, still staring at the ground.

'She'll be all right, miss, if she's just left in peace. That's all she wants. Just to be let alone for a bit. I'll look after her,' Maria Peat stated forcefully.

Liddy sighed unhappily. She was genuinely concerned for the girl, yet at the same time did not want to badger her.

'Very well,' she accepted reluctantly. 'But if this sick stomach persists, then you must report it to the matron.'

'All right, miss. She will,' Maria Peat promised, and led her friend away.

Liddy returned to her own room and dressed herself in readiness to accompany the paupers to the church for their once-monthly morning service.

She was dreading the trek through the town. On several occasions in the past she had witnessed the pauper procession along the High Street and heard with disgust the insults and jeers directed at them by the town's riff-raff. And now she herself was to be part of that procession, and a target for those jeers and insults.

I'll just hold my head high, and look straight in front of me, she decided. I'll not let the roughs provoke me into answering them back.

Half an hour later, the long crocodile file of paupers shambled two by two down the High Street. At their head strode Henry Melen, glowering at the onlookers as if daring them to shout at him personally. His tall, strong build and hard-etched features exuded a menace that kept him free from insult. Amelia Melen walked by her husband's side, her rosy handsome face deliberately impassive and ignoring all around her. At intervals along the column, overseers kept a watchful guard on their charges. The paupers knew that any interchange of words or signals with those whom they passed would bring down savage punishment on their heads so they took care to keep their eyes downcast.

Today the hooligans were concentrating their attention on the rear of the column where Liddy walked alongside her files of children, her face burning with angry embarrassment under the barrage of jeering catcalls and lewd shouts and invitations.

'What's a piece of sweet meat like you doing in the fuckin' bastille?'

'I'll bet that's why her's in there. Her's bin fuckin' too much.'

'Suck my dick and I'll let you come and live wi' me.'

'By Christ, I'd make you scream if I got between your legs, my pretty.'

By the time she had travelled fifty yards along the High Street, Liddy's temper was near to flashpoint, and when one of the ruffians darted forwards and tried to lift her skirts, she exploded.

'You filthy beast!' she shouted and slapped him across his stubbled face with all the force she could muster. He was so shocked that he stumbled backwards, tripped and fell, and a roar of mocking laughter and cheering greeted this.

The smaller children, alarmed by this sudden violence, began to mill about fearfully, and Liddy was forced to turn from her attacker to calm them. The ruffian sprang to his feet, bellowing in fury.

'You fuckin' cow! I'll put your fuckin' lights out!'

He started towards her, but before he had covered more than two steps, a horseman suddenly charged out from an alleyway and the horse's shoulder cannoned into the man, sending him sprawling again.

Liddy stared up in shock at James Kerr.

'Take the children on, I'll deal with this scum,' James ordered, and she gratefully obeyed. Shepherding the children in front of her, she urged them to hurry to catch up with the rest of the column.

James interposed his horse between the gang of hooligans

81

and the column. He pointed his horsewhip at the face of the now-risen ruffian.

'Any more trouble from you, John Powell, and I'll have you brought before the magistrates.'

The legger – a member of a gang of ne'er-do-wells – recognised his assailant, and although he lusted for revenge he knew that to attack a gentleman would almost inevitably bring the retribution of the law down on his own head.

'I was only having a bit o' fun,' he blustered.

'Well, take your fun elsewhere,' James warned. 'And one more word from you will be a word too many.'

Scowling and muttering beneath his breath the legger turned away.

A tremor of nervousness struck through James as the rest of the gang glowered up at him. For a moment or two he thought that they were going to swarm on to him, but then they also turned away, and with relief he kneed his mount to follow after the pauper column.

When he caught up with Liddy he dismounted and walked beside her leading his horse.

She smiled at him gratefully. 'Thank you for what you did, James. I don't know what might have happened if you hadn't saved me.'

He felt ill at ease at meeting her again. The memory of her previous rejection of his advances still rankled, even though since the start of his passionate affair with Mercedes Wybergh he had not thought of Lydia Landser very often.

'I was sorry to hear of your mother's death.'

'It was a happy release for her,' Liddy answered. 'I'd expected to see you at the workhouse. You come there sometimes, don't you? Did you know that I'd become the schoolmistress there?'

'Yes, I knew that,' he replied brusquely.

Liddy was puzzled by his manner, not understanding why he was behaving so stiffly when they had previously so enjoyed each other's company.

As he got over his initial surprise at this meeting, James

found himself looking at her appreciatively, enjoying her pretty face, and the glossy ringlets escaping from her bonnet. He realised that she still exerted a powerful attraction over him and her friendly attitude caused him to wonder if after all she might be regretting her previous rejection of him. His rancour abruptly disappeared, and his customary good humour gained ascendancy. He noted that she appeared tired: there were dark shadows beneath her lucent eyes, and, concerned, asked her, 'Are you in good health, Liddy?'

'Indeed I am, I thank you,' she assured him, while inwardly examining her own pleasure at meeting this young man once again. I feel so pleased to see him, she thought. He must have made a deeper impression on me than I realised. He is looking very handsome, is he not.

Aloud she asked, 'Tell me, James, why did your uncle cease treating my mother? Was it because of money, or rather the lack of it?'

He shook his head. 'No, Liddy. The parish would have paid our fees. I regret to have to tell you that your father refused my uncle, myself and Mr Fitzgerald any access to your mother. I fear that . . .'

He hesitated uncertainly, until she urged him to continue.

'. . . I hope that you will take no offence, because I do assure you that none is intended. But your father's mental and physical condition has sadly deteriorated. However, he is not legally a madman, so we have no legal powers to treat him against his will. Likewise, of course, we couldn't force entrance to the cottage or force your father to give us access to your mother.'

He examined her delicately freckled features anxiously.

'I truly pray that I have not distressed you too much by speaking so frankly, Liddy.'

'You haven't, James.' She looked fully at him and told him levelly, 'I won't play the hypocrite by claiming that my mother's condition, or her death, grieved me deeply. There was no love between her and me. It's my father I'm grieved for. We were always so close and loving towards each other. I can't bear to see him as he has become. I'm hoping that Dr Burman will cure him of the drink mania.'

'I've heard of Burman. He has a sound reputation. But he charges high prices, does he not?'

She grimaced wryly. 'He does indeed. But Edward Harcourt has insisted on loaning me sufficient money to pay Burman. And he refuses to charge any interest on the loan.'

James was surprised by this, knowing Harcourt's reputation as a hard-headed avaricious man of business.

'He has proved to be a true friend to me.' Liddy smiled. 'He's become my guardian angel.'

James nodded non-committally, but silently wondered if Edward Harcourt's kindness to her had hidden strings attached.

By now the column of paupers was beginning to climb up the short steep entrance pathway of the church burial ground.

'We must part now, James.' Liddy was reluctant to finish this conversation, and on impulse asked, 'Would you think me shamefully forward if I told you that I would like to see you again?'

'No, indeed,' he replied eagerly. 'I was about to ask you if I might call on you at the workhouse.'

A glow of happiness suddenly lightened Liddy's spirits, and she could not help but coquette a little.

'I'm not sure if the Melens would approve of me receiving a gentleman caller.'

He chuckled, and told her, 'Then I shall make my call an official one as part of my medical duties. The Melens will not be able to object to that, so their approval is of no consequence.'

He took her hand, and pressed it warmly. 'Until we meet again, Liddy, which hopefully will be in the very near future.'

Liddy continued on up the pathway, and James stayed watching her until she disappeared from view, both of them experiencing a sense of pleasurable anticipation towards their next meeting.

James rode back to Tardebigge happier than he had been for some time. His affair with Mercedes Wybergh had had an aftermath. She had left her house and gone to Spain, and James was troubled with ambiguous feelings. He missed their passionate love-making, and also he discovered that he had become more emotionally attached to her than he had realised. Her departure had left him feeling to some extent bereft.

Back at the house his uncle told him, 'Our patient is waiting for you, Nephew. He's eager for a game of chess.'

'Very well. By the way, I met up with Lydia Landser in the town. She seems happy enough even though she's been forced into becoming the workhouse schoolmarm.'

'I'm glad to hear that. Poor child.' Septimus Nairn showed his sympathy. 'By God, that family has been brought low. She must have suffered a deal of heartbreak these last months.'

'Well, she hasn't let it break her spirit.' James was admiring. 'In fact she appeared to be in remarkably good spirits. I'm going to call on her next week.'

A smile hovered momentarily on Nairn's grim features. 'You still find her attractive, do you, Nephew?'

'Yes, I do,' James admitted readily.

Nairn shook his head in mock despair. 'By God, Nephew! You have a positive talent for being attracted to totally unsuitable women. First of all, it's a widow old enough to be your mother, and now it's a young girl whose family is ruined, and is to all intents and purposes a pauper herself.'

James knew that he was being bantered, and took it in good part. 'I haven't expressed any intention of marrying Lydia Landser, have I? I merely said that I find her attractive.'

Nairn became serious. 'I confess that I hope for you to some day marry a wife who can bring money and property with her. Better a plain face and wealth, than a pretty face and poverty . . . Now, go and play chess with our patient. He's taken a great liking to you, and to gain the patronage of such a powerful man would serve you well in your future career.'

In his bedroom, Humphrey Chamberson, Earl of Allesley, was sitting at the chessboard with the pieces placed ready for play.

'I heard your arrival, Jamie.' His eyes shone welcomingly.

Thick plastering covered his forehead, the middle of his face and upper lip, from which a small sliver had been resected four days before to form the columna for his new nose.

James smiled. He had conceived a reciprocal liking for Chamberson during the weeks the man had lived at the house. Chamberson had borne his considerable pain and discomfort without complaint, had been an undemanding guest, and had proven to be an erudite and pleasant companion. He and James had spent many hours in each other's company, talking, playing chess, walking out during the hours of darkness to avoid the prying eyes of neighbours.

Once a day James mixed a solution of cyanide of mercury and water, and using a camel-hair brush rubbed it into the syphilitic rashes and sores on Chamberson's throat, tongue, anus and penis. He also at intervals of several days administered mercurial steam fumigations of camphor because this method did not affect the functions of the patient's stomach and intestines as deleteriously as other modes of treatment might.

As he came to know James, and to trust him, Chamberson had confided the identity of the woman he believed had infected him, who was the young wife of a prominent colonial bishop. Chamberson also asserted, and James believed him, that he had not indulged in any sexual relations since he had first discovered that he had syphilis.

James greatly admired Chamberson's courageous acceptance that his infection was by now incurable, and that he faced a future filled with suffering which could even include eventual blindness or the onset of insanity before he died.

'I draw much comfort from the fact that I never married, Jamie,' he would say frequently. 'I could have infected my wife, or any children we would have had before realising that I had myself become infected.'

'What will happen to your title, my lord?' James asked one day.

'It will pass on to my cousin, Timothy, together with my houses and lands and other property, and of course my money. He's a cretin, but a good-hearted one.'

James could not suppress pangs of envy for the fortunate Timothy, cretin though he might be.

They were both strong chess players, and now they won one game each and drew the third, before Chamberson tired of playing.

He leaned back in his chair and stared speculatively at the younger man.

'Do you have ambitions, Jamie? For high position perhaps?'

'Not really, my lord. I sometimes imagine how it would be to become a great figure in the land, but my main ambition is only to become as skilful a surgeon as my uncle.'

'You admire your uncle greatly, don't you?'

'Oh yes,' James stated emphatically. 'He is a wonderful man. A great man, even.'

'Something of a Radical as well, I believe.' Chamberson's eyes twinkled mischeviously.

'He believes in speaking the truth concerning the injustices that abound in this country,' James declared with fervour. 'And if that causes him to be thought of as a Radical, then I must be considered to be a Radical also. Because I respect and admire him for it.'

'To be considered a Radical could well harm your prospects of advancement in your profession,' Chamberson said gravely. 'There are many people in society who look askance at Radicals. They regard them as being dangerous revolutionaries.'

'It does not appear to have harmed my uncle's practice,' James countered. 'After all, my lord, are you not a pillar of society yourself?'

Chamberson's eyes hardened, and for a moment James expected an angry riposte. Then the man chuckled. 'You have scored a good hit, Jamie. You should take up fencing. I'm sure you would prove adept with the rapier.'

'I did not intend to cause you any offence, my lord,' James told him apologetically.

'You did not.' Chamberson stretched and yawned. 'I feel like sleeping now, my boy.'

'Then I'll say goodnight, my lord. Do you wish for anything?'

'No, thank you.'

When James went to leave, Chamberson said, 'Hold a moment, Jamie. As you know I shall be leaving here shortly. I want to assure you, that if at any time in the future I can help you in any way, then my door will always be open to you.'

'Thank you, my lord.' James felt very gratified.

Later that night, when James told his uncle of what Chamberson had said, Nairn grinned in huge satisfaction.

'Excellent, Nephew! You have gained what every young man needs above all else if he is to succeed in life. A friend in high places.'

Twelve

O ld Bridie Harper was being made ready for burial when James Kerr arrived in the workhouse sick ward for his weekly visit. In the beds on each side of her, the other women, girls and small children watched the laying-out process with apparent unconcern, and those women who were well enough to make any comment merely made obscene jokes as Nurse Kings and her pauper helpers carried out the necessary offices for the corpse.

James made no remonstrance against this callous display, even though he personally found it distasteful. He had come to know all too well that pauper inmates, who in life were regarded as being of less value than the beasts of the field, could not expect to be treated with any degree of reverence or respect when dead.

'That's it then, sir.' Nurse Kings completed her task and smiled with satisfaction. 'She looks too neat and tidy for burial in the Potters Field, don't she, though I say it meself.'

The small corpse lay on its back clad in a coarse white shift, jaws strapped shut with a bandage, pennies on its eyes, arms crossed on withered breasts, big toes tied together.

'Indeed she does, Nurse Kings. Perhaps we might ask the Guardians to buy a private plot for her,' James suggested ironically. 'At what time did she die?'

He had no real interest in the answer. There was nothing he could have done to prolong Bridie Harper's life. She was too old and worn-out, and had once told him how much she longed for what to her would come as a happy release.

'Round about three o'clock. Same as most of the old 'uns do.

I came to have a look at her at midnight, and she was plucking the blanket and rambling on that her mam had come to fetch her. So I left Old Susan to keep the death watch. There was no point in me losing any more sleep over her, was there.'

'No, there wasn't,' James agreed equably. He was feeling in very good spirits. His typhus patient, Annie Clears, had now survived for nearly three weeks, despite suffering attacks of convulsions and delirium. When he had examined the woman in the death shed on his earlier arrival this morning, he found that her burning temperature had fallen dramatically and the fever appeared to have left her. She was very weak and torpid but he was now confident that she would live.

'You can bring Annie Clears back into the ward now, Nurse Kings. She'll need careful feeding. Start her with beef tea, and some rice pudding and arrowroot three times daily, and a glass of port wine four times daily, and a quart of good ale.'

The stocky woman smiled wryly. 'I don't know as how the matron 'ull agree to that diet, sir. The Board don't take kindly to us giving the inmates costly delicacies. And you know the rules against giving them any strong drink.'

'I'll speak to Mrs Melen about it before I leave.'

James was not prepared to brook any interference with his prescribed diet. He was proud to have saved Annie Clears, and had no intention of losing her now. Her strength must be built up with good nourishment and he meant to ensure that she should receive this, no matter how strongly the Board might object.

Other inmates were now coming into the ward to gawp at Bridie Harper. James made no remonstrance; it was an established custom here, but he never ceased to marvel at the macabre fascination that death in its multitudinous aspects held for the inmates.

He continued his round of the ward, moving from the female side to the male. The vast majority of the beds were filled with the old and the very young, and James had long since accepted that there was little he could do for the aged men and women except to try to relieve their pains and make them as comfortable as he was able. It was a similar case with most of the young children, the majority of whom had been born rickety-bodied, bronchial-chested, sickly in constitution, many with congenital illnesses. In this day and age, four out of five of the children of the slums died within the first few years of life. James did not allow himself to agonise over it. It was a fact of nature.

He considered himself fortunate to have Nurse Kings as his helper here. Although harsh and brusque-mannered, she was a conscientious woman who ensured that the patients were kept clean, their bedding changed regularly, their medicines and treatments administered to order. He thought himself fortunate as well in his relationship with the Melens. They were always pleasant with him, allowing him a virtually free hand, and normally accepting without demur his instructions about medication and diet for the sick inmates.

His rounds completed, he told Nurse Kings, 'I'll go and see Mrs Melen concerning Annie Clears' diet. Will you have her brought up here as soon as possible?'

'I will, sir,' the nurse assured him. 'She can have Old Bridie's bed.'

'Thank you.' James smiled and left the ward, his thoughts turning towards Lydia Landser. After I've spoken with the matron I'll go and see Liddy, he decided.

'Now, children, repeat after me . . . I believe in God the Father Almighty . . .'

'I believe in God, the Father Almighty . . .'

'Maker of heaven and earth . . .'

'Maker of heaven and earth . . .'

'And in Jesus Christ, his only son, Our Lord . . .' Liddy recited the Creed automatically, and paid little or no attention to the responses of the children.

Instead her eyes were drawn again and again to Hannah Kearns' thin, pallid face. She was convinced that something was badly wrong with the girl. This morning she had again found Hannah retching in the privy. When she asked her what the matter was, she had been met with a storm of tears, and a stubborn refusal to answer her questions.

I'm going to have to do something, Liddy determined. Hannah could be seriously ill.

'. . . Who was conceived by the Holy Ghost . . .'

'Who was conceived by the Holy Ghost . . .'

'Suffered under Pontius Pilate . . .'

'Suffered under Pontius Pilate . . .'

'Oh God!' Liddy gasped in dismay as Hannah Kearns suddenly swayed and fell headlong from the wooden bench.

Liddy rushed to her side, and as she knelt to examine the girl she heard one of the elder girls mutter, 'I bet her's up the duff. Me mam's always being sick and passing out every time she's up the duff.'

'You shut your fuckin' trap, Emma Taylor. Or I'll close it for you.' Maria Peat rounded furiously on the speaker.

She can't be pregnant! Liddy thought incredulously. She can't be! But even as she told herself this, memories crowded of the pregnant women at the salt works forever complaining of morning sickness and dizzy spells.

Hannah Kearns' eyelids fluttered and opened, and as the girl stared blankly up at her, Liddy said firmly, 'Stay still, Hannah. Don't try to get up yet. Maria, go and fetch Nurse Kings.' She spoke sharply to the excited children clustering noisily around her. 'And the rest of you be seated, and keep quiet. Do as I say.'

By the time Mrs Kings arrived Hannah had recovered sufficiently to sit up in Liddy's arms.

'What's ailing her?' the stocky-bodied nurse asked suspiciously. 'Trying it on, is she?'

'No, Mrs Kings, she's not trying it on,' Liddy told her firmly. 'The child's been poorly for weeks now. She'll have to be seen by the doctor. He's here now, isn't he?'

'It's for the matron to say who sees the doctor, not you,' Mrs Kings retorted.

Hannah Kearns tried to struggle free of Liddy's restraining arms. 'I'm all right, miss. I'm all right now.'

'No, Hannah, you're not all right. And you must be seen by

the doctor,' Liddy insisted, and the child began to sob heart-brokenly.

'Mrs Kings, let us have a word in private.' Liddy released the girl and gestured to the nurse to follow her into the corridor out of earshot of the children.

'I think that she might be pregnant, Mrs Kings.'

The other woman suddenly looked wary, and made no answer.

'She must be examined by the doctor,' Liddy insisted.

The nurse's weather-beaten features frowned with uncertainty.

'I'm going to see the matron myself.' Liddy was not prepared to argue further. 'And I'm going to see her now. Where is she?'

'I think she's talking with the young doctor. But she'll not take kindly to you going and pestering her while she's busy with him.'

'Then she'll just have to take it unkindly, won't she,' Liddy snapped, and hurried away.

Liddy met Amelia Melen on the stairs.

'I must speak with you, ma'am.'

'I'm very busy just now, Miss Landser. Can't it wait?'

'No, ma'am, it can't.'

The matron betrayed a momentary irritation at Liddy's presumptuous insistence. 'What is it then?'

'It's Hannah Kearns. She's not well at all.'

'I see. Well, thank you for bringing this to my attention, Miss Landser. You may leave it for me to deal with.'

'The medical gentleman is here now, is he not? He could examine the child,' Liddy suggested.

'That won't be possible.'

'But why not? She needs to be examined, ma'am. She's ill.'

Amelia Melen felt near to exploding in fury at this irritating human gadfly. But she knew that she must act warily. She could not risk berating this young woman who was becoming so close to Edward Harcourt.

She smiled sweetly. 'I'm on my way to speak with Mr Kerr.

93

I'll tell him about the girl. I take it that Hannah Kearns is not in any danger of dying at this very moment?'

'Well, no, I don't believe so,' Liddy admitted. 'But she is ill, ma'am. And I really do think it necessary that she is examined by the doctor as soon as possible. I fear that she could be pregnant, and it's making her ill.'

'Pregnant? That's not possible!' the matron denied emphatically.

'I think it is, ma'am,' Liddy asserted firmly, and briefly stated her reasons for believing this.

Amelia Melen's thoughts were racing. Hannah Kearns was little more than a child, and if she had become pregnant then the Board would demand explanation. Amelia Melen knew of cases of young girls becoming pregnant in other workhouses which had resulted in the dismissal of the Masters and Matrons for failing in their duty to protect the female children in their charge. She was not prepared to risk such an outcome for herself and her husband. If the girl was pregnant, then the matter must be kept as quiet as possible until she could take whatever measures were necessary to rectify the situation.

'Send the girl to her dormitory, Miss Landser, and I'll bring Mr Kerr there to examine her. And it's best that you don't talk of it to anyone else. At least not for the time being.'

'Very well, ma'am, I'll bring her directly.'

'No, you'd best stay with the others. Have Nurse Kings bring her.'

James was waiting in the Melens' private quarters, and when the matron came to him he first of all told her of his wishes concerning Annie Clears' diet.

She promised that his instructions would be carried out.

Then he requested politely, 'While I'm here I'd like to have a word with Miss Landser. We're old friends so I trust that there is no objection to my talking to her privately?'

This information took Amelia Melen by surprise, but as always she was quick to regain her mental balance. The last thing she wanted at this moment was for Lydia Landser to have

94

an opportunity to tell the young man about Hannah Kearns' possible pregnancy.

She exclaimed with regret, 'Of course there is no objection, Mr Kerr, but what a pity you didn't tell me of this sooner. I'm afraid Miss Landser isn't here at this time. She went out earlier on some business of her own.'

James experienced a sharp disappointment. 'Oh, I see. When will she return?'

'That's very hard to say. She told me that her business might take several hours. It could be nightfall before she comes back.'

The matron had noticed his disappointment and concluded, So, this one's smitten with the little bitch, just as Harcourt is.

This discovery of another prospective suitor of Lydia Landser was a welcome one to Amelia Melen. She might at some future opportunity be able to use it to create a breach between Lydia Landser and the powerful Edward Harcourt.

'I shall tell Miss Landser that you were asking for her, just as soon as she returns, Mr Kerr.'

'Thank you, Mrs Melen.'

In the dormitory Amelia Melen found to her displeasure that Lydia Landser had disobeyed her, and was sitting gently talking to the stubbornly silent Hannah Kearns who sat staring at the floor. The matron hid her anger, however, and asked, 'Where is Nurse Kings?'

'One of the boys cut his hand; she's dressing it for him.'

'Has the girl told you anything, Miss Landser?'

'No. She refuses to even speak to me.' Liddy was wondering where James Kerr was, and she could not resist asking, 'Is Mr Kerr coming?'

'No. He was late for an urgent appointment and had to leave.'

Amelia Melen's sharp gaze detected the shadow which passed across the younger woman's expressive features, and she told herself, the little bitch likes him. I'll have to make sure that Harcourt finds out.

She smiled at Liddy. 'You may leave Kearns to me to deal with now, Miss Landser.'

'Perhaps I can be of help, ma'am?' Liddy felt a reluctance to abandon the girl to the matron.

'No, Miss Landser, I think not.' Amelia Melen ordered Hannah Kearns sharply, 'Come with me, girl.'

The girl stared with mute appeal at Liddy who could only shrug helplessly and tell her, 'You must go with the matron, Hannah.'

Amelia Melen pushed Hannah through the door of her own private quarters and roughly ordered, 'Lift your skirt and lie down. Get your legs open.'

She roughly pushed and prodded deeply into the girl's frail body for several minutes before straightening and declaring, 'I think you are pregnant.'

She bent and grabbed the weeping girl by the hair. 'Who have you been whoring with, you little bitch?' She shook Hannah's head backwards and forwards and the girl cried out in pain. 'Tell me! Tell me his name!'

Frightened as she was of the matron, Hannah was even more terrified of Daniel White, believing implicitly his threats to kill her should she ever speak out about their liaison.

'Who is he?' The matron's hand whiplashed across the girl's face. 'Who is he?' She slapped the thin pallid cheeks until they burned bright red, and her hand was sore, but Hannah only sobbed and cried out in pain.

'All right then, you'll go down into my cellar and stay down there until you tell me. Down there with the rats.'

The matron dragged the weeping child into the scullery, lifted the trapdoor and forced her down the stone steps into the blackness, savagely threatening, 'And if I hear you shrieking, if you make any sound at all, I'll flay the hide from you.'

The trapdoor slammed shut and, shivering with fear of the rats, Hannah crouched against the damp greasy wall, trying to stifle her whimpers.

Amelia Melen spent the next hour going about her normal

duties in the house, but behind the facade of normality, she was thinking hard. Eventually she returned to her private quarters, poured herself a glass of gin and sat sipping it, deciding on what she must do. The Board of Guardians was to meet in a few days and one of the items on their agenda was the adoption of Katie Kennedy. She had prepared long and carefully for this and had no intention of allowing anything to put its successful conclusion at risk. She knew that by now the news of Hannah Kearns' suspected pregnancy would already have been circulated among the paupers. She also was almost certain who had made the girl pregnant. But she needed confirmation from Hannah Kearns. And she needed it now. Her fierce fury erupted, causing her to clench her fists and grit her strong teeth.

'I'll get the truth from the little bitch!' she exclaimed.

She drained her glass, lit an oil lamp and carried it down into the blackness of the cellar.

An hour later she emerged, breathing heavily, her rosy face pale now, and sheened with sweat. She drank straight from the bottle of gin, gasping as the fiery spirit hit her throat. The clock on the wall whirred and chimed, and she knew that she must act quickly and decisively. Her husband had gone into town, and he would be ensconced in his favourite ale house for at least another two hours.

Her breathing was easier now, and her cheeks were regaining their colour. She examined herself in the looking glass, and adjusted her mobcap and bonnet, tucking in the tendrils of hair which had escaped from confinement. Then she went to the porter's lodge.

When Daniel White opened the door of the porter's lodge she hissed, 'I need to have words with you, about one of the girls.'

'Words wi' me, Missus? About one of the girls?' His pustular, dirty-red face betrayed a flicker of alarm.

'Shut your mouth.' She pushed him back into the room and closed the door behind her.

Inside she scowled and hissed threateningly, 'Hannah Kearns has told me everything that you've done to her, and I'm going to see you hung for it.'

'I'se done nothing to her,' he blustered. 'Her's lying. Her's a lying little whore. I'se never touched her . . .'

Amelia Melen let him go on with his blusterings for several minutes, then abruptly silenced him with a hard slap across his mouth.

'Shut your rattle, you bloody animal!'

He gaped in soundless shock.

'Now you listen well.' She spoke in a low voice, that throbbed with threat. 'I know all about you. I know that you've had carnal connection with girl children before this time. I know that you've raped little girls. Well, you'll not be able to get out of it this time, like you did before at Shrewsbury Workhouse. I'll get you hung this time.'

He shook his head violently, his features writhing in terror.

'Don't anger me, White,' she warned, 'by keeping on denying what I know to be true. I can get you hung for raping Hannah Kearns and the others. Nobody will believe you this time. Not when I tell the magistrates what happened at Shrewsbury Workhouse.'

The man's nerve broke. 'I never forced her. It was her who kept coming to me and offering herself. She 'udden't give me any peace until I done it to her. It was her who wanted it. She 'udden't leave me be until I shagged her. Don't have me done for it, Missus! It wasn't my fault. It was all her fault. She kept on and on at me until I shagged her. She 'udden't give me no peace. Please don't have me done for it, Missus! Please! I beg you!'

She smiled triumphantly. 'Just think what it'll feel like when the rope's tight around your neck.'

He emitted a wail that sounded like an animal caught in a trap.

She deliberately waited, savouring his terror, then snapped sharply, 'Be quiet now. I've a mind to save your neck.'

Hope flickered across his brutish face, and he opened his mouth to speak, but before the words could come she slapped him viciously hard across the lips.

'Keep your mouth shut. You'll only answer when I tell you

to. For now you attend to your duties as normal. And say nothing to anyone. Do you understand? Say nothing to anyone.'

Relief glistened in his blood-shot eyes as he realised that he might have escaped from mortal danger. He began to snivel loudly, tugging his greasy forelock, repeatedly bobbing his head in grovelling obeisance.

'Yes, Missus. Thank you, Missus. Thank you. Thank you. You won't regret this, Missus. I swear you won't. I swear it.'

'From this moment on, you're my dog, and you'll do whatever I tell you to do. Whatever! Understand?'

'Yes, Missus. I'll do anything you tell me. Anything at all.'

'Keep away from the girls,' she warned.

'I will, Missus. I will. I swear it.'

Satisfied that she had him under absolute control, Amelia Melen left without another word and made her way into the main building. She went to the room where the girls and children were picking oakum, and stood looking at them for some seconds before asking the female pauper overseer, 'Where's the Kearns girl?'

'I don't know, Missus. She never come here with the others. I never seen her at dinnertime neither.'

Amelia Melen frowned and directed the question to the rest. 'Do any of you know where Hannah Kearns is?'

No one answered, and the matron berated the overseer, 'Why didn't you report it when she didn't come to work?'

'Well, the girls said that you was talking to her, Missus.'

'That was hours since,' the matron retorted. 'When you see her tell her to report to me. She'll get punished for this. And so will any of you if I find you're keeping her whereabouts from me.'

From the oakum room the matron went to find Lydia Landser in her room. She rose and questioned anxiously, 'How is Hannah Kearns, ma'am?'

'She was very well when she left me. Where is she now?'

'I don't know, ma'am. I haven't seen her since I left her with you.'

99

Amelia Melen clucked her tongue in exasperation. 'She didn't go to her work or to her dinner apparently.'

'Did she tell you anything, ma'am? About her condition, I mean?' Liddy asked.

'She just kept on repeating that nothing was wrong with her. In the end I lost patience and sent her from me.' The matron shook her head and added wearily, 'Do you know, Miss Landser, there are times when I grow tired of the constant aggravations these girls cause me. She'll be hiding somewhere, not a doubt of it. Hiding and laughing at the vexation she's giving to everyone. Anyway, I can't waste any more time looking for her. I've other work to be doing. If she comes to you, then bring her to me immediately. I've a mind to give her a whipping when she deigns to show her face again.'

Liddy nodded reluctantly, pitying the girl with all her heart for what awaited her.

Thirteen

'Miss, miss! Wake up, miss!'

Liddy opened her eyes and peered dazedly up at the lined face of Eliza Duggins.

'What is it? What's the matter? Has the rising bell sounded?' Even as she spoke the bell began its clanging.

'The Missus wants you downstairs straightaway. Everybody's got to go to the main hall.'

'What's happened?' Liddy was still drowsy with sleep.

'One of the wenches has run off in the night.'

'Who?' Liddy jolted into wakefulness, already fearing that she knew the answer to that question.

'It's young Hannah Kearns. Her's nowhere to be found in the house. Her's run off.' The woman's toothless mouth twisted in a grin. 'And good luck to the little wench, I says. Her's better off away from here, wherever her's run off to. If I was younger I'd run off meself, and that's a fact, that is.'

Liddy dressed quickly, brushed her teeth and hurried downstairs.

In the main hall, where the paupers took their meals, the women and girls had gathered, and the atmosphere was excited, almost festive. Any runaway from the workhouse was admired by the paupers as being someone who had sufficient courage to defy the hated authorities. By escaping from this 'Bastille,' Hannah Kearns had suddenly become transformed from just another helpless, useless nonentity into a daring heroine.

Chattering and laughter surrounded Liddy as she pushed through the mass of women and children, her eyes seeking for Maria Peat.

101

'Come here, Maria.' Liddy drew the snub-nosed girl away from her classmates. 'Now tell me, where has Hannah run off to?'

The girl's face was sullen as she shook her head. 'I dunno, miss.'

Liddy was deeply worried about Hannah Kearns, fearing that the fragile child would not be able to survive unharmed in the harsh world outside the workhouse walls.

'You must tell me, Maria,' she urged. 'Hannah's unwell. She will come to harm unless she's found quickly and brought back here.'

'She'll come to more harm if she's fetched back,' Maria retorted defiantly.

For a brief instant Liddy felt like shaking the girl. 'Can't you understand, child, that a girl like Hannah can find herself in terrible danger if she's wandering the countryside without money or friends to help her. There are bad people out there, child. People who will harm her.'

Maria's teeth displayed in a feral snarl. 'There's bad buggers in here who 'ull harm her as well. There's bad buggers in here who's already harmed her.'

Liddy's patience was strained to breaking point. 'Then tell me who they are!'

The sullen glare that met the question brought the depairing realisation to Liddy that nothing she could say would convince this young girl that she, Liddy, wanted to be a friend, wanted to help Hannah Kearns. In Maria Peat's world, Liddy was one of the enemy, an adult in a position of authority.

Liddy sighed heavily, and entreated gently, 'At least will you tell me at what time she went?'

Maria shook her head. 'I dunno, miss.'

'But you must have some idea of the time she went?' Liddy challenged. 'You're her bedmate, and her best friend. She wouldn't have left without your knowing?'

'She never come to bed, miss. I never saw her since she was with you in the classroom.'

The answer shocked Liddy into brief silence. Then she questioned, 'Are you telling me the truth, Maria?'

'O' course I am, miss,' the girl retorted indignantly. 'Why should I lie about it? I never seen Hannah since when she was left in the classroom with you.'

Before Liddy could ask anything else the Melens came into the hall. Amelia Melen shouted to her,

'Miss Landser, come here, if you please.'

'We'll discuss this later, Maria,' Liddy said.

The girl shook her head. 'That won't serve nothing, miss. I dunno more than what I's told you already.'

Amelia Melen greeted Liddy with a question. 'Have you seen anything at all of Hannah Kearns?'

'No, ma'am.'

The handsome, rosy face betrayed a hint of suspicion. 'Are you sure?'

Resentment that her word should be doubted caused Liddy to reply sharply. 'Of course, ma'am. I'm not in the habit of lying.'

'I'm sorry, Miss Landser. I don't doubt you –' the matron was instantly apologetic '– but I'm greatly concerned for the girl. She should be here where she can be cared for. Not roaming about God only knows where.'

Henry Melen shouted for silence, and glowered about him. 'Listen well, all of you. The girl, Hannah Kearns, has run away during the night.

'You may be certain of one thing. That is that sooner or later she will be caught and brought back here. Notices of reward for her capture will be posted throughout the entire Midlands, and when she's brought back, if I find out that any of you helped her to run away, then you'll pay a heavy price. Now get your breakfasts and then go to your workplaces.'

Liddy went back to her room and completed her toilet, her mind filled with concern for Hannah Kearns. When Eliza Duggins brought her her breakfast of rice gruel and bread, she found that she had no appetite for it and told the woman.

'You can eat it, if you wish, Duggins.'

'I can ate it, all right, miss.' Duggins beamed. 'And another half-dozen like it.'

103

I wonder if poor little Hannah has had any breakfast to eat, Liddy thought sadly, and went down to the classroom.

As she waited for the children to come from their breakfast she kept on thinking about Hannah Kearns, and wondering if the girl was in fact pregnant.

Liddy found herself beset by a dichotomy. Girls of Hannah's age who became pregnant were very often committed to lunatic asylums as being moral degenerates. Liddy feared for Hannah's safety outside the workhouse yet also feared that if Hannah were found to be pregnant when brought back, she could well be committed to the madhouse, and if so would in all probability remain incarcerated there for the rest of her life.

Is there nothing I can do to help the poor little soul? Liddy thought, racking her brains in a fruitless search for inspiration. Until, seemingly inevitably, Edward Harcourt came into her mind: I'm sure Edward would not allow Hannah to be committed if I was to tell him how good and intelligent she is. And that I'm sure she's not a loose girl by nature. She must have been forced into submission by whoever made her pregnant.

She heard the clattering of wooden-soled clogs from the corridor and the sounds of children's voices.

There was nothing she could do for Hannah at present, Liddy accepted, but if it became necessary she would go to see Edward, and ask him to help.

Greatly comforted by this resolve, she was able to smile in welcome at the first child who entered the classroom, little Katie Kennedy.

'What do we tell the Board about this talk of Hannah Kearns being pregnant?' Henry Melen was a very worried man.

His wife, however, appeared unconcerned. 'We tell them that as far as we know there was no truth in it.' Her teeth gleamed as she gibed mockingly, 'Just look at you, husband! Where's the big bold soldier gone that I used to be married to? He wouldn't have been feared of facing a bunch of self-serving hypocrites and telling them the plain truth.'

104

There was both doubt and fear in his eyes as he demanded, 'Is it the truth though? Might you be hiding something from me?'

'What do you mean?' she countered aggressively, and when he made no quick reply, burst out angrily, 'Just what are you getting at? What are you accusing me of?'

Alarmed by her outburst he tried to mollify her. 'I wasn't accusing you of anything, my dear.'

'Oh yes you were, and I want to know what!' She furiously rejected the attempt to soothe her. 'Come on! Spit it out!'

'Well, I was just wondering if maybe you hadn't sort of encouraged her to run away,' he muttered uneasily.

'Encouraged? Encouraged? How do you mean, encouraged her?' As always during their rare disputes, her speech became stridently foul. 'Come on, you fuckin' bastard, tell me. Tell me just what you're getting at! Tell me what you mean, you fuckin' bastard!'

Faced with this raging virago who dominated him, not only with her sexual desirability but also with her stronger will and greater intellect, he surrendered abjectly.

'Don't let us quarrel, my love. I meant nothing. You just tell me what to say to the Board. Just tell me what I must do.'

With victory achieved her fury disappeared as quickly as it had appeared.

In a softer voice she asked, 'Did you wake up in the night and find me gone? Is that what you're upset about?'

He nodded gratefully. 'Yes, that's all, my love. I lay awake for ages waiting for you to come back. I couldn't help but wonder where you was. But then I fell asleep again.'

Of course you fell asleep again, you fuckin' great lummox, she thought scornfully. You drank enough laudanum in that last glass of brandy I gave you to make you sleep all night. You must be getting used to the stuff if you woke up. I'll have to increase the dose next time.

She smiled and said affectionately, 'Oh, you great donkey, you. I only went to use the privy, that's why I was so long away.'

She came and kissed him. 'Don't you fret about the Board,

my sweetheart. They know well enough that there's always runaways from any Bastille. We can't chain the paupers to their beds, can we, or watch them every minute of the day. It's not our fault that Kearns ran off. All you have to do is to tell the Board what I tell you to. They'll accept it without question, you see if they don't.'

'Very well, my love. If you say so.' He smiled with the relief of getting his loving partner back in place of that savage virago.

'Oh, I do, Henry. I do say so.' Her voice contained a warning note. 'That's all you have to remember . . . that I do say so.'

Fourteen

'Well, gentlemen, now that we have heard Mr Melen's report I'm sure that, like myself, you accept that no blame can be ascribed the Master or the Matron in the case of this wicked and unnatural girl, Hannah Kearns. And indeed, Mr Melen is to be commended for his promptness in having reward notices posted throughout this district and even further afield.'

Edward Harcourt paused to allow his fellow Guardians to voice their concurrence, then asked the clerk: 'Is there any other business on the agenda, Mr Pethwick?'

'There is the application for the adoption of the Kennedy girl, sir. Miss Agnes Farquar is waiting to be interviewed by the Board.'

Edward Harcort frowned in recollection. 'Oh yes, I do believe that the matron spoke to me of this matter,' and told Henry Melen: 'Be good enough to ask your wife to attend upon us immediately. There is no need for you to return here yourself.'

'Thank you, sir, gentlemen.' Behind an impassive mask, Henry Melen was greatly relieved at escaping any censure. He was also surprised at how the few Board members present had seemed completely uninterested in the absconding Hannah Kearns, and had not queried his report in any aspect.

The elderly clerk cleared his throat meaningfully, and Harcourt looked questioningly at him.

'Is there something you wish to bring to our attention, Mr Pethwick?'

'Yes, there is, sir.' Pethwick tapped his ink-stained forefinger on the papers in front of him. 'Gentlemen, concerning this application for the adoption of the Kennedy girl, I would like to point out that no visit has been made on behalf of the Board, to the home of this lady, Miss Agnes Farquar, and no enquiries made in Manchester concerning her antecedents, social standing, or character.'

Harcourt gusted a sigh of irritation. Pethwick was challenging his authority yet again. Without bothering to hide his impatience with the clerk he explained, 'Gentlemen, I did not order either visit or enquiry, because it has not been necessary to do so in this case. The lady in question is personally vouched for by the matron, who has known the said lady for many years. This is why I have sent for Mrs Melen now, so that she may give us a full acounting of Miss Farquar.' Now he challenged the clerk in his turn. 'Do you not trust the matron to be able to judge whether or not this Miss Farquar is a suitable applicant, Mr Pethwick?'

Pethwick was more than willing to cross swords. 'We have a procedure laid down which we are obliged to follow, Mr Chairman. And that procedure behoves us to have full enquiries made about any individual who applies to adopt a child in our care. In this particular case I am also greatly concerned because the girl's mother, Megan Kennedy, has not given her permission for this proposed adoption.'

Harcourt feigned an amused incredulity. 'Are you seriously suggesting that the Board needs to obtain the permission of a lunatic who is an inmate of the Powick Asylum, Mr Pethwick?' He beamed at his fellow Guardians, inviting them to share his own amusement at this preposterous suggestion. 'I fear you will next be proposing that we appoint one of our pauper inmates to advise us on the administration of this workhouse?'

Pethwick's features reddened angrily at the shout of laughter which went up from the men around the table. But before he could make any reply, Amelia Melen came into the room.

Today she was looking particularly fresh, rosy, and sexually desirable.

She curtsied demurely. 'Good morning, gentlemen.'

'Good morning, Mrs Melen.' Harcourt smiled warmly. 'Will you please give the Board a full account of your acquaintance with Miss Agnes Farquar, and the reasons why you believe her to be a suitable applicant for the adoption of Kennedy.'

Amelia Melen spoke for a considerable time, radiating absolute sincerity and conviction, and was then asked to bring Agnes Farquar into the room.

If any Board member had harboured even the slightest doubt of the middle-aged, Miss Agnes Farquar's respectability and probity, then one look at her would have served to dispel that doubt. Her gentle pale face was framed by white hair which just edged from beneath her bonnet and fine lace mobcap, and was devoid of any hint of rouge or powder. Her clothing was subdued in colour, yet patently expensive. She wore no jewellery and carried a small leather-bound Bible in her gloved hands. Tall and slender, she moved with a regal grace, and when invited to sit on the chair placed ready for her, she smiled her thanks and sank down in a rustling of starched petticoats from which wafted a faint scent of lavender.

Edward Harcourt led the questioning and she answered without any hesitations, confirming the salient points of Amelia Melen's previous account of her. Her soft voice and diction was that of an educated gentlewoman.

After a time Edward Harcourt requested, 'Might I ask you, ma'am, one final question, which may sound rather impertinent, I fear?'

'You may ask me anything that you please, sir.'

'I cannot help but wonder why you should chose to adopt . . .' He hesitated. 'Please forgive my bluntness, ma'am. But with the choice of any healthy child, I cannot help but wonder why you should choose to adopt a deformed monster?'

Sharp indrawn breaths from some of the Board members greeted this brutal frankness.

Agnes Farquar's pale blue eyes glowed lucently. 'It is the Lord's will that I take this poor afflicted child and care for her, sir. I try to do His will in this, as in all other things pertaining to my life.'

'I'm sure that I speak for these other gentlemen as well as myself when I say that I heartily applaud that sentiment, ma'am.' Harcourt seemed genuinely touched.

There was a general murmuring of agreement and muted applause.

Harcourt looked at his fellow members with eyebrows raised in silent question. Each man nodded firmly.

Harcourt rose to his feet and bowed to the seated woman. 'The Board is delighted to accede to your application to adopt Kate Kennedy, ma'am. The necessary papers shall be drawn up as soon as possible.'

The pale gentle face showed disappointment. 'I was hoping, sir, that I might take the child with me today. I have important family affairs to deal with in Manchester, and cannot afford further delay in returning there.'

Harcourt didn't hesitate. 'But of course you may take the child with you today, ma'am. We can have the papers drawn up within the hour for signatures and witnessing.' He turned on Pethwick with a warning frown. 'There will be no difficulty with that course of action, will there, Mr Pethwick?'

The clerk knew that he had already lost today's skirmish with the chairman, and that if he raised any objections now the Board would all be ranged against him. With bad grace, he muttered, 'Within the hour, Miss Farquar.'

Agnes Farquar smiled with gratitude. 'My heartfelt thanks to you all, gentlemen, and the Lord's blessing be upon you, for today you have surely carried out His will.'

When she and Amelia Melen had gone from the room, Harcourt observed jocularly, 'This was a fortunate manifestation of the Lord's will, gentlemen. It's saved the parish a deal of expense, because we'd have been supporting the little Kennedy monster for the rest of its life. I only wish that we could find a hundred more Miss Farquars to take our other expensive little burdens from us.'

'Hear, hear!' a member agreed vehemently while others chuckled and smiled.

'Well then, that concludes the business for today, I believe,' Harcourt told them. 'Let us now adjourn to the Crown Inn.'

'Get that bleedin' gin bottle out, Amelia. I'm dying for a gargle.' Agnes Farquar flung herself down on the chair in the Melens' parlour.

Grinning broadly, Amelia Melen hastened to take the bottle out of the cupboard and fill two glasses with the neat spirit.

'Here's to you, Aggie. You were brilliant.' She toasted the other woman. 'I've never seen you perform better. You even had me believing you before it was over.'

Agnes Farquar smiled complacently. 'Yes, it's a part I've always played well, you know. I got eight curtain calls the last time I played it.'

'We'll have something to eat and then I'll fetch the monster. Where's Cull at now?'

'Wolverhampton, so I haven't got to go far to deliver her.'

'Well, this will make the journey seem all the shorter.' Amelia Melen took a small leather pouch from her pocket and handed it to Farquar. 'Twenty sovs, as agreed.'

'Bobby Shafto's gone to sea,
    Silver buckles on his knees,
    He'll come back and marry me.
    Bonny Bobby Shafto.'
The childish treble was pure and sweet-toned.

'That was wonderful, Katie.' Liddy applauded delightedly. 'Who taught you to sing that?'

'I think it was me mam who did, miss,' the small child informed her gravely. 'But I can't remember.'

'And do you know any more songs?'

Liddy and Katie were alone in the children's dormitory in the early afternoon. Because of her deformity the child could not work at picking oakum or any other manual labour, and so after the morning classes she was left by herself in the dormitory, and forbidden to stir from there, passing the long lonely hours without toys to play with or any other means of distraction.

Liddy, whenever opportunity offered, would sneak into the dormitory to keep the child company and try to entertain her. This had to be done stealthily because the Melens frowned upon any close, friendly relationship between inmates and staff.

Now she asked Katie, 'Sing me another song then, my dear.'

'Ba ba black sheep
Have you any wool?
Yes, sir, yes, sir
Three bags full.
One for the master.
One for the maid.
And one for the little girl
who lives down the lane.'

'That's wonderful. How well you sing.' Liddy again applauded, and the child's face glowed with pleasure at this praise.

'Hannah learned me that song, miss. Hannah who's run away.'

The mention of Hannah Kearns marred Liddy's mood of well-being. It was now nearly two weeks since Hannah had disappeared, and nothing had been heard of her, despite the widespread offers of reward for her recapture.

'Did you like Hannah?' she asked, and Katie nodded forcefully.

'So did I.' Liddy smiled sadly. 'I wish she'd come back safe and well.'

Katie shook her head. 'She won't come back here, miss. Maria says that Hannah will never come back here, because the man hurts her all the time.'

Liddy was instantly alert, sensing that here there might be an opportunity for her to penetrate the secretive world of the pauper children. She controlled her immediate impulse to pressure Katie with eager questions and instead was deliberately casual.

'It's a shame that the man hurts Hannah. But if she came back, then I'd make the man stop hurting her.'

'You couldn't stop him, miss. He'd kill you. He's killed lots of the kids.'

'How do you know that?' Liddy asked gently.

'Please, miss, Maria told me.'

'I wonder who the man is? I bet nobody really knows.' Liddy forced herself to smile. 'I don't know who he could be.'

'I do, miss, and some of the other girls do as well,' Katie stated solemnly. 'But it's a secret. And if we tell, Maria says that the man will kill us.'

'No, he won't. I'll make sure of that. So can't you tell me the secret?' Liddy encouraged. 'I shouldn't tell anybody else the secret, if you told me.'

'Somebody might hear me telling you,' the child pointed out with grave logic.

'Nobody would hear if you whispered it to me. If you whispered into my ear, then nobody but me could hear, could they? So nobody will know that you've told me.'

Katie considered this for some moments, and Liddy pointed to her own ear and coaxed, 'Nobody can hear if you whisper.'

Katie's blue eyes were wide as she looked from side to side, then she stepped to Liddy, beckoning for her to bend down.

Liddy felt the child's warm breath against her ear, and then came the whispered words.

'It's Mr White, miss.'

Liddy's immediate reaction was a horrified disgust. But she knew that to display it would only frighten the child unnecessarily. So she forced a smile and whispered back, 'You're a very good girl to tell me this secret.'

'You shan't tell anybody, shall you, miss?' Katie begged anxiously. 'Because Mr White will kill us if you do.'

'No, I shan't,' Liddy assured her. 'Because it's a secret, isn't it?'

Her mind was in turmoil and she couldn't marshal her thoughts. She needed to be alone in order to think clearly about the horrific information Katie had given her.

'I'll have to leave you now, Katie. Be a good girl and wait quietly for the others to come back.'

Liddy returned to her attic room and sat for a considerable

time at the single small window which overlooked the main gates. She was trying to evaluate the true import of what Katie had told her, going over it again and again in her memory. Daniel White had been hurting Hannah Kearns! Did hurting mean raping the girl? But how could he have continuously raped her without being discovered?

Katie's voice sounded in her mind: 'He's killed lots of the kids . . . Please, miss, Maria told me . . . and if we tell, then Maria says the man will kill us . . . It's a secret . . . It's a secret . . . It's a secret.'

The sharp visual image of Maria Peat's sullen features denying any knowledge of Hannah Kearns' whereabouts kept on overlaying the previous thoughts, until finally Liddy shook her head in dismissal. It can't be true, she thought. It's just Maria Peat filling Katie's head with nonsense.

She rose from her chair to leave the window, and then was brought to a halt as she saw the diminutive figure of Katie Kennedy, wearing her brown outdoor cloak and bonnet, walking towards the gates in company with a well-dressed woman.

Where can you be going, Katie? Liddy wondered, and stayed watching as Daniel White hurried from his lodge to open the gates for the oddly matched pair to pass through, bowing to the woman and knuckling his forehead in a slavish obeisance.

As the gates closed again, hiding Katie and the woman from her view, Liddy was suddenly attacked by a sensation of foreboding. Who was that woman? And why should she be taking Katie out of the house?

The sense of foreboding intensified, until Liddy could bear it no longer. She went downstairs and searched for Amelia Melen. In the oakum-picking room she was told that the matron was in the laundry.

Thick clouds of steam enveloped her as she opened the door and went into the heat. She saw the matron watching the toiling women at the great dolly-tubs and went to her.

'What are you doing here, Miss Landser?' Amelia Melen smiled bleakly. 'Have you come to offer your services as a laundress?'

114

'No, ma'am. I wanted to ask you where little Katie Kennedy is being taken, and by whom?'

The matron frowned. 'I don't think that that need concern you, Miss Landser.'

Her fondness for the child impelled Liddy to ignore the threat of the matron's displeasure.

'It does concern me, ma'am. I take great interest in her welfare.'

'Her welfare is the concern of the Board. So I'll thank you not to pry further into matters which are none of your business.'

Liddy became stubbornly determined not to give way.

'With all respect, ma'am, Katie is one of my pupils, and as her teacher her welfare is my business.'

Amelia Melen's dark eyes glinted with fury, but when she spoke her voice was cold and controlled.

'Very well, Miss Landser. The Board has decided that Kennedy is to be adopted. The lady who has taken her is a gentlewoman who is now in the position of her guardian.'

Liddy was completely taken aback with the shock of this news.

The other woman took shrewd note of this reaction, and went on. 'It's a wonderful stroke of good fortune for the child, Miss Landser. Since you are so interested in her welfare I would hope that you will be happy on her behalf.'

A dozen questions clamoured in Liddy's mind, but before she could begin to ask them Amelia Melen said brusquely, 'And now I must leave you. I have the running of this house to attend to.' With that she swept imperiously away.

Liddy walked slowly from the laundry and along the corridor. Somewhat to her own surprise she found that she was experiencing a painful sense of loss, and ruefully acknowledged that she must have been much fonder of little Katie than she herself had realised.

Back in her room, the secret Katie had whispered began to nag at her once more, and despite her previous dismissal of the story as a fabrication of Maria Peat's, she still wondered if there could possibly be a grain of truth in it.

Shall I report it to the Melens, she asked herself. Even as the idea occurred she accepted its futility. Without proof the story would be rejected as the lies of a pauper girl wickedly attempting to get an innocent man into trouble, and Maria Peat would be savagely punished for doing so.

What an awful place this was. Liddy felt utterly wretched and depressed.

The poignant visual memory of little Katie in her shabby brown pauper cloak and bonnet walking by the side of the tall well-dressed woman brought a lump into Liddy's throat, and she felt a terrible sadness. It seemed that everyone she came to care for was inevitably taken from her. Her father, her brother, and now poor little Katie.

Liddy sank down upon her hard narrow bed and burst into tears.

Fifteen

W hen the rising bell clanged, Liddy had already been awake for several hours. For weeks now she had not slept well, tormented as she was by the disappearance of Hannah Kearns, and the memory of what little Katie Kennedy had whispered to her. No matter how hard she tried to dismiss it as childish fantasy, to thrust it from her mind, still it dominated her thoughts, giving her no respite day or night.

I'll know no peace of mind until I do something about this . . . Today! she determined. I'll tackle Maria Peat today.

The dinner bell rang and Liddy told the children, 'Go and get your dinners. Not you, Maria, stay here.'

'I'll get into trouble if I'm late for me dinner, miss,' Maria Peat protested.

'No, you won't. I shall explain to Mrs Melen that I kept you back.'

'Oh but, miss . . .' the girl whined.

'Be silent!' Liddy snapped sharply, her irritability fuelled by strained nerves and lack of sleep.

As soon as she was alone with the girl she said, 'I know for certain that Daniel White is the man who made Hannah pregnant, Maria. So I think it's time you told me all that you know of the matter.'

The snub features became a sullen mask. The small mouth clamped in a stubborn line.

Liddy felt like taking hold of the girl and shaking the truth

117

from her, but knew that violence was not the way to obtain the truthful answers she wanted. The workhouse children were well used to being threatened and beaten, and well-versed in telling lies convincingly enough to satisfy any questioner.

'Come here, child.' She took the girl's grimy hand and led her to sit down on the bench. Sitting down beside her, Liddy said gently, 'Maria, I'm your friend, and Hannah and Katie's friend as well. If someone is misusing you then you can tell me, and I shall do my very best to help you. Katie told me about how Daniel White has been hurting Hannah. Has he been forcing her to . . . to . . . to . . .' She stumbled over the words, all the long indoctrinating years of her respectable upbringing making it difficult for her to speak freely or easily of sexual intercourse.

Maria Peat suffered no such constrictions, however. 'What's you trying to ask me, miss?' The sallow pug face was expressive with contempt of such ladylike inhibitions. 'Am you trying to ask me if Daniel White has been shagging Hannah?'

Liddy felt herself crimsoning with embarrassment, but she nodded doggedly. 'Yes, Maria, that's what I'm asking you. I want to know if Daniel White has been forcing Hannah to have sexual connection with him. And is he forcing any of the other girls to do likewise. Is he forcing you?'

'No.' Once more Maria's face became a sullen mask, and her lips tightened into the hard line.

Liddy was beginning to feel a sense of desperation. 'Maria, if you won't tell me the truth, then I can't help you, or Hannah.'

'I am telling the truth.'

Liddy was convinced that the girl was not. She persisted.

'Hannah is pregnant, Maria. She's alone and friendless. Her life is ruined. If Daniel White isn't stopped he will make other girls pregnant and ruin their lives also. He could make you pregnant, and then what will become of you?'

'Nothing worse than what's become of me already!' Maria retorted bitterly, and in her youthful face her eyes for a brief instant were those of a much older woman ground down by the misery of her life.

'Let me help you, child,' Liddy begged.

118

'Nobody can help me.' Maria shook her head, her voice charged with hopeless conviction. 'Now can I go and get me dinner, miss?'

Liddy knew that she would extract nothing more from the girl, and sighed in defeat. 'Very well, Maria.'

The girl ran, clogs clattering on the flagstones, and nearly collided with James Kerr in the classroom doorway.

'Whoa, steady there, girl, you nearly trampled me down,' he scolded jovially. Then he saw Liddy's pale strained face and asked with concern, 'Are you feeling unwell, Liddy?'

'A little tired, that's all.' Although she was pleased to see him, yet she was annoyed that he had not been near her for weeks now, and this annoyance provoked her to barbed sarcasm. 'I suppose that I should feel honoured that you've at last deigned to come and speak to me. After all, you're a gentleman and I'm only a workhouse schoolmistress.'

He was stung by this unjustified gibe. 'I've been away from home for some weeks, Liddy, attending a course of lectures in York. Sean Fitzgerald covered my duty here. I only came back yesterday.'

'Then I apologise,' she said wearily, her low spirits still weighing heavily upon her.

James was sensitive to her mood. 'If something is troubling you, then perhaps I can help?'

Liddy shook her head doubtfully. 'I'm not sure if you can, or anyone else for that matter.'

'Try me.' He smiled coaxingly.

Liddy hesitated for only a moment, then she related at length all her suspicions about Daniel White and the girl inmates.

It was James's turn to shake his head doubtfully. 'I find this very hard to believe. Surely this girl, Hannah Kearns, would have told the matron if White was sexually abusing her.'

'She was too frightened to speak of it. He was threatening to kill her if she said anything.' In the face of his doubt Liddy felt impelled to argue even more stubbornly for what she believed to be the truth.

'Liddy, are you not giving too much credence to the prat-

119

tlings of a small child? Katie Kennedy is little more than an infant. How could she know of such things?'

'That is precisely why I give it credence,' Liddy insisted, fast becoming exasperated by what she perceived to be his wilful refusal to face unpleasant facts. 'An innocent child like little Katie is not able to fabricate elaborate lies.'

'Innocence is very quickly lost in here,' he retorted. 'It's well known that workhouse children lie with great facility, as you yourself must have discovered by now.'

The longer this argument was continuing the more James's own patience was becoming strained. He really could not credit that such abuses could take place here under the strict and vigilant regime of the Melens.

'No, Liddy, I fear you are mistaken in this. You have been sadly deceived.'

Liddy's resolve only hardened in the face of his disbelief. 'No, I'm not mistaken. You must examine Maria Peat. If Daniel White is having sexual connection with her, then surely you'll be able to discover it from your examination.' She flushed as she forced herself to voice further indelicacies. 'Her maidenhead will have been destroyed, will it not? And there will surely be other signs as well.'

'I'm not sure that I would be able to recognise the true import of any signs I might discover.' He suddenly became angry with this pushy young woman for forcing him to reveal his own medical shortcomings. 'I've not had any experience in such things.'

'Then ask your uncle to make the examination,' Liddy urged impatiently. 'I'm sure that Dr Nairn will be able to make a judgement.'

'Mr Kerr? Nurse Kings said that you had arrived.'

They were both startled by the voice of Amelia Melen, who had come silently to the classroom door.

Her rosy face stared questioningly at James. 'On what must Dr Nairn make a judgement?'

Before he could formulate any reply, Liddy answered for him, her tension making her challengingly aggressive.

120

'I want Dr Nairn to examine Maria Peat. I believe that Daniel White has been forcing sexual connections upon her, as he did with Hannah Kearns and perhaps other girls as well.'

Amelia Melen's mind raced. She noted the young man's obvious discomfiture, and decided that he presented no immediate threat. The young woman was quite another matter, however. She was obviously determined on confrontation, and the matron knew that she herself must now tread very carefully. The first necessity was to ascertain how much Lydia Landser actually knew, and if she possessed any hard proof.

'Miss Landser, these allegations greatly shock me.' She assumed an air of deep concern. 'Please, let we three discuss this matter quietly, and in detail. I must know what grounds you have for laying such serious charges against Daniel White.'

Liddy had been steeling herself to face a virulent verbal onslaught, and this almost placatory reaction from the matron disarmed her.

The matron sat down on a bench facing Liddy, and nodded encouragingly. 'Now, my dear, tell me everything.'

She listened to Liddy's words without interrupting or displaying any reactions other than an occasional doubtful frown.

When Liddy fell silent Amelia Melen told her with apparent sincerity, 'I'm very glad that you've brought your suspicions to my attention, Miss Landser. I shall certainly bring this matter to the attention of the Board as soon as possible.' She then requested, 'Could I ask you, Mr Kerr, to examine Maria Peat before you leave here today? If the girl has been raped then there will surely be lacerations and bruises on her private parts and thighs, will there not?'

'I would assume so, if force was used,' James agreed, while desperately racking his brains to recall the sections in *Taylor's Medical Jurisprudence* which dealt with rape. 'But I confess I'm reluctant to submit her to an intimate examination which could cause such a young girl considerable distress. She's made no allegations of being raped, after all.'

'Nevertheless she will have to submit to an examination, no matter how much it may distress her,' the matron insisted

121

sternly. 'Miss Landser is accusing Daniel White of committing a very serious crime, for which he could well be hanged. He is entitled to have his innocence proven if he is innocent, and if he is guilty then he must pay the penalty.' She turned to Liddy. 'Who are these other girls you spoke of that Daniel White has allegedly been forcing to have carnal relations with him? They must be examined also.'

Liddy was forced to confess that she had been told no other names except Hannah Kearns.

'Well, Hannah Kearns is not here to be questioned, is she, and you say that Maria Peat denies any such offence being committed against her?'

Liddy felt that she was being manipulated into unwilling retreat. 'Yes, she denies it, ma'am.'

'Then why do you not accept her denial?'

'Because I believe that she's lying.'

'But why should she lie? Why should she want to protect a man who is raping her?'

'I really can't say unless she has been made too afraid to speak out,' Liddy admitted.

'Would you like me to whip the truth from her?' Amelia Melen's voice abruptly hardened.

'No, of course not!' Liddy protested.

'Will you come with me, Mr Kerr,' the matron requested brusquely. 'I want you to examine Maria Peat immediately. Will you please wait in your room, Miss Landser.'

'Wouldn't it be better if I were present at the examination?' Liddy questioned.

'I fail to see how your presence could serve any useful purpose since you are neither a doctor nor a midwife. Please wait in your room,' Amelia Melen snapped and ushered James out of the classroom with her.

Liddy went back to her room, troubled by a rapidly burgeoning sensation of dismay. If no lacerations or other wounds were discovered on Maria Peat's body, and if the girl continued in her denials, then she, Liddy, would appear guilty of making false accusations against an innocent man.

122

Duggins came in to tell her, 'I've left your dinner in your room, miss. It's potatoes and beef broth today. Only you'll not find much meat in the broth, nor potatoes neither.'

Liddy was uncaring of the food. She immediately asked her, 'Have you heard stories about Daniel White and the young girls?'

Duggins' careworn features became instantly wary. 'What sort of stories, miss?'

'That's he's forcing the girls to have sexual connection with him?'

Duggins' eyes became shifty and evasive, and this reaction served to convince Liddy that Duggins knew something.

'He is, isn't he?' she pressed. 'Come now, Duggins, you must tell me what you know. You must.'

'I don't know nothing about such stories,' Duggins denied. 'And if the Missus was to know that you was saying such things, her'd be spitting mad.'

'She does know. I've already told her. And Maria Peat is being examined by the doctor this very minute. So you'd better tell me what you know. Because if you're hiding anything you could get into trouble yourself,' Liddy warned sternly.

'I don't know why you're picking on me like this, miss. I aren't never done nothing to you, has I,' Duggins whined complainingly. 'I don't know nothing.'

'You're lying,' Liddy accused heatedly. 'You do know something about Daniel White and the girls, I know that you do.'

The older woman would not meet Liddy's eyes. Instead she shook her head violently and cried out, 'I'm going to tell the Missus what you're saying. And I'm going to tell her that you're picking on me.'

Disgust for this woman flooded through Liddy. 'Have you no pity for the young girls here?' she demanded. 'Their lives are miserable enough without having an animal like Daniel White abusing them further.'

'I'm going to tell the Missus of what you'm saying,' Duggins wailed, and ran from the room.

As the sound of Duggins' clogs died away, a sense of hope-

123

lessness assailed Liddy. What if James Kerr found no wounds on Maria Peat's body, and she continued her denials, where would that leave her?

She went to her room, and there stood looking down at the shallow tin bowl in which three grey sodden potatoes were half-submerged by grease-filmed watery broth.

Liddy smiled mirthlessly and told herself, I'll probably be accused of trying to bring a scandal upon the workhouse. I could lose my position here. So I might as well eat the condemned prisoner's last meal.

She took her spoon and severed one of the coarse potatoes into pieces. 'I wish it was your neck, Daniel White,' she muttered with virulent loathing.

Some time had passed when Duggins came to inform her, 'The Missus says that you're to come to her parlour this instant.'

'What have you told her?' Liddy asked.

The woman's face reddened, and she hurried away without replying.

Liddy could not help but feel a tremor of apprehension as she faced a scowling Amelia Melen, a dour-faced Henry Melen, and an unhappy-looking James Kerr.

'There are no lacerations or bruises on Maria Peat's private parts, Miss Landser,' Amelia Melen stated without preamble. 'And the girl denies absolutely that she has had any sexual connections with Daniel White.'

'I still think that she is lying,' Liddy asserted stubbornly.

'Why did you try to force Duggins to make false accusations against Daniel White?' Henry Melen glowered. 'Why are you trying to bring a scandal upon this establishment, and my wife and myself into disrepute?'

Liddy's fiery temper erupted. 'Because it's a scandal that young girls can be so wickedly abused.' She rounded on James Kerr, unreasonably angry with him for his failure to discover injuries on Maria Peat's body.

'Are you sure that you examined Maria Peat thoroughly, Mr Kerr? Could you have missed any evidence?'

Because he was strongly attracted towards Lydia Landser, James had been unhappy that she was getting herself into trouble for no good reason that he was able to perceive. But now she was attacking his own professionalism, and that annoyed him.

'My examination was thorough, and I resent your questioning my competence.'

Her temper was fuelling upon itself, and she riposted heatedly, 'I mean't no insult, Mr Kerr. But you did say, did you not, that you lacked experience in this field. Perhaps it might be better if Dr Nairn or Mr Fitzgerald were to examine the girl.'

His own anger flared, and he retorted with equal heat, 'I find your words insulting. You're attacking my professional competence.'

'I'm merely saying that you should be able to recognise the causes of bruises and lacerations.' She was beginning to regret her hasty words.

'I can recognise the causes of lacerations or bruises, Miss Landser,' he said gritting his teeth. 'But only when those bruises and lacerations are there to detect. In this case there are none. But it seems that my word isn't acceptable to you any more.' He turned to the Melens. 'It will serve no useful purpose for me to remain here any longer. I bid you good day.'

Ignoring Liddy, he walked out, his face hard with anger.

Liddy was dismayed at his abrupt departure and mentally cursed her own temper. It now seemed she had made an enemy of a man that she had long wanted to become closer to.

Amelia Melen's next words forced all thoughts of James Kerr from her mind, however.

'You've behaved disgracefully, Miss Landser. You've shown wicked malice towards myself and Mr Melen in attempting to bring scandal upon us. I've no other choice but to report your conduct to the Board, with the strongest recommendation that you be discharged from your position here.'

Liddy's fierce pride flared. 'The Board will not discharge me.'

'Oh yes it will.' Amelia Melen's face was ugly with rage. 'I'll make sure of that. You've tried to bring trouble on our heads, and you'll pay for it. I'll make sure that the Board discharges you, and without a character as well.'

'The Board will not discharge me, because I'm resigning this instant. I don't want to stay in this foul place a moment longer.' Liddy refused to give the Melens the final word, by immediately walking out of the room.

As she packed her pitifully few possessions into the carpetbag, Liddy was glad that she had not allowed them to humiliate her before the Board. But at the same time she was fearful of the future. She realised that she was in a dire predicament.

'I've no money. Where can I go now? What can I do?'

She could find no answers.

'We could find ourselves on the wrong side of Harcourt for this day's work,' Henry Melen told his wife unhappily. 'Why couldn't you wait and let the Board deal with her, instead of driving her away like this?'

'Don't you lay all the blame on me, my buck!' His wife rounded on him furiously. 'You opened your fuckin' mouth wide enough as well.'

Her fierce attack immediately forced him on to the defensive, and he because flustered. 'I'm not laying all the blame on you. I'm only saying that we could find ourselves on the wrong side of Harcourt for driving her out like this. You keeps on saying that he's got a fancy for her.'

Amelia Melen went and lifted her cloak from its hook and threw it over her shapely shoulders, then tied her large-poked bonnet on her head.

'Where are you going?' her husband questioned.

'I'm going to see Edward Harcourt, of course, you great fool,' she hissed angrily. 'I'm going to get our side of the story in first, before that little bitch gets to him and lies our jobs away.'

Edward Harcourt sat behind his desk listening to Amelia Melen's indignant account of Lydia Landser's wicked ingratitude towards her benefactors, namely himself, the Board of Guardians, and the Melens.

When the voluble outpourings ceased, he gravely thanked Amelia Melen and assured her that in his opinion she had acted correctly, and he would ensure that the Board concurred with that opinion. Then he courteously showed her to the door and returned to his capacious leather chair. Only when he had reseated himself in its comfortable embrace did he permit a smile of satisfaction to curve his lips. He felt absolutely certain that Lydia Landser would once more be forced to come to him for help. There was no one else she could turn to. And he would help her. But from now on she must start to pay the price for that help.

Sixteen

Daniel White unlocked the gates and opened them for Liddy to pass through. He grinned triumphantly at her. 'That'll teach you for trying to get me into trouble.'

Liddy glared at him and could not restrain herself. 'Some day you'll pay for what you've done, you filthy animal.'

He spat contemptuously on the ground before her feet, and used both hands to make an obscene parody of sexual intercourse.

'This is what you needs, you bloody bitch. A bloody good fuckin'.'

She lusted to hit him, but realised that he was trying to provoke her to attack him physically so that he could use his vastly superior strength to overpower and humiliate her still further.

'I'll make sure you pay for what you've done,' she promised him.

'Go on. Piss off!' he growled and slammed the gates shut behind her.

Rain was falling and as she trudged along the road her bonnet and cloak were quickly becoming penetrated by damp. When she reached the junction where the High Street commenced she took shelter in a shop doorway, and stood for a long time gazing despondently at the rapidly spreading puddles on the muddy roadway.

Despair engulfed her. Where could she go? She had no money for lodgings.

Edward Harcourt would help her. Even as the thought came, her fierce pride forced her to thrust it away: I can't trouble him

128

again, after all he's done for me and my family. I've got to find my own way out of this.

'You can't stay here all bloody day, young woman. Haven't you got no home to go to?'

She turned to find the shopman glowering suspiciously at her.

'I was only sheltering from the rain,' she told him defensively.

'Then go and shelter somewhere else, if you please. You're blocking my doorway from my customers.'

What customers? she felt like asking, but instead picked up her carpetbag and stepped silently out into the falling rain.

The hems of her long skirt and petticoats soon became thickly plastered with mud, her cracked bootees let in the water and began to squelch audibly as she followed a narrow twisting lane which led into the surrounding fields. She had no plan or destination, but was hoping to find a barn or shed in which she could take refuge. She walked for more than two miles before seeing a tumbledown shack on the edge of a field. By now she was soaked to the skin and thankfully she hurried towards the building. Her heart sank when she reached its sagging walls and found that most of its rotted thatched roof had fallen in and its interior was a thick morass of liquid mud and manure. She was suddenly bone-weary and totally disheartened as she huddled against the wall seeking the scant protection it afforded from the keening wind and gusting eddies of rain.

Seventeen

D usk fell early, aided by the dark shroud of clouds, and with its coming the wind and rain seemed to intensify their assaults upon the sodden land.

Liddy's clothing was saturated, her skin wet and chilled, and she shivered uncontrollably, her teeth chattering.

If I don't get shelter I'll catch pneumonia. I could even die from exposure, she realised miserably, and accepted that she had no real choice other than to swallow her pride and throw herself on Edward Harcourt's mercy yet again.

She left her pitiful shelter and began to trudge wearily back towards the town.

The bank was shuttered and closed but lights shone from the bowed windows of Harcourt's adjoining house.

She stood outside the front door for many minutes, unable to bring herself to lift the lion's-head knocker. He had helped her so much already. How could she impose further upon him? What would he think of her now?

Finally, with a heavy heart, she took hold of the iron door-knocker.

The manservant saluted her politely and invited her in, and Harcourt came smiling to greet her.

'Lydia, my dear girl, come in quickly out of this awful weather.'

The manservant took her cloak, bonnet and carpetbag, and Harcourt led her into the drawing room, insisting that she seat herself close to the blazing fire.

'What brings you here on such a terrible night?' he asked.

'I've resigned from my position,' she told him.

'Resigned?' Edward Harcourt exclaimed in feigned shock. 'But why?'

Liddy dejectedly related all that had occurred that day at the workhouse.

The man listened intently, outwardly serious, inwardly exultant.

When she had finished, depression whelmed over her and she sat with her head downcast.

Once more it was her air of vulnerability which powerfully excited Harcourt's lust and he felt his manhood engorging.

He touched her hand to make her look at him, and frowned. 'You have acted very foolishly, Lydia. You realise of course that you now have no character reference to offer any other potential employer?'

Desperation made her plead, 'Can you not speak to the Board on my behalf? Persuade them to at least give me a reference?'

He shook his head with feigned regret. 'It would serve no purpose, my dear. I must confess that the majority of the Board did not want to employ you in the first place. I had to browbeat them into doing so. Now, of course, they will point the finger of blame at me and sneer that I was mistaken in you.'

Guilt assailed her. 'I'm sorry, Edward. Truly I am.'

He took her hand and pressed it between his own, telling her, 'It makes no matter, Lydia. Their sneers can do me no harm. But now we must think about you and what's to be done to help you.'

Relief and gratitude brought tears to her eyes. 'You would be perfectly justified if you were to abandon me to my own devices,' she told him sincerely. 'I've let you down so badly.'

Releasing her hand, he leaned forward and cupped her face between his palms. 'I'll never abandon you, my dear.'

He hungered to crush his mouth against her soft moist lips, to tear the clothes from her, to feel the heat of her flesh against his own.

I've got to have her. I've got to have her now, his lust clamoured, but another voice in his mind warned repeatedly, Wait! Wait! Wait!

He withdrew his hands and smiled. 'I'll have a room prepared for you. You must change out of these wet clothes. There are some lady's gowns and other clothing which once belonged to my sisters. Make use of them until your own clothes are dried. You shall stay here tonight, and tomorrow we'll see what can be done.'

Liddy experienced a moment of hesitation. A young woman staying unchaperoned in the house of a bachelor would cause many respectable eyebrows to be raised.

'What will people think if I stay here in your house? It will offend against propriety.'

He waved her objection aside. 'I don't give a damn what anybody might think, and anyway no one need know. My servants will say nothing.' He gestured towards the window where the rain was lashing against the panes. 'You can't go out into such a storm, Lydia, and where could you go if you did?'

Liddy didn't want to go out into the cold and rain again this night. She felt safe here in this warm room, protected by his friendship.

'There's nowhere,' she admitted truthfully. 'I've no money to pay for lodgings or even an inn room.'

'I don't want to hear another word about propriety,' he warned jocularly. 'You shall stay here as my guest, and that's that. I've a fine cut of beef already roasting for our dinner.' He smiled avuncularly. 'After a good meal and a restful night, then life will seem a great deal rosier for you. I'll guarantee that by this time tomorrow, your present troubles will all be behind you.'

Now the tears did fall from her eyes, and she told him, 'You're the best friend I've ever had, Edward. I don't know what I would do without you. There's no one else who would help me as you have done.'

'That's what friends are for.' He smiled and patted her shoulder as he rose to his feet. 'Come with me now, my dear, and I'll show you your room. You can change out of those wet clothes while I go and give my servants their instructions.'

Eighteen

Septimus Nairn sighed with exasperation, and looking up from the book he was reading entreated wearily, 'For pity's sake, Nephew, will you give over prowling around the room like a beast in a cage. Why can't you sit quietly for a few moments at least?'

James halted his rapid pacing and apologised. 'I'm sorry, Uncle. I'm thinking about something.'

'What you really mean is that you're troubled about something,' the older man observed perceptively.

James nodded unhappily.

Nairn laid his book aside. 'You'd better tell me.'

James related the events of that day at the workhouse, and when he had done so appealed, 'What do you think? Could there possibly be some truth in Lydia Landser's accusations?'

'You discovered no physical evidence of assault upon Maria Peat, and furthermore she denied having any type of sexual relationhip with the porter. Therefore you can only accept that there is no truth in the accusations.'

'I realise that, but at the same time Lydia gave me the impression that she believed implicitly in what she was saying.'

'She's a young woman, and young women have fevered imaginations, Nephew. And frankly, with her family background and recent history it is quite understandable that she has become a trifle unbalanced herself, and has convinced herself that her figments are indeed facts.'

James was horrified by what his uncle was imputing. 'Are you saying that she's gone mad?'

Nairn shook his head and answered soberly. 'Oh no,

134

Nephew. I'm merely saying that she is a young woman who has suffered a great deal of trouble and disturbance and stress during these last years, and this has resulted in her becoming unbalanced in her emotions and thoughts at this time. Thus we find her making such wild and irrational accusations, without a single iota of proof.' He sighed regretfully. 'But I think she has undoubtedly brought fresh troubles upon herself by making these accusations.'

'How so?' James asked with concern.

'Well, she will certainly be dismissed from her position. The Board cannot permit a scandalmonger to remain in their employment.'

'But she was only doing what she considered to be right. Protecting the workhouse girls,' James protested.

'I'm in no position to judge her motivations.' Nairn picked up his book. 'And I've no real interest in discovering them. And furthermore it would appear that the workhouse girls have no need of her protection.'

'But her parents were your patients?' James challenged.

'Indeed they were, to my sorrow.' His uncle snorted irascibly. 'There are still two bills for her mother's treatment remaining unpaid. I think that I've already been over-generous to that family.'

'But if she is dismissed, then where can she go? I doubt that she has enough money to enable her to find lodgings even.'

'That's not your concern.' Nairn was unsympathetic.

'I could try and persuade the Board not to dismiss her.' James spoke as if to himself. 'I can go and speak to Edward Harcourt. He wields much influence over the Board, does he not? They will do whatever he tells them to do.'

Nairn's eyes were kindly as he studied his nephew's worried expression, but his voice betrayed none of that kindliness.

'If you intervene on her behalf, then perhaps your own motivations might well be misconstrued. My advice to you is to keep out of it entirely.'

'How can I do that, when she is in such sore need of a

friend?' James said quietly. 'No, Uncle, I can't abandon her so callously.'

'Then be it on your own head,' Nairn snapped curtly.

'I'll go directly and speak with Edward Harcourt,' James told him.

'It's pouring with rain, blowing half a gale, and the night is as black as pitch. You'll end up in a ditch. Wait until tomorrow when you'll at least have daylight to see by,' Nairn objected.

'No, I won't be able to rest until I've done what I can to help her,' James protested and hurried out.

'Silly young fool, letting his heart rule his head again,' Septimus Nairn grumbled aloud, then his hard-set mouth softened into an affectionate smile. 'But I'd not have him any different.'

Nineteen

The food was succulent, the wine sweet and heady. Harcourt plied Liddy with drink, while exerting every atom of his considerable charm to entertain her, and Liddy's cares and worries eventually floated away on a alcoholic stream of enjoyment. As she became increasingly tipsy, so did her trust in Edward Harcourt increase, until she was talking to him without restraint about her personal feelings, hopes and dreams.

These artlessly given confidences touched a softer chord in Edward Harcourt's character, as he remembered the hopes and dreams and ambitions he had nurtured in his own youth. He also began to regard this young woman in a rather different way and toyed with the idea of her as wife, rather than mistress. Fuelled by alcohol, the notion of marrying such a desirable young woman became increasingly inviting as the time passed.

He knew from previous experience that a mistress always retained some degree of freedom. A man could never be sure if she had some other secret lover. A wife, however, was the absolute property of her husband. If Lydia Landser became his wife he could make sure that she would never have any opportunity to indulge herself with a lover.

He was tired of buying woman-flesh, and knowing that that flesh had been used by other men perhaps only hours previously. This girl before him was fresh, untouched by other men. She was still young and malleable enough to be moulded into whatever he chose. She would come to his bed as a virgin, and he could train her to satisfy his sexual desires no matter how perverse those desires might be. As his wife she would have no choice but to do as he required.

Yes, perhaps I might marry her, he thought.

Just as he came to that decision she innocently admitted how attractive she found James Kerr, and how at times she had entertained fanciful thoughts of marrying him.

Sudden fury surged through Harcourt. That young bastard! he cursed silently. I mark down a woman for myself, and he comes into the picture. He's like a bad penny. First Mercedes Wybergh, and now Lydia.

He betrayed nothing of what he was feeling, however, and instead gently encouraged Liddy to go on confiding in him.

The sound of loud and sustained hammering on the front door carried to the room, and Liddy giggled.

'Whoever that is seems very determined to get in.'

A sudden premonitory instinct caused Harcourt to tell her, 'I'll not be long.'

He went out into the passage closing the door behind him just as his manservant was opening the front door to the visitor.

Rainwater was dripping from the brim of James Kerr's top hat and running down his gutta-percha riding cloak.

Harcourt's instinct had been correct.

He smiled and went forwards with his hand outstretched in greeting.

'Mr Kerr, what brings you out in such filthy weather? Come into my study and take a glass of something to warm you up. You're in need of it, I'm sure.'

In the study James refused the proffered drink. 'No, I thank you, sir. I've come to ask you a personal favour. It concerns Miss Lydia Landser, the schoolmistress at the workhouse.'

'Please ask whatever you will of me, Mr Kerr,' Harcourt invited.

James related his own version of the events of that day. It quickly became obvious that he didn't know that Lydia had already left the workhouse, and it also became equally obvious as James began to plead for leniency for Lydia that the young man was more deeply emotionally involved with her than perhaps he himself realised

Harcourt's expression of kindly interest and concern masked a fierce rage against this young interloper who it seemed was once again threatening to thwart his own plans for a woman.

Not this time, Kerr, Harcourt promised himself silently. You'll not thwart me this time.

Eager now to be rid of his visitor, Harcourt promised James that he would do all in his power to keep Liddy in her position, and ushered the young man from the house.

He stood for some moments considering what he should now do. He was convinced that James Kerr would offer Lydia shelter and protection himself as soon as he discovered that she had left her employment. Harcourt feared that if this should happen, then she would be lost to him for ever. His compulsive sexual obsession with the girl, all the long months of planning and waiting, now served to harden his resolve, and in his alcohol-fevered brain all the risks of retribution were now of no matter. His own overwhelming sexual desire was all that drove him. His need to possess her body was absolutely paramount and could no longer be controlled.

He went down the stone steps to the cellar kitchen where the manservant and his wife the cook were sitting sharing a bottle of gin.

'I don't want to be disturbed again tonight, on any matter,' he told them.

As Harcourt went back up the steps the manservant winked at his wife, and whispered, 'He's going to be shagging that young piece, that's why he don't want to be disturbed.'

The woman chuckled lewdly. She was well aware of her master's voracious sexual appetite.

'He's risking his reputation, aren't he, by entertaining a whore in his own home. What'll people say if the news gets out that he's having whores here? He must be hot for it tonight.'

The manservant frowned warningly at her. 'If the news does get out, then you and me 'ull be for the chop. And I don't want to lose me place here. We'll never find a better situation than this 'un. So you just keep everything shut, like them wise monkeys does.'

'Don't you worry about me saying anything,' the woman hastened to tell him. 'I knows which side me bread's buttered on, don't you fret.'

She took a swig of gin, belched loudly, and asked curiously, 'Where's he brought her from?'

Her husband shook his head. 'I dunno. She just come to the door, dripping wet. She don't look like a flash girl. She's too shabby dressed.'

'Perhaps she's only just starting at the game,' his wife suggested sagely, as she lifted the bottle.

'You could be right,' her husband agreed, then complained, 'Hold on, you greedy cow, leave some of that for me . . .'

Harcourt next went upstairs to his own bedroom where he took a small glass phial from a drawer and put it into his inside pocket.

When he returned to the dining room Liddy smiled drowsily at him.

'I was almost falling asleep.'

'Then I think it time for a final nightcap, my dear.' He smiled back. 'And then you must get some rest. It will be a busy day tomorrow for both of us. I'm going to give you a glass of my finest sherry wine. It's been likened to nectar.'

He went to the drink cabinet, while Liddy sat enveloped in a glow of blissful contentment. He opened the fresh bottle and poured out two glasses of the golden liquid. Shielding the glasses from her view he took out the small phial of laudanum, and emptied its contents into Liddy's glass.

When she took the glass from him, he lifted his own high in the air.

'I propose a toast, my dear.'

Her white teeth gleamed as she giggled. 'I fear a toast will make me even dizzier than I am now, Edward. I hardly dare take another drop.'

'I insist.' He chuckled, and clinked his glass with hers. 'To your future happiness, success and prosperity, Lydia. Now you must drink it all up for good fortune to follow.'

He watched her with greedy anticipation in his eyes.

Within a brief span of time Liddy's eyelids began to flutter, and as she slipped into unconsciousness he moved quickly to prevent her falling from her chair.

A moment later, Harcourt was breathing heavily from the exertion of carrying Liddy's limp body upstairs and placing her on his bed, and he waited to catch his breath before beginning to strip her clothing from her. But as he uncovered her firm ivory-white breasts, rounded thighs, smooth belly, his breathing again quickened to a harsh panting. He tore his own clothing off, spread her legs and knelt between them, gloating over her beauty, until unable to restrain himself any longer he lowered himself upon her and thrust deep into the tight moist flesh between her thighs.

Twenty

During the night the storm had passed over and now the skies were clear and the rays of the early morning sun lanced through the leaded casement of the bedroom and fell across the bed where Liddy still lay sleeping.

Edward Harcourt, fully dressed, sat on a straight-backed chair by the side of the bed staring at the girl. The alcohol-fuelled sexual madness that had driven him to violate her unconscious body had drained from him, and now he was a worried man, racking his brains in a desperate search for some way of escape from this predicament.

His breath caught in his throat as Liddy stirred, murmured indistinctly, and opened her eyes.

Liddy's initial awareness was of how dry her mouth was, and then of the painful throbbing in her head, and finally of the man's tense face only a yard distant from her own.

'Edward?' She was shocked into wakefulness, and the horrified realisation that she was naked. Instinctively she clutched the bedclothes tightly to her while trying to comprehend what was happening here.

Now the moment of crisis had come, Harcourt's native nerve and cunning did not desert him. He suddenly saw the way of escape opening wide. Shaking his head he told her regretfully, 'I don't wish for you to blame yourself, my dear. We are both equally to blame. But I will behave honourably and marry you.'

'Blame? Equally to blame? Marriage?' The words were swirling in the maelstrom that was Liddy's mind.

'I shall have the banns called this very Sunday.' Harcourt's confidence was increasing with every moment that passed. 'Or if you prefer I can apply for a special licence, and then we can wed within days only.'

Liddy's confusion was total, the dazing effects of alcohol and laudanum still lingering, and she shook her head in a fruitless attempt to clear her thoughts.

Harcourt's shrewdness told him that this was the moment to leave well alone, and so told her, 'You stay in bed and rest for a while longer, my dear. We'll have ample time later to talk about the wedding. And don't reproach yourself for what has happened. We should both have been stronger to resist temptation.'

He didn't touch her, only walked quietly out of the room leaving Liddy staring bemusedly after him.

Suddenly in dismayed comprehension, she sat up and threw back the coverings. The faint smears of blood on her inner thighs and on the sheets, the soreness of her intimate parts, told their own story.

Liddy was a tough-minded young woman, never prone to hysteria, but in this moment she came perilously near to losing control of her emotions. She stayed motionless for many minutes trying desperately to recall what had happened between herself and Edward Harcourt, but only vague recollections of taking food and wine, of sharing talk and laughter with him came to her.

'Did I really give myself to him? Did I?'

Liddy had for several years been conscious of her own strong and healthy sexual desires and her eager expectations of one day meeting a lover who would satisfy them. Had she given in to those tormentingly strong desires?

She couldn't bring herself to believe that she had done so, and yet the evidence appeared irrefutable. Edward Harcourt's manner towards her had been that of a confident lover, and there were no bruises or scratches on her body to suggest that any force had been used. Self-disgust suddenly assailed her. If she had given herself to a man she was not in love with, then she'd behaved like a whore.

She burst into tears of utter mortification.

*　　*　　*

143

In his office Edward Harcourt indulged in brief self-congratulation. I've handled it brilliantly, he told himself.

The memory of her firm smooth body, the warm fresh scent of her flesh, the white globes of her breasts, roused him yet again to a heat of sexual desire. He was determined now that she should marry him as soon as possible, and he was feverishly anticipating the fleshly delights he would experience night after night when she became his virtual chattel.

She has no choice now. She has to marry me!

Twenty-One

'She's gone? But when? Where?' James Kerr reacted with shocked dismay to Amelia Melen's news.

'Three days since. She resigned her position and walked out on that same day, Mr Kerr.' The matron sighed regretfully. 'She's a foolish young woman acting like she has. I told her that I forgave her for her wickedness; and that I'd speak to the Board on her behalf and ask them to give her another chance. But in her temper she'd not listen to me at all. She's got a very bad temper, I have to say.'

'I can't say that I thought her to be a wicked or ill-natured girl myself, Mrs Melen,' James replied sharply.

The rosy features smiled understandingly. 'Well, of course, she always showed her sweeter side to you.'

'Did she say where she was going?'

'No. She just stormed out.'

'Do you know of any person she might go to for shelter?'

'Well, not really. Mr Harcourt has befriended her in the past, but I can't think that she'd go to him after abusing his trust so badly.'

'How so? How has she abused his trust?' James found himself becoming angry, and in one part of his mind was marvelling how he felt so strongly driven to take Lydia Landser's side.

Amelia Melen's amiable manner didn't falter. 'Why, by making such wicked allegations, and trying to cause trouble and scandal here when none existed, Mr Kerr. I'm only an ignorant woman, but I should think myself that that was an abuse of trust, wouldn't you?'

James innate sense of justice forced him to acknowledge that

145

there was some force to this argument, and he unhappily accepted it without further dispute.

'Is there anything else you're wanting, Mr Kerr? Can I offer you some tea perhaps?' she enquired politely.

'No, I thank you, ma'am. I have to meet someone at the train station. I'll bid you good day.'

Sean Fitzgerald was returning from Ireland and it was he whom James was to meet from the train and take back to Tardebigge.

James drove the pony and trap from the workhouse with his mind full of Lydia Landser. He was surprised himself by the acute anxiety he was experiencing about her.

She must mean a deal more to me than I've ever realised, he surmised ruefully, even though I've seen little enough of her.

The newly constructed station lay half a mile south-east of the High Street and the train had already arrived when James reached there.

Sean Fitzgerald, even ruddier faced and plumper than when he had left, greeted James like a long lost son, and for his part James was delighted to have his genial friend back.

James was so happy to be in the company of Sean Fitzgerald once more that he was temporarily able to put his worries about Liddy to the back of his mind, and the Irishman's anecdotes about his extended holiday in Ireland kept him in fits of laughter all the way back to Tardebigge.

There was a surprise awaiting him at his home where a smart horse and gig were standing outside the front door.

His uncle was waiting for them in his study, accompanied by a tall, broad-browed man with a shock of iron-grey hair.

James looked searchingly at him as the man asked, 'Don't you know me now that I've grown a nose, James?'

'It is you, isn't it, my lord!' James exclaimed in shock, and then apologised in acute embarrassment. 'Forgive my rudeness, I beg you. I didn't recognise you at first.'

Humphrey Chamberson, Earl of Allesley, roared with delighted laughter. 'That doesn't surprise me.'

James could not help but stare in wonderment at Chamberson's nose. It was very snub, certainly, and paler than the rest of his complexion, and there was scarring where it merged with his face, but it was undoubtedly a real nose.

'Well? What do you think of your uncle's handiwork?' Chamberson demanded jovially.

'It's marvellous, my lord.' James was overcome by admiration. 'It's wonderful!'

He now noted the scarring left on Chamberson's forehead, but in comparison to the hideous spectacle prior to the operation he considered Chamberson to be now almost handsome.

James smiled broadly. 'It's like a miracle.'

'And I owe it all to this wizard who performed that miracle.' Chamberson put his arm around Nairn's broad shoulders and hugged him.

'My lord, may I present Mr Sean Fitzgerald, who is my chief assistant and trusted confidant.' Nairn introduced Sean, and the irrepressible Irishman immediately asked, 'If you please, my lord, Dr Nairn wrote to me concerning this operation. Could I make so bold as to closely examine your new nose?'

'Please do, Mr Fitzgerald,' the earl invited readily, and endured good-humouredly for several minutes Fitzgerald's peering and poking and prodding and twisting.

'Jasus!' The Irishman finally exhaled a great gust of air. 'This is tremendous stuff. It's a work of art, so it is, and may God strike me down if I tell a lie. Haven't I always said that Dr Nairn is the finest surgeon in this kingdom, and in the world as well, I shouldn't wonder. And here's the living, breathing, snot-box proof of it!' Realising what he had said he became instantly flustered. 'Begging your pardon, my lord, for calling it a snot-box. I meant no disrespect to your lordship. It's just that I was entirely carried away by me admiration for a moment there.'

Chamberson laughed heartily and clapped the Irishman's shoulder, then told James, 'I've already explained to your uncle why I am here today. Tomorrow I'm going to London to re-enter society. I want you to accompany me and remain as my house-guest for as long as you wish. I intend to introduce you to

147

some powerful and influential people there, who can be of great service to you in furthering your future career.'

James was taken aback by this offer. He instinctively turned to his uncle, who nodded and said enthusiastically, 'His lordship is giving you a wonderful opportunity, Nephew. An entrée to the highest society in the land. I trust that you are as grateful for it as I am myself.'

James's mind raced. He recognised that this could open doorways which otherwise would always remain firmly closed to him. It could bring him a future of glittering success in his chosen profession. It was a chance that he should seize with both hands . . . And yet . . . he could not bring himself to voice instant grateful acceptance of the invitation. Before he went anywhere he wanted to be sure that Liddy Landser was safe and well, and had shelter and sustenance.

'I am indeed very grateful, my lord,' he said unhappily, searching for some credible excuse to make for refusing the invitation. 'But I have patients to care for here. I'm acting as the resident physician in the workhouse.'

'It makes no matter.' Septimus Nairn, irritated by what he perceived as his nephew's inexplicable ingratitude, brusquely dismissed the argument. 'Sean will look to the paupers.'

'That's settled then.' Chamberson took James's hesitance to accept as a natural diffidence, and beamed happily at the young man. 'I shall send my carriage for you and we'll meet at the railway station in Birmingham. I can promise you a gay time of it in London.'

'I shan't be able to stay for too long, my lord,' James told him. 'I can't neglect my work here.'

'Your conscientiousness does you great credit.' Chamberson smiled. 'But I warn you, I shall be loath to let you leave me and I shall do my utmost to persuade you to extend your stay for as long as possible.'

Nairn and James accompanied the earl to his gig and waved him farewell as he drove away at a spanking pace.

As the gig disappeared around the bend of the road, Nairn rounded irritably on James.

'What the devil was the matter with you? Why did you behave so oafishly?'

'I'm sorry, Uncle. I intended no offence,' James apologised guiltily. 'It's just that there is something that is worrying me greatly, and if I'm in London . . .' His voice trailed away.

'It's that damned Landser girl, isn't it?' his uncle accused.

'Yes. She's gone from the workhouse, and I'm worried what might have become of her,' James admitted unhappily. 'That's why I've no wish to go to London at this time.'

'You're not her keeper, boy,' Nairn snapped.

'No, I'm not. But I hope that I'm her friend.'

His quiet reply deflated the older man's anger and his voice quietened, became placatory.

'Yes, I know you are, and I'm pleased that you show loyalty to your friends. But you owe a greater loyalty to your own kinfolk.'

'But I am loyal to you!' James exclaimed. 'Have I ever given you any cause to doubt it?'

'No, but hear me out now. Chamberson is much taken with you. He wants to make you his protégé. I don't think that you fully understand what that can mean to your future. You have the intelligence, and all the other talents necessary to become a truly great surgeon. But without the patronage and support of the rich and powerful you will never gain the recognition that should be your due. You will be doomed to remain an obscure, virtually unknown country sawbones, as I have been doomed to so remain.'

'But you're not obscure, or unknown,' James objected spiritedly. 'You are asked to operate all over the Midlands.'

'But never in London, or Paris, or Edinburgh or Vienna.' There was bitter rancour in Nairn's expression and voice. 'Liston, Taylor, Snow, Cooper, Spence, Civiale, Dieffenbach, Graefe, Maisonneuve, these are the names that are known in those cities . . . And I am a finer surgeon than any of them. But because I was born poor, and lacked rich and powerful patrons, I've never received the recognition I deserve. I remain a country sawbones, whom those fine gentlemen

149

would sneer at and despise for lacking the good fortune they've enjoyed.'

His thick fingers grasped James's upper arm in a painfully bruising grip, and his voice throbbed with intensity.

'I'll not allow that to happen to you, Nephew. I'll make sure that you take your rightful place in the sun. Tomorrow you're going to London, and while there you must take full advantage of the chances you'll have to make yourself known to the rich and powerful. Because the only way that a poor man can even hope to achieve his rightful due is to curry favour with the arrogant bastards who rule over us.'

Twenty-Two

'**M**r Harcourt, how do you do, sir? To what do I owe the pleasure of this visit?' Dr Aloysius Burman was his usual affable, plump and glossy self as he greeted this unexpected visitor in the skull-lined study of his asylum.

Harcourt wasted no time on courtesies and demanded abruptly, 'What condition is George Landser in?'

Burman became instantly guarded and answered cautiously. 'He is doing as well as can be expected. I'm making satisfactory progress in his treatment, which of necessity is long-drawn-out and arduous in application.'

Harcourt frowned and hissed impatiently, 'Spare me your bullshit, Dr Burman. We both know what your treatments consist of. Shall we speak frankly with each other?' He waited for the other man's acquiescence.

Although Aloysius Burman was something of a charlatan in his dealings with his patients' friends and relatives, he nevertheless had a genuine interest and much experience in treating the mentally afflicted, and he resented Harcourt's implied derogation of his professional practices. But he was in considerable financial debt to the banker, and could not risk a quarrel with him, so merely replied subversiently, 'As you wish, sir.'

'Is George Landser of sound enough mind to sign a legal document, and is he fit to be seen in public?'

'George Landser is much improved as a result of my treatment.' Burman could not keep an inflection of resentful acid from his tone. 'And is certainly sane enough to sign any legal documents.'

'I would like to see where you keep him, and to have words with George Landser.' It was an order, not a request, but Burman was slow to comply. Harcourt knew the reason for the other man's hesitance, and he grinned mockingly.

'Don't worry, man. I know well that you're not keeping him in the style that I'm paying for him to be kept in. You'd cheat your own mother out of her last farthing, wouldn't you, so why should you think that I don't accept that you cheat me also?'

Burman grimaced unhappily, but knew better than to make any denials.

'I'll take you to him, sir,' he mumbled and led Harcourt out of the study.

The large cellars were below ground level but an adjoining courtyard had been dug from the earth and doors and windows let into the thick walls to admit light and air. As the two men came down the stone steps, a bizarre medley of sounds enveloped them: wailing and moaning, cackling laughter, voices talking, shouting, muttering.

When Harcourt entered the first cellar he sniffed distastefully. It reeked of stale flesh and human wastes, mingled with which was another smell, somehow reminding him of the feral stench of wild animals.

'What is this peculiar stink?' he questioned.

'It is madness,' Burman replied simply.

The inmates of the cellar were all wearing long white canvas smocks, their heads close-cropped, and at first glance Harcourt was hard put to recognise their sexual gender as female. They were immersed in their own fantasies and griefs, some rocking backwards and forwards moaning and sobbing, others laughing and gesticulating, others holding conversations with invisible companions, still others merely motionless, silently gazing at the walls, their eyes empty of any spark of human emotion.

One small elderly woman came to stand close and stare at Harcourt, her red-rimmed eyes puzzled as if he were some strange apparition. She reached out to touch him and a large black-clad female attendant appeared and interposed herself between them, telling the woman not unkindly, 'Get away now, Martha, leave the gentleman alone.'

Martha remained where she was, and the attendant told her more sharply, 'Do as I tell you,' and pushed her backwards, but without using undue force.

'As you see, Mr Harcourt, we practise humanity here,' Burman said with some pride. 'We follow the precepts of Pinel and Esquirol and treat all our patients with kindness. This is the female day room, and in fine weather we allow them into the courtyard there also.'

'Is it a kindness to crop their heads and dress them like convicts?' Harcourt queried ironically.

'It is hygienic, sir,' Burman stated positively.

Burman and Harcourt passed through a door at the far end of the cellar which opened into a dormitory, lined on both sides with wooden cots. On one of the cots a woman was lying on her back, mouth gagged, wrists and ankles shackled and a heavy chain fastened around her waist, its other end padlocked to an iron ring set into the wall.

'We sometimes have to restrain the violent ones, Mr Harcourt, to prevent them injuring themselves or others,' Burman explained. 'But I do not believe in isolating them unless their violence is constant. This poor creature will be released when her fit has passed and she is no longer a danger to herself or to the rest.'

The male day room was a replica of the female: the men wore the same white canvas gowns, had their heads close-cropped, and were under the watchful guard of a burly, black-clad male keeper.

Harcourt could not see George Landser among the patients, however, and he looked interrogatively at his companion, but Burman only beckoned him through the room and adjoining dormitory and on into a smaller room beyond.

In this room there was a cot, a small table, and a chair on which a man wearing ordinary clothing was sitting, intent upon the large opened Bible on the table before him.

'You have a visitor, George,' Burman announced.

Harcourt was momentarily taken aback. George Landser looked clean and sober, was freshly shaven, his greying red hair neatly dressed and not cropped short like the other patients.

Burman glanced sideways at Harcourt's surprised expression, and smiled smugly.

'This is not what you expected to find, I take it, Mr Harcourt?'

Harcourt could only shake his head.

Landser rose to his feet and bowed gravely.

Harcourt quickly recovered his composure. 'I'm happy to find you so well, George.'

'Yes, I'm very well, and for that mercy I thank the Lord my God.' There was a quality in Landser's eyes, a gleam, an expression, which disturbed Harcourt. He felt he had encountered this same look before, but could not remember where or when.

'The Lord has blessed me exceedingly, Edward. He has shone his light into my soul.'

Remembrance flooded into Harcourt's mind. Landser's eyes were those of the religious fanatics that he had known, and despised, when he was still only a youth.

'So, you've found religion, have you?' he involuntarily uttered aloud.

'I've found salvation through the grace of the Lord!' Landser declaimed sonorously.

Harcourt was hard put to hide his contempt. 'I'm sure that Lydia will be happy to hear of it. Though she might well wish it had come sooner.'

'My salvation has come when the Lord has so desired it,' Landser declared with absolute conviction. 'His ways are inscrutable to us who are merely the dust of His Creation.'

'Well, sir, what do you think to my mode of treatment now?' Burman's pink face shone with pride. 'Mr Landser is almost cured of his affliction. Almost cured of his enslavement to strong drink.'

Harcourt smiled sardonically. 'You have my sincerest congratulations, Dr Burman. You have indeed triumphed in this case. Would you now please leave us alone? I have certain private matters to discuss with Mr Landser.'

When Burman withdrew, Harcourt told Landser, 'Sit down, George, we have much to talk about . . .'

Twenty-Three

I t was dusk when Edward Harcourt returned from Henley in Arden, and as he entered his house he immediately asked his manservant, 'Where is the young lady?'

'She's still in her room, sir. She refused breakfast, and asked not to be disturbed, so I haven't been near her since.'

Harcourt nodded. 'Very well. Lay the table for two for dinner.'

Liddy sat on the side of the bed, immersed in her thoughts. She was calm now. The period of bitter self-recrimination had passed. After three days and two nights of anguish and self-reproach she was beginning to come to terms with what had happened. She had seen very little of Harcourt during that period, and had remained in her room, only leaving it to perform the unavoidable bodily functions.

She had tried desperately to remember the actual physicality of love-making, but her memory remained a blank. Her own ruthless self-honesty forbade her from trying to excuse what she had done, by telling herself that she had been helpless to resist Harcourt's advances. She knew that if she had not wanted to make love with him, then she would have fought to the death to prevent it. So she was not blaming Edward Harcourt for what had happened between them. How could she blame a man for succumbing to a temptation to which she had obviously suc-cumbed herself. A man, furthermore, who had only ever treated her with great kindness.

Now she sadly accepted the fact of her own drunken im-morality, and was taking stock of her situation. She realised

156

that any fanciful imaginings of romance and marriage with James Kerr must now be banished from her mind. In her world a gentleman would never marry a woman who had so shamelessly given herself to another man out of wedlock . . . But what was she to do now?

Her lips twitched in a fleeting mirthless smile . . . What could she do? She was homeless, penniless, characterless, her father in a lunatic asylum, her brother, God only knew where. To all intents and purposes she was materially totally bereft and facing a very bleak future; and above all else she had lost her self-respect. She had behaved like a drunken whore.

She thought about Edward Harcourt's talk of marriage. Could she bring herself to marry him? She liked him and was deeply grateful to him, but she didn't love him, and also he was old enough to be her father.

Could she grow to love him? She doubted that. Love was not something that could be forced into growth from a sense of obligation or any other motive. One either fell in love, or one didn't.

Harcourt tapped on the door and called softly, 'Lydia, may I come in?'

With a sinking heart she stood up and told him to enter.

When she faced him, she felt her cheeks reddening with embarrassment. Since her infancy this was the only man who had ever seen her naked, and the only man who had known and penetrated her intimate body.

Harcourt saw the dark circles beneath her eyes, her drawn, worried expression. He sensed her tension and momentarily she touched some softer chord in his character. To his surprise he found he was not looking at her solely as a sexual plaything.

'Are you feeling unwell, my dear?' he questioned with genuine concern.

'No, I'm perfectly well, I thank you.' Her voice held a tremor, but she met his searching gaze levelly.

'Please, sit down,' he requested. 'I want to talk to you.' She acquiesced, seating herself on the side of the bed. He drew up a chair and sat close to her. Now the softer chord in his character

157

was being rapidly overlayed by his powerfully dominant pre-datory instinct. And experienced predator that he was, he stalked his prey carefully.

'Can you ever forgive me for what happened between us?' he asked gravely.

She hesitated, then said slowly, 'Any blame there is must be apportioned equally between us, Edward. I feel that I behaved shamelessly.'

He shook his head vehemently. 'No. I should have been stronger.' Then he spread his hands in a gesture of helplessness. 'But I am so much in love with you, that I couldn't help myself.'

She opened her mouth to speak, but he prevented her.

'No, please, hear me out. Today I've been to see your father. I'm happy to tell you that he is well and will soon be able to resume a normal life.'

A sharp pang of guilt struck Liddy. She had hardly given a thought to her father these last days. Am I wickedly unnatural? she asked herself, but found no answer.

'I've asked your father for his permission to marry you, and it's made him very happy.'

Liddy was stung into protesting, 'Aren't you taking it all too much for granted, Edward? I haven't yet agreed to marry you.'

He ignored her interjection, and went on, talking earnestly. 'I want to marry you as soon as possible and raise you once more to your rightful position in society. I'm a very wealthy man, and by marrying me you will not only be assuring your own future, but also the future of your family. I can provide your father with his own home and servant, and you will be able to visit him every day should you so wish. Also I can try to discover what has become of your brother, and should he agree I can establish him in any business he might wish to pursue.'

He paused, hoping for some reaction from her to enable him to gauge how to proceed. But she stayed silent, regarding him with solemn eyes.

He decided to cast fresh bait, and went on. 'From what Mrs Melen has told me at times, it seems that you are unhappy with the arrangements made for the education of the pauper children.

Well, when we are married you will be a woman of much influence and authority. You will be able to make whatever arrangements you wish concerning the education of the paupers.'

He smiled warmly. 'In fact you will be empowered to do much good for the poor of this parish, my dear.'

As she listened she fully appreciated how much she could gain by marrying him. Security and comfort for herself and her father. A finding of her beloved brother. An end to the bitter social humiliations she had endured. Opportunity to help those poor, benighted workhouse children whom she pitied so, and had in some cases become very fond of.

'Will you marry me then, my dear?' he asked quietly. 'I'm sure that we can be very happy together.'

Her head told her to accept his offer, but her heart rejected it.

'I don't know,' she told him. 'I need to think about it.'

'But don't you have any feelings for me?' he questioned.

'Oh yes, I do have feelings for you, Edward. I like you a great deal. But I'm not in love with you,' she answered honestly.

'When we're married you will come to love me, I'm sure of that,' he said confidently.

'I can't be sure of it.' Her uneasiness caused her to speak more sharply then she intended, and guilt assailed her at her own churlish attitude.

She stood up abruptly. 'I must have time to think on this.'

He rose also. 'Of course you must. Now come downstairs and have dinner with me.'

'No, I'm not hungry. I'd prefer to stay here. I need to think.'

'Very well. I know when I'm not wanted. I shall leave you alone.' His demeanour became noticeably cooler, and she misunderstood the reason for it.

Thinking she had wounded him, not realising that his coolness was masking his fury at being balked, she apologised. 'I'm sorry, Edward. I've no wish to hurt your feelings. But I really do need to be on my own. I must have some time to think.'

He forced a smile. 'We'll talk tomorrow, my dear. I'll say good night.'

'Good night, Edward,' she answered with patent relief.

Outside her closed door he balled his fists in anger. He had expected some show of maidenly coyness, but she was proving much more difficult than he had anticipated. Despite her reluctance he was, however, still confident that she could be pressured into marrying him.

And then I'll bring the little bitch to heel in very short order, he promised himself grimly.

After he had eaten his solitary dinner he sat drinking and smoking until he was disturbed by a loud knocking on the front door.

His servant came to tell him, 'There's a young gentleman wishes to speak with you, sir. It's a Mr James Kerr. He says it's a matter of urgency.'

'Show him in,' Harcourt ordered irritably. The last thing he wanted at this moment was to have James Kerr in his house and so close to Lydia Landser. But when the young man entered the room he rose and smiled.

'How are you, Mr Kerr?'

'I'm very well, I thank you, sir.' James wasted no more time in polite preamble but immediately told the other man of Liddy's disappearance.

'I came to see you, sir, to ask if you knew of her whereabouts?'

'No, Mr Kerr. I've no idea.'

'Did you not know that she left the workhouse three days since?'

'No, and I must say that I feel I should have been informed of it. It was on my recommendation, after all, that the young woman was appointed to her position there.'

'But where can she have gone to, sir? She has little or no money from what I've been told.'

'I've no idea where she might be, Mr Kerr.'

'Could I ask a favour of you?' James entreated.

'But of course.'

'I have to go to London tomorrow morning, and shall be absent for some time. Could I leave this packet with you to be given to Miss Landser?'

160

Harcourt frowned doubtfully. 'I'm happy to oblige you, but as I said before, I've no notion of the young lady's whereabouts.'

'But you have been her benefactor, sir. I'm confident that she will contact you if she is to contact anyone hereabouts.'

Harcourt pursed his lips and agreed judicially. 'Yes, that may well be. Very well then. I'll keep the packet here in case she should contact me. Although I doubt that she will.'

James clutched at this straw. 'I'd be most grateful if you would do so, sir. Thank you very much.'

'It's London you go to then? Is there an address at which I can contact you should I have news of Lydia Landser?'

'Yes, I shall be staying at the house of the Earl of Allesley. It's in Handley Square, Mayfair.'

'Then you will be moving in exalted circles.' Harcourt seemed impressed. 'Will not our rustic society be too dull for you to return to, when you've experienced the gaieties of London in company with the *bon ton*?'

'No, sir, for I am a rustic at heart and city life has no great appeal for me.' James smiled. 'Now I'll not intrude upon you longer, for I know that you are a busy man.'

'It's always a pleasure to see you, Mr Kerr,' Harcourt assured him graciously.

When James had left Harcourt sat pondering for some moments. He turned the sealed packet over in his hands, then broke the seal and unwrapped the cloth covering to discover a folded sheet of notepaper and a purse which contained twenty golden sovereigns. He scanned the message written on the notepaper. As he had feared, James Kerr was offering help and protection, and despite the stilted formal phrasing it was glaringly apparent that James Kerr was as attracted towards Lydia Landser as she to him.

Harcourt threw the notepaper on to the fire and watched it curl and flame.

Twenty-Four

In the late afternoon sunlight Liddy stood gazing at the front of Septimus Nairn's house. She knew why she had walked to this place. She wanted to see James Kerr, in the wholly irrational hope that he could somehow solve the quandary that faced her. Yet now that she was here, she could not bring herself to call at the house and ask for him.

I'm acting like a whore again, she thought with scathing self-disgust, coming from one man's bed to seek out another man.

Despondency whelmed over her and she turned and walked away.

A horseman was riding up the steep incline that crossed over the canal tunnel. When he saw the young woman walking with her head bent, he recognised her instantly and as he neared her he reined in his mount.

'How are you, Miss Landser? What brings you here?'

Startled, she looked up to find the ruddy features of Sean Fitzgerald beaming down at her.

She couldn't admit that she had come to find James Kerr, and instead lied. 'I was taking the air, Mr Fitzgerald, and walked further than I'd intended.'

He asked after her father, and brother, and when she told him of them, grimaced sympathetically.

'Life can be very cruel, Miss Landser. But Dr Burman bears a good name as a humane man. I'm sure that your father will be getting the best of treatment with him, and will soon be entirely well again. And I'm sure that your brother is well and hearty also. He's a young man, and young men always roam, and neglect to write and so cause their family heartache. He'll turn up again, just wait and see.'

'I pray so,' Liddy murmured fervently.

'It's a shame I didn't meet you earlier this week, you could have wished Jamie good luck in London.'

'London?' she queried.

'Yes, London. He's the house-guest of the Earl of Allesley,' the Irishman announced proudly. 'It's Jamie's chance for fame and fortune, you know, being introduced into high society by the earl himself. It's a great honour, so it is, and the chance of a lifetime for him.'

A sharp dismay struck through Liddy, and she could only nod agreement, while trying to come to terms with this totally unexpected and unwelcome news.

'Well, I must get on. Enjoy your walk, Miss Landser.' Fitzgerald lifted his hat in salute and rode on.

Liddy walked slowly, one emotion above all dominating her: a sense of loss so deep that it felt almost like a bereavement . . . James Kerr was gone, to seek fame and fortune in London. He was lost to her for ever and no amount of fanciful daydreams would bring him back.

As she neared the town she forced herself to accept the seemingly inevitable fact that her family's only chance of achieving any security, any decent standard of living, any quality of life, was for her to accept Edward Harcourt's offer of marriage. Her ruthless self-honesty enabled her to admit that she was considering herself as much as her family. She was sick of living in poverty, sick of being powerless and dependent on others for even the slightest of advantages. Even if the Board of Guardians could be persuaded to give her a character reference, she would still be doomed to spend her days in ill-paid, servile employment, being ordered about by those whom she had been brought up to regard as her social, moral and mental inferiors.

By the time she reached Bromsgrove she had made her decision. She would marry Edward Harcourt.

Twenty-Five

July 1843

I t was Saturday afternoon and Liddy was feeling somewhat apprehensive as she waited for the arrival of her father, uncertain what effect his sojourn at Dr Burman's establishment might have had on him.

Over two weeks had passed since she had accepted Harcourt's offer and she was to marry him this coming Monday. They were going to Birmingham to be married by licence, and up to now the coming union had been kept a secret, known only to themselves and her father, who was coming to stay with her and give her away. Although not relishing the prospect of being married, she had pragmatically accepted that there was really no other viable course open to her. And Edward Harcourt would prove to be a fond and complaisant husband, she had no doubts on that score. He had accepted without complaint when she had refused to sleep or make love with him until after they were married.

Her lips twisted in a mirthless sardonic smile at her own prudery. He's already physically been husband to me, so why do I still play the nervous virgin? she asked herself. Then admitted, because in my heart I still am a nervous virgin.

A pony cart came to a halt on the road outside and she went to the window and saw her father alighting.

Liddy hurried to open the front door and go outside to greet him.

'Hello, Pa.' She wanted to hug him but was unsure of how he would react. Then he held out his arms, and she went gladly into his embrace.

'Oh, Pa, it's so good to see you.' Tears stung her eyes.

She wiped her eyes as he released her, and then stared closely at him. He was thinner now, his features heavily lined, almost haggard, and little trace of his old flamboyance of manner and dress remained.

'Are you feeling perfectly well, Pa?'

'Oh yes, the Lord is my shepherd, so how could I not be well? Blessed be the Name of the Lord.' He declaimed the last sentence in sonorous tones and made the sign of the Cross.

He had always been an irreligious man, and for a moment Liddy thought that he was joking, then with a frisson of unease she noted the fanatical gleam in his eyes.

The driver of the pony cart was one of Dr Burman's burly assistants, and he had been taking a close interest in the exchange between father and daughter.

He grinned mockingly and informed Liddy, 'Your feyther's found the Lord, missy. He's took to religion like a duck takes to water. Aren't that so, Mr Landser?'

'Indeed it is. The Lord has shone His Light into the darkness of my soul. Blessed be His Name.'

Disconcerted, Liddy took her father's arm and led him into the house.

In the drawing room George Landser's manner became increasingly frenetic. He began muttering prayers and pacing rapidly up and down the room, three paces, turn, three paces, turn, three paces, turn, while Liddy watched with escalating unease.

'Won't you sit down, Pa?'

He ignored her, until she spoke more sharply. 'What is it, Pa? Is something wrong?'

He halted and faced her.

'I can do nothing without your help, Liddy. I must depend upon you for even the bread in my mouth and the shelter over my head.'

She wryly acknowledged how their relative situations had changed. She was now the protector and provider. She was now in the role of parent.

165

'Of course I'll always help you, Pa. I'm happy to do so.'

'And this proposed marriage, are you happy about it also?'

She shrugged. 'I'm content enough with the prospect.'

'You're very fortunate to be making such a fine match, Liddy. The Lord has blessed you.'

'I'm sure he has,' Liddy agreed dryly.

George Landser recommenced his frenetic pacing, and began to wring his hands and beg aloud, 'Give me the strength to confess all, Lord. I beg you to give me the strength to confess. To make amends.'

Liddy stared at him with concern.

'What is troubling you so, Pa? Sit down and tell me.'

He abruptly sat down on a chair and, leaning towards her, said brokenly, 'I'm carrying a grievous burden of sin upon my soul, Liddy. I must have your help to lift it from me.'

Momentary exasperation irked her. 'Then tell me how I can help you, Pa.'

'You must save your sister. I must atone for the wicked wrong I've done to her, and become a father to her.'

Shocked alarm kept her silent. She feared his mind had gone. Explanations, excuses, pleas for forgiveness babbled from him in a torrential jumble of words and Liddy could only try desperately to make sense of what he was telling her. Slowly she pieced together the various threads of his story and could only shake her head in bemusement.

'You say I have a young sister? But where is she? Who is her mother? What are their names?'

Her reaction to his answers was horrified disbelief.

'It can't be true! It can't be!'

'May the Lord strike me down this instant if I'm lying. Indeed I deserve to be struck down for this sin,' George Landser said fervently, then his face seemed to crumple and he broke into harsh, stomach-wrenching sobs.

Liddy was filled with a furious disgust, but as the moments passed and the genuine depth of his remorse and grief became apparent, a sense of pity for him and for the tragic mother and child gained strength and gradually overcame her anger.

She went to him and cradled his head against her breasts as if he was a child.

'There now, Pa, don't grieve so,' she comforted. 'I shall do whatever I can for the girl. I promise I will. Don't grieve so.'

As his sobs slowly eased and died away, she was struggling to come to terms with what she had heard. She could still not fully accept it as the truth, even though her instincts told her that her father was not lying.

She found that she could not entirely condemn his immorality. She had behaved immorally herself with Edward Harcourt, had she not?

Obviously her father didn't know of Katie Kennedy's adoption, or that Meggie Kennedy was incarcerated in Powick Asylum. He thought that they were both still inmates of the workhouse.

When she told him what had happened to them, harsh sobs were once again torn from him.

'It's all my fault,' he choked. 'I deserve to rot in hell for this. The child is lost to me, and it seems that I've destroyed poor Meggie. What can I do, Liddy? What can I do?'

At this moment Liddy couldn't even begin to accept that little Katie Kennedy was her sister, although such a relationship might be an explanation for how strangely familiar the child had seemed to her, and how quickly she had grown fond of her. It could have been blood calling to blood. All she could do at this moment was to try to comfort him.

'I'll speak to Edward, Pa, and see if he can suggest anything. But it must wait until after the wedding. I can't burden him with this knowledge now.'

In fact she was doubting if she could ever bring herself to tell Edward Harcourt about this further disgrace to her family. Kind and forbearing though he is, how will he react to this, she wondered with foreboding.

Edward Harcourt was at Tardebigge waiting in Septimus Nairn's house when the surgeon returned from his rounds on this same Saturday afternoon.

'Edward? What brings you here?' Nairn greeted. 'And why do you have a face like thunder?'

'Because my damned clap has flared up again, and it's damned sore. I swear that I'm pissing broken glass, and every erection I get is like a crucifixion.' Harcourt's mood was vicious.

Nairn frowned. 'Have you been indulging yourself with the whores again?'

'Two nights only.'

'Come into the study and let me take a look at you.'

Examination completed, Nairn said, 'I'll give you an injection to soothe the heat and pain, and prescribe a fresh course of powders.'

Harcourt didn't reply, only stood scowling, while Nairn mixed some mucilage of gum arabic and olive oil, drew the mixture into a syringe and carefully inserted the syringe nozzle into Harcourt's uretha.

Harcourt hissed with pain as the blunt metal nozzle penetrated halfway down his uretha and the liquid was injected.

Nairn smiled grimly and remarked with heavy irony, 'After bought sexual pleasure, pain is almost inevitable, Edward. You of all people should know that very well by now.'

While the other man rearranged his clothing, Nairn made up a powder mixture of Glaubers salts and nitre and subdivided it into small portions which he wrapped individually.

'Take one of these packets three or four times daily dissolved in linseed tea. You'd best come and see me every day for injections.'

'How long will it take to clear up?' Harcourt wanted to know.

'It will be gradual, Edward. You have a severe infection. Keep away from the women or you'll be spreading it far and wide.'

'It was a woman who gave it me to begin with, wasn't it, damn and blast her!' Harcourt grumbled.

As he rode back to Bromsgrove, Harcourt was cursing his bad luck, and the impulse that he had given way to ten days previously on a business trip to Hereford. He had met a pretty young prostitute there and spent two nights with her.

Perversely he now began to blame Lydia Landser for this resulting infection: If she hadn't refused to let me fuck her, then this wouldn't have happened. It's her fault for being so prudish. She should have given me what I needed.

After riding on a while longer he calmed, and consoled himself, Never mind, she'll not be able to refuse me come Monday night. She'll be my lawful property then. And I don't care how sore I'm feeling, she'll be fucked that night as many times as I can manage.

Twenty-Six

There was no music, no bridesmaidens or grooms, no flowers, no guests at the wedding of Edward Harcourt and Lydia Landser. The ceremony took place at midday in a dingy Birmingham chapel and was conducted by an elderly, half-drunken clergyman. The witnesses were George Landser and the clergyman's decrepit housekeeper.

Liddy wore a new gown and bonnet which Harcourt had bought for her, but carried no bridal posy. The day was darkly overcast with storm clouds, and the weather was in concert with Liddy's mood. Even as she voiced the responses during the marriage service she wanted to run from this chapel and this wedding, but she forced herself to face the bleak reality that there was no one and nowhere to run to. She had no realistic choice other than to become Edward Harcourt's wife. No matter how she might wish that it were James Kerr standing here beside her, the fact was that she was fated to be with Edward Harcourt.

I just have to accept that this was destined to be, and try to make the best of it, she told herself over and over again.

Edward Harcourt was in buoyant mood, and impatient for the service to finish so that he could take Liddy to the hotel room he had reserved and begin to satisfy his hunger for her body. He intended for them to stay for some days at the hotel so that he would be undisturbed by any business or domestic matters while he commenced her education in the duties of being his wife.

As Liddy signed the register her face was pale and her hand was trembling and Harcourt's lust quickened at these indications of her vulnerability.

As soon as they left the chapel he told George Landser, 'Go back to my house. You may stay there until we return. Come, Lydia.' He took her arm and pulled her along with him before she could even kiss her father goodbye.

The hotel was only a few hundreds yards distant, and as they neared it Liddy's apprehension was increasing with every hurried step. Harcourt's grip on her arm was tight, his face unsmiling, and he hardly looked at her.

At the hotel the two clerks behind the reception desk obviously recognised Harcourt. While he was checking that their luggage had arrived and other arrangements made, they both kept on sneaking sly knowing glances at Liddy as if they somehow recognised her also, and it deepened her uneasiness.

When the couple followed the porter towards the broad staircase, the senior clerk grinned pruriently at his colleague, and whispered, 'She don't have the look of a gay girl, does she? She looks too nervous. Do you think he might really be married to her?'

'Could be. But I feel sorry for the poor little cow if he is her husband. D'you remember what that last slut he brought here told us?'

'Oh yeah.' The senior clerk leered. 'She reckoned she wouldn't sleep with him again if he offered her double the price. It makes you wonder what he gets up to, don't it?'

His colleague chuckled lewdly. 'Well, whatever it is, he'll be getting up to it again directly, I'll bet me life on that. She's a nice-looking wench as well. I'll bet he'll be shagging the arse off her in two shakes of a donkey's tail, the lucky bastard.'

He bowed and smiled obsequiously at an oncoming guest. 'Good afternoon, sir. How may I help you?'

A bottle of wine stood on the table in the ornately furnished room. Harcourt opened it and poured two glasses, handing one of them to Liddy.

'To us, my dear.' He clinked his glass with hers, and then drank it down in quick gulps. He was still unsmiling, his manner tense, his eyes feverish.

Liddy drank, grateful to moisten her nervously dry mouth and throat. She was finding his manner strange, and it did nothing to lessen her apprehension.

He refilled his glass and again gulped it empty. Then he put the glass on the table, removed his hat and came to take her still half-full glass from her. He undid the ribbons of her bonnet and removed it, then pulled her hard against him, his mouth clamped on her mouth, crushing so hard that her inner lips were bruised against her teeth. He dragged her to the bed and thrust her down upon it, his hands scrabbling to lift her gown and petticoats, tearing at her drawers. She felt that she was suffocating and panic made her begin to struggle against him, but he was too strong, too heavy and she felt a tearing pain as he thrust brutally into her. His teeth bit into the side of her throat and his pounding body drove the breath from her lungs. Each savage thrust sent agonies lancing through her intimate flesh. She could hear his loud animal-like grunting and she prayed desperately to God to make this bestial onslaught end, and sobbed with relief when he cried out and the pounding stopped, and he lay slumped upon her, gasping hoarsely.

This is a nightmare, she wanted to scream in anguish. This is a nightmare.

After what seemed a long, long time, he rolled off her, and she lay with spread thighs, feeling degraded, irredeemably soiled. She stirred and came to a sitting posture, pulling her skirts down. She felt physically nauseated, yet at the same time her fury was rising, tears of anger stinging her eyes, blurring her sight.

He rose to stand up, pulling his trousers closed, and she attacked him fiercely.

'How dare you treat me like this! You have no right to do so.'

'I have every right.' He scowled down at her. 'You're my wife now. My property. And I can do whatever I want with you.'

172

'Oh no you cannot!' she contradicted heatedly. 'I'll not accept such treatment.'

The next instant his hand whiplashed backwards and forwards across her face, and she cried out in pain. Then he was on her again, forcing her on to her back, punching her breasts and stomach, muffling her cries with a pillow. She struggled frantically, but stood no chance against his weight and strength. She couldn't draw air into her lungs and blackness threatened to drown her. Then the pillow was lifted and she dragged in air.

He was sitting straddled across her stomach, knees pinning her arms, one hand squeezing her throat, the other bunched into a fist held threateningly in front of her eyes.

'Listen very carefully to what I say,' he hissed venomously. 'In law you are now my chattel, my property. You belong to me in body and soul, and I can use you as I wish. Thrash you, work you, keep you hungry, ragged and shoeless if I choose. And no one can prevent this, because you're my wife and I am your lawful husband and master. Even God cannot come between us. He cannot stop me killing you this instant if that is what I want to do.'

The cruel pressure of the fingers on her throat suddenly increased, cutting off her breath, and waves of blackness shot through with red flashes overwhelmed the light of day.

The pressure eased and she sucked in strangled gasps of air. With that life-giving air there came fear. A terrible fear of this man, and what he might do to her. A fear that made her feel utterly helpless. Utterly at his mercy.

'Now, my dear,' his tone became silkily coaxing, 'my inclination is to treat you kindly. To be a fond husband to you. To help and support your family. But if I am to do that, then in return you must be an obedient and dutiful wife to me. You must behave as I wish you to behave, and do whatever I ask of you. Not grudgingly, but willingly.'

Again the fingers tightened viciously, and again red-flashed blackness overwhelmed her with the sickening terror of death.

The fingers drew back, and pain-wracked, terrified awareness slowly returned.

'Do you understand, my dear? Are we in agreement?'

Despite her terror, despite her physical agonies, Liddy knew that she wanted to live and that she would do whatever was needful to survive.

'I agree.' The words were not able to be voiced, her throat and mouth paralysed by dryness and pain.

'I shan't ask you again,' he warned. 'Are we in agreement?'

She nodded.

He smiled warmly, then bent to kiss her, his lips gentler now.

He levered himself backwards, drawing her with him off the bed. He poured out more wine and told her, 'We'll drink a toast to our future happiness, my dear.'

Despite her fearful anguish Liddy relished the relief of the cool liquid on the painful dryness of her mouth and throat.

He sat in the armchair by the fireplace and pointed to a spot in front of him. 'Come, my dear, stand there to face me.'

She wordlessly obeyed.

'Finish your drink. No need to gulp it. We have all the time in the world before us.' He was smiling, sitting completely at ease.

When she had emptied her glass he told her, 'Take your clothes off.'

She hesitated, and he frowned. 'Do as I say, and don't turn away from me.'

Too afraid to protest, weeping with anguish and shame, Liddy began to undress.

Twenty-Seven

London
October 1843

A t the beginning of August James Kerr received the news of Liddy Landser's marriage in a letter from his uncle, and it hit him hard. Shock, disbelief, pain, anger, regret crowded one behind the other as the dominant emotion, while to the outer world he was forced to show a smiling face. Her marriage was also the reason that he was still here in London, because he had not felt able to return home until his heartache had soothed. He was surprised himself by the force of his emotional reaction, but now midway through October he had weathered that emotional storm and was ready to return. He still thought about Lydia Landser a great deal, but now the dominant emotion was of regret for what might have been, and he was confident that he would be able to see her, even talk with her, without betraying any deeper emotion than friendship.

London and its society had not proven to be the glittering entrée to fame and fortune for him that his uncle had envisaged. Humphrey Chamberson was a generous host and true to his word did introduce James to some powerful and influential men, but as soon as those men ascertained that James possessed neither land, wealth or title they immediately lost any interest in furthering the acquaintance. James went to several balls but did not enjoy them. The affected mannerisms and drawling speech of the languid young bloods irritated him, and although he danced with some pretty girls he found himself wishing that it was Lydia Landser he was partnering in the polkas and gallopades and waltzes.

In September Chamberson was forced to leave London to attend to urgent business at his estate in Hampshire, and so James was left very much to his own devices. He visited the museums, art galleries, theatres, and also managed to tour the capital's hospitals. On one memorable day he gained access to view an amputation of the leg performed by the great Robert Liston himself. James was not overly impressed by the famous surgeon's manner or technique; he thought that Liston displayed a little too much of the showman playing to his audience, and lacked his Uncle Nairn's finesse with the knife and saw.

Tiring of museums and galleries, James had begun to spend hours each day wandering through the length and breadth of the city. This was a pastime which he thought could never pall for him: the streets were like a living theatre pulsating with drama, incident and constant change. But now James was more than ready to return home. However, Chamberson had specifically asked him to remain until he, Chamberson, should return from Hampshire, which would be any day now.

James was wandering around Whitechapel, a grimy slum swarming with rude and boisterous life. He loitered to read a wall display of garish posters advertising a host of dubious panaceas, never-to-be repeated bargains of every description, and a myriad entertainments. One poster immediately took his attention: PROFESSOR PARR PROMISES PAINLESS EXTRACTIONS OF TEETH AND ROOTS. DEMONSTRATIONS PERFORMED AT PROFESSOR PARR'S PHARMACY.

Another lying quack, James thought dismissively, then realised that he was in the same street as the address given at the bottom of the poster.

He sauntered on, seeking for the professor's premises and soon spotted the crude tar-painted lettering on the greasy wall of a tumbledown shopfront which proclaimed 'PROFESSOR PARR'S PHARMACY'.

176

James halted and examined the premises, peering through the filthy panes of the leaded windows, some of which had been broken and stuffed with rags. From what he was able to see, the jars, bottles and packets strewn on the window shelves were the typical medicinally-worthless stock in trade of a cheapjack.

Ragged barefoot street urchins came capering around him, turning cartwheels and shouting, 'Spare a copper, guvnor. Spare a copper.'

He threw some small coins on to the ground and the urchins scrambled for them with raucous cries of delight.

'You've made a rod for your own back now, sir. The little bastards will come swarming around you like wasps around molasses.'

The vulpine-featured, middle-aged man in the shop doorway was seedily flashy in his broad-check trousers, blue frock coat, high beaver hat and ruffled shirt. His garish cravat was secured with a huge false diamond pin, rings glittering on all his fingers. His greying hair was long, hanging to his shoulders, and oiled so that it glistened in the sunshine.

'Professor Parr, at your service, sir.' He bowed gracefully. 'Can I be of any assistance to you?' His accent had the nasal twang of America's north-eastern states.

'I saw your poster concerning the painless extraction of teeth and roots, sir,' James told him. 'I'm curious as to what method you use to achieve this.'

'Do you wish to have some of your own teeth extracted?' Parr questioned, his dark close-set eyes shrewdly appraising the quality of James's clothing.

'No. Fortunately my teeth are sound.'

'Spare a copper, guvnor, spare a copper!' The urchins clustered around James once again, and Parr gestured an invitation.

'Step inside, sir. They'll give you no peace otherwise.'

The interior smelled damp and musty and was as grimy and unprepossessing as the exterior. A sturdy ancient wooden surgical chair was bolted to the centre of the floor, leather straps fastened to the arms, headrest and legs, and on a table next to it was strewn a selection of pliers, scalpels, sponges, pieces of dusty cotton wadding, and some rusting surgical instruments.

'How long have you been practising these painless extractions, Professor?' James made polite use of the title, although strongly doubting its entitlement.

'For several years.'

'It's strange then that I haven't heard of you, since I take great interest in such matters.'

The dark eyes became wary. 'I've been practising in my own country, the good old US of A. I've only landed here some weeks past. I haven't even had time to find suitable premises for my pharmaceutical business yet, let alone advertise my dental practice widely.'

'I'd much appreciate seeing a demonstration. Will there be one today?' James had already decided that the man was a charlatan.

'It can be arranged. But it will cost you a fee.'

'How much?'

'Ten pounds.'

'That's too much.'

'Shall we say seven pounds ten shillings then?'

'Five pounds,' James offered.

'Very well.' Parr held out his hand.

James smiled and shook his head. 'Money to be paid when I've witnessed the demonstration.'

Parr grinned broadly, displaying a discoloured set of gutta-percha false teeth. 'I like your style, sir. I see that you're no simpleton to be gulled by large promises. So allow me to propose a wager to you.'

James was intrigued by this suggestion. 'Let me hear it.'

'I will extract a tooth painlessly and you will then pay me ten pounds. If the patient feels any pain, then I will pay you ten pounds.'

'Agreed.'

'Wait here, sir, I'll not be long.'

Despite his scepticism James could not help but feel a

178

burgeoning excitement. Could he really be on the verge of witnessing a veritable miracle? A tooth drawn without pain? No. It was impossible. If he could do it then he'd be treating the crowned heads of Europe, not living here in this slum.

When Professor Parr returned he was accompanied by an elderly tramp, who stank rancidly, and whose rags were visibly verminous.

'Sit in the chair, Billy,' Parr ordered brusquely, 'and open your mouth so that this gentleman can see your teeth.'

The tramp's open mouth was a hideous spectacle of broken, blackened fangs, and the stench of his breath even caused James's long-hardened stomach to heave involuntarily.

'Select a tooth, sir,' Parr invited James. 'Any one you wish.'

'That one, the canine.'

'Very well.' Parr disappeared into an inner room and returned within moments carrying a flask and a piece of rag.

'You know what to do now, Billy.'

The tramp sat docilely while Parr poured some of the flask's contents on to the rag, then held the rag tight over the tramp's nose and mouth.

James found he was silently counting the seconds, and as he reached the half minute the tramp's head fell forward as he became unconscious.

Parr laid aside the rag and flask, snatched up a pair of pliers and clamped the long canine tooth. He wrenched brutally, loosening it in its socket and twisted it out of the tramp's jaw. The tramp remained still, eyes closed, breath snorting stertorously, blood trickling from his mouth and into the tangled mass of his beard. Beneath the grime his face was an ashen grey and his lips were blue.

James stared wide-eyed, held motionless in wonderment by this unbelievable event he had witnessed.

Parr stepped back and picked up the discarded flask and rag, and as he did so James caught a whiff of a sweetish pleasant smell. His memory instantly ranged back to his holiday in Birmingham, and the ether party he had shared with his companions.

It's ether. He's used ether, he thought, dumbstruck.

The tramp began to regain consciousness, blinking blearily around him.

'That's it done with, Billy.' Parr pressed some coins into the filthy paw. 'Off you go now.'

He lifted the tramp bodily and propelled him outside the door, leaving him squatting against the wall, vomiting helplessly.

'Ten pounds, I think was the sum wagered, sir.' Parr presented his open palm and James counted out ten gold sovereigns on to it with good grace.

'It's ether you've used, isn't it?' he exclaimed excitedly.

'No, it isn't,' Parr denied.

'Yes, it is,' James insisted firmly. 'I'm a medical man myself, and I know how ether smells.'

'It has some ether contained in it, I'll admit. But the other ingredients are my own secret compounds. Here, smell it properly.'

He proffered the flask, and James cautiously sniffed. It smelled like ether, without a doubt, but mingled with the sweetish odour there was a second positive scent which he could not identify, as well as traces of others. Also, instead of being colourless as was pure ether, it was a pale green hue.

'How long have you been using this? How did you come to discover it?' James questioned eagerly.

A calculating gleam came into the dark eyes.

'I discovered this formula some years since. I haven't quite perfected it yet, I confess. But a little more experimentation will readily accomplish that, and as you've seen for yourself it serves magnificently as it is.

'When it's perfect I intend to patent the formula, and set up in business. But it's very expensive to produce the compound, and necessitates much time and trial. I confess that some recent family misfortunes have left me a virtual pauper, so I can't carry out my plans immediately. I fear I might even be driven to sell the formula in order to save my family from imminent ruin. I've just received one offer which I'm feared I'll be forced to accept.'

180

'Might I know for how much?'

'The last offer was a thousand pounds,' Parr informed. 'But he might go higher if I can hold out a little while longer.'

'A thousand pounds! Perhaps even more! That's a fortune!'

'It might be for you or me, but there are those to whom it's only a drop in the ocean.' Parr looked and sounded wistful. 'You say that you're a medical gentleman, sir, and I've already judged that you're a decent, honest man. Someone like you would be my ideal purchaser for the formula, because you'd use it for the benefit of mankind and not solely to enrich yourself, like this other one who's made the offer intends to do. It's a shame that someone like you can't afford to buy it from me.'

Temptation blossomed in James's mind. A dazzling vista of fame and success opened wide before him. With this formula, once it was perfected, he could banish pain completely, and with that banishment the practice of surgery would be transformed beyond men's wildest dreams. He could become the greatest surgeon in history.

'Supposing I could raise the necessary sum, Professor, would you be prepared to give me some time to do so?'

The vulpine features assumed an expression of deep consideration.

'I would, if circumstance permitted, sir. But as I said before, my family is in sore straits and time is at a premium.'

James's thoughts were racing, ideas flashing through his mind, yet simultaneously his deeply ingrained honesty and sense of justice still impelled him to point out, 'This formula could be worth a vast fortune to whoever patents and produces the compound, Professor. But as you said yourself it will take much expense, time and trial to produce it in quantity, and it needs some further experimentation to bring it to an absolute perfection. To speak frankly, I've no money myself, but I have a friend who is very wealthy indeed. He might be persuaded to invest in such a venture as this, and might also be persuaded to give you and me both a share in future profits.'

'By God, sir, but you've a shrewd old head on your young shoulders!' Parr exclaimed in admiration.

181

James could not help but preen a little. 'Well, I'm not altogether a fool from the country, Professor.'

'And I'm no fool from the country myself, sir.' Parr grinned. 'And can recognise an honest man when I meet him.' He held out his hand. 'Might I have the privilege of knowing your name?'

James grinned happily as he shook hands.

'My name is James Kerr.'

'And I am Reuben Parr, so let us be familiar. I shall be Reuben to you and you shall be James to me. Now we'll go and find a snug little tavern and have a drink while we discuss this further.'

Twenty-Eight

T his evening the ballroom of Humphrey Chamberson's house was thronged with well-dressed men and fashionably gowned women seated on rows of chairs facing the raised stage at one end of the long room, on which another chair had been placed to face the audience. The air was filled with loud voices and laughter, and stuffy from the heat of the myriad-candled chandeliers and the close proximity of so many bodies.

James Kerr and Humphrey Chamberson stood together at the open double doors of the ballroom. Chamberson was completely at ease, greeting the guests that were still arriving, James stood stiffly, tense and very nervous.

Tonight he was going to demonstrate a painless extraction of teeth in front of an audience among which were numbered some powerful and influential members of the medical profession.

As each new guest came towards him James anxiously sought for the vulpine features of Reuben Parr, who was supposed to be here by this time.

Chamberson noted his unease, and intuiting its cause smiled reassuringly.

'If Parr does not arrive in time then you're perfectly capable of performing the demonstration yourself, Jamie. Have I not seen you do so with my own eyes?'

James forced a smile. 'Indeed you have, my lord.' A rush of gratitude drove him to continue. 'I can never thank you enough for what you have done for me, my lord.'

183

'Nonsense. I'm grateful to you for giving me this opportunity to contribute towards the relief of suffering. It's a great thing we are doing here, Jamie, and will ensure us both a page in history.' He patted the younger man's shoulder and winked roguishly. 'And of course the fact that we shall all make a deal of money from it is even more reason to celebrate, is it not?'

Because of his own physical ordeals beneath the surgeon's scalpel Humphrey Chamberson had not needed any persuasion to go with James into Whitechapel and witness a demonstration of painless extraction performed privately for him by Reuben Parr. Over the course of a week he had witnessed a total of five demonstrations performed by both Parr and James, which had left the hapless tramp, Billy, virtually toothless but with sufficient money to stay drunk for a month.

Chamberson had been so impressed that he had readily agreed to buy the formula from Parr, and have a contract drawn up which guaranteed both Parr and James a share in future profits when the miraculous analgesic should be patented, produced in quantity, and sold to a public desperate for any promise of relief from the agonies of surgical procedures. Parr had been paid his one thousand pounds that earlier day, and had handed over the formula, plus two flasks of the prepared elixir.

James had only had time to briefly study the formula and directions for manufacture. He recognised most of the ingredients, but there was one which was new to him. A dried shrub-root which could only be obtained in the southern states of America. Parr said that he had used up his existing stock of this shrub-root, but that he was expecting more to arrive from America within the next week or so, when they could immediately commence the manufacturing process.

James had written to Septimus Nairn to tell him of his discovery, and to invite him to this public demonstration, but because of a prior commitment to perform an operation in Worcester, Nairn had been unable to make the journey.

'I wish my uncle could have been here tonight,' James said wistfully.

'I don't doubt but that Dr Nairn will hear soon enough of your triumph, Jamie,' Chamberson consoled. 'In fact the whole world will come to hear of it in due course. You're going to be famous, my boy.'

Despite his anxiety sudden exultation surged through James. Yes, he told himself. After tonight I really am going to be famous.

In his mind's eye he pictured the face of Lydia Landser and experienced a poignant yearning to see her once more. God, I wish you could be here, Liddy, he thought. I'm sure it would make you proud of me. Then, with a touch of pique which he could not control, And make you regret that you didn't wait for me, but rushed to marry Harcourt instead.

The last guest to arrive was a tall man with grey hair and mustachios and a military bearing. Chamberson introduced him to James as Dr Alexander Hall, a high-ranking army medical officer.

The newcomer frowned suspiciously at James. 'So, you are the young man who claims to have discovered this miraculous elixir that banishes pain?'

'No, sir, I make no such claim for myself. The elixir was discovered by Professor Reuben Parr while he was practising in America.'

Hall's manner became scathingly contemptuous. 'Oh, it's another of those Yankee dodges, is it? Well, I'm of the opinion that it's all humbug, young man.'

'Indeed it is not humbug!' Chamberson intervened indignantly. 'I have seen it work with my own eyes.'

'I don't doubt that you have seen what you believed to be the banishment of pain, my lord,' Hall countered dismissively. 'But you have been humbugged. There's not a doubt in my mind about that. You have been sadly deceived, my lord, by yet another Yankee dodge.'

With an effort James controlled his own angry reaction to this accusation, and merely said quietly, 'I trust that you will be as ready to offer an apology when you have witnessed this demonstration, as you have been to offer insult, Dr Hall.'

'I'll do more than offer apology, young man. If I am satisfied that you have banished pain, then I will kiss your arse and allow you to kick mine as hard as you may.' With that the choleric doctor passed on into a ballroom now packed with sitting and standing people.

Chamberson scowled after him. 'I've clashed with that man before, Jamie. I shall take the greatest pleasure in watching you kick his arse.'

He pulled out his pocketwatch to check the time, and announced decisively, 'We can't wait for Parr any longer. And to be truthful, I much prefer having you carry out this demonstration alone. Parr's appearance bears too much resemblance to a cheapjack, and the people I've invited here tonight would not be impressed with him, as they will be with you.'

He turned to the hovering manservants and ordered, 'Go and fetch the man, Sorenson, here. And you, bring the implements.'

Then he smiled encouragingly at James. 'By this time tomorrow the whole of London will be clamouring to meet you.'

Sorenson was the man on whom James was to demonstrate. He joined them now and presented a woebegone spectacle, one side of his face grotesquely swollen as a result of abcessed teeth, his red-rimmed eyes watery with pain, his speech a virtually unintelligible mumbling. He was hugely fat, with a massive paunch and great globular buttocks that strained his trousers almost to splitting point.

A hubbub of excited talk followed the progress of the small procession to the stage, and there was an outbust of laughter when Sorenson could not manage to mount the stage by himself, and was manhandled up on to its boards by several manservants.

The chair groaned audibly as Sorenson seated himself, and provoked another outburst of laughter, which only stilled when Chamberson stepped to face the audience, holding his hands up for silence.

'Ladies and gentleman, I have the honour to present to you Mr James Kerr, who is going to perform a painless extraction of teeth. He will demonstrate that the banishment of pain is no longer a dream, but a reality.'

James looked nervously across the rows of faces, and his mouth felt dry and stale. Then his gaze momentarily locked upon the choleric features of Dr Aexander Hall, who was visibly sneering, and anger drove out nervousness. He cleared his throat and told the audience, 'Tonight, ladies and gentlemen, I am going to prove that pain can be banished. That surgical procedures can be performed without inflicting agony upon the patient.'

He lifted up the half-full flask of pale green liquid and held it high so that all could see it.

'I make no claim to be the discoverer of this elixir. The credit for that must go to Professor Reuben Parr, who unfortunately could not be here this evening to receive his due.'

He paused, and once more locked eyes with Hall. On sudden impulse he said, 'Could I request Dr Alexander Hall to be kind enough to step up on to the stage and examine our subject, Mr Sorenson, in order to satisfy himself that Mr Sorenson is labouring under the affliction of abcessed teeth, and that this demonstration will be no humbug.'

Hall's features reddened cholerically, but he rose and came to the stage. He made a brief examination of Sorenson's mouth, and nodded brusquely.

'Yes, the teeth are undoubtedly abcessed.'

'Would you care to remain on the stage so that you may have a close view of all that I shall do?' James challenged.

'That won't be necessary,' Hall sneered. 'Your failure will not necessitate a close view.'

His words created a stir among the audience, and one man remonstrated loudly, 'Shame on you!' But others only laughed.

James waited until Hall had resumed his seat before telling the audience, 'As you have just heard, ladies and gentlemen, all progress must struggle to overcome the obstacle of ignorance.'

His riposte brought appreciative laughter, and Hall's red face almost purpled.

James examined his implements. He had decided to use strong forceps to pull the teeth because of the greater leverage they afforded.

He placed them to hand, and then bent to tell Sorenson, 'There will be people supporting you so that you need not fear falling from the chair. I want you to breathe in the fumes from this flask. Take deep breaths and draw the vapour fully into your lungs. Don't be afraid. You will merely fall briefly asleep, and when you wake your sufferings will be ended.'

He positioned two of the manservants so that they could support Sorenson and then pinched the man's nostrils closed with his left hand, and held the flask to his mouth.

Sorenson sucked in the vapour, and started to cough. James urged, 'Don't stop. Keep on breathing it in.'

The fat man obeyed, and James began to count silently. The man's sweaty features slowly took on a greyish hue, and his lips began to turn blue, but he was not yet unconscious.

James's count reached ninety and anxiety attacked him. Billy, the tramp, had always fallen unconscious within a count of thirty-five.

Then Sorenson's head fell sideways and his jaw dropped slackly.

James gusted a sigh of relief as he put aside the flask and snatched up the long-handled forceps. He pushed Sorenson's head back, and quickly locked the forceps on to the nearest of the abcessed molars.

James levered, twisted and pulled. To his shock and dismay, Sorenson bellowed in agony and heaved against the restraining grip of the men holding him.

James stepped back, the bloody tooth gripped in the forceps jaws, and as he did so he heard Hall's triumphant shout, 'It's humbug! Didn't I tell you that it's all humbug!'

Sorenson's bellowing struggles abruptly ceased, his huge body collapsed, and despite their efforts the two men could not hold his weight as the chair slipped from under him and he fell to the floor.

James stared down in horror at the open red-rimmed eyes as uproar erupted throughout the room. Shouts, jeers, laughter filled the room, while at his feet the last rattles of dying breath came from Sorenson's gaping mouth.

Twenty-Nine

J ames had not gone to bed. Tortured by guilt, blaming himself for the death of Sorenson, he had spent the night pacing his room, hardly daring to even think of how he would face his uncle and tell him of what had happened.

As the grey dawn lightened the eastern skyline he left the house and hurried through the city to Whitechapel. There the mean streets and alleys were already bustling with the start of the new day and the main thoroughfares were choked with carts and wagons passing to and from the docks.

The shop door was wide ajar and James entered to find that the premises were empty, every bottle, jar and box had gone, as had the ancient surgical chair. The only token of Reuben Parr that remained was the tarred lettering on the outside wall.

He went back into the street and was accosted by a ragged urchin. 'Are you looking for the bloke who had the shop, mister?'

'Do you know where he's gone?'

The urchin held out his filthy hand, rubbing fingers and thumb together in the age-old signal for a payment.

James impatiently fumbled in his pocket for coins which he gave to the urchin. 'Where's he gone?'

'A n'orse and cart come and shifted the stuff. It went down that way.' The urchin pointed towards the docks. 'But the bloke who had the shop wasn't with it.'

'Do you know whose horse and cart it was?'

Again fingers and thumb signalled for payment, and James gave over more coins.

'I ain't got the foggiest notion, mister.' The urchin grinned, and scurried away, whooping with laughter.

James was forced to confront and accept the dread that had continuously assailed him throughout the tormented hours of the night. Reuben Parr had marked him as a country fool, and had snared him with ease.

James wasted no energy in futile raging against the man. He only blamed himself for being so stupid. Unwilling to let Parr escape so easily James began to knock on neighbouring doors and make enquiries. But all he met were suspicious glares, shrugs of indifference, and invitations to, 'Hook it quick, why don't you!'

Finally, after two fruitless hours of searching and questioning, James admitted defeat and steeled himself to return and face Humphrey Chamberson. The previous night the earl had curtly requested James to go to his room and leave him to deal with the immediate aftermath of the catastrophic death of Sorenson.

Masters the butler met James at the door on his return to the house.

'His lordship wishes to speak with you immediately, Mr Kerr. He's in the Green Room. I would suggest that you do not keep him waiting any longer for your appearance.'

James experienced a frisson of foreboding. The butler's manner was noticeably frosty in comparison to his previous obsequious warmth.

Chamberson's attitude was also cold and his greeting a demand: 'Where in hell's name have you been?'

James told him of his unsuccessful quest for Reuben Parr.

'I can't say that this surprises me.' Humphrey Chamberson shrugged. 'However, I shall still have efforts made to trace him. I don't appreciate being cheated out of a thousand pounds and being made to look a fool.'

'I intend to repay you every penny, my lord. It's all my fault.'

'No, you will not give me a penny,' Chamberson said firmly. 'I don't hold you to blame for my own greed and stupidity. I do blame you, however, for involving me in this damned farce. It's made me the laughing stock of society.'

'I know I'm to blame, my lord, for introducing Parr to you without checking into his background,' James insisted miserably. 'And I'm to blame for killing that man yesterday.'

'We do not know yet what killed Sorenson. It could be that his heart was diseased, or he suffered a fatal apoplexy. The autopsy will discover the cause of his death. And by tomorrow we shall also discover whether or not the preparation was poisonous. I'm having it analysed by the most knowledgeable chemist in London. So until we do know all, I suggest that you stop blaming yourself.'

James could draw no comfort from this argument. 'The truth of the matter is that I was so eager for fame and fortune that I neglected taking the simplest of precautions. I should have taken the preparation to a reputable chemist and had it analysed for its poison content. I deserve to go to prison because Sorenson died as a result of my failings.'

Chamberson lost patience and said sharply, 'All you were trying to do was to relieve his sufferings. So let us have no more of this nonsense about going to prison. I shall make sure that you don't. And now kindly spare me from any more of your self-pitying maunderings.'

'Is that how I sound? As if I'm pitying myself?' James questioned in dismay.

'Yes, you do,' Chamberson snapped curtly.

James's pride was hurt by this accusation. 'No, I do not pity myself at all, my lord. I blame myself, which is an entirely different emotion.'

The older man sighed irascibly. 'If you wish for a self-inflicted martyrdom, then so be it. But I have no intention of sharing that martyrdom with you. As I said before, I intend to make sure that no blame will fall on either of us. I have some connections which I can use to ensure that. Since you must remain in London until all these matters are settled, which should be very soon, I propose to allow you to remain here in my house Then I think it best if you return to your uncle's home.'

'As you wish, my lord,' James agreed miserably.

'I shall write to your uncle and inform him of what has happened here. I shall also inform him that by ensuring that no blame falls on you for this unfortunate death, I consider that I shall have amply repaid the debt of gratitude that I owe him.' He paused momentarily, then with the merest hint of discomfiture in his eyes, added, 'While you remain here I would appreciate you keeping to your room as much as possible, and taking your meals there.'

'Very well, my lord,' James answered with what dignity he could muster. 'There is one further thing that I must ask you though. What of Sorenson's family? I would like to try and make some compensation to them for what I've done.'

'Fortunately he has no dependants. His wife is dead and they had no children. I believe he has a brother somewhere, but they have long been apart. You have no need for any concern on that score. And now I'll bid you goodbye, Mr Kerr.'

Thirty

It was ten days before all the legal procedures following Sorenson's death were completed. The analysis of the elixir proved it to be simply ether, with added non-toxic colourants and perfumes to disguise its smell and appearance. The autopsy on Sorenson's corpse revealed that he had died from a massive brain haemorrhage and the inquest jury had brought in a verdict of natural death from apoplexy.

The coroner had stated that no blame attached to James, but James still blamed himself. His last days at Chamberson's house waiting for the outcome of the verdict had been an ordeal, made harder to bear by the overt hostility displayed towards him by his host and the servants.

But he could accept that there was justification for that hostility. The Sorenson debacle had redounded as badly upon Humphrey Chamberson as it had upon himself. They were both being jeered at as gullible fools for allowing themselves to be so easily deceived and cheated by a cheapjack who promised the unattainable. The banishment of pain.

James travelled back to Birmingham by train, dreading the moment when he would have to face his uncle. He had written to Nairn to tell him what had happened, but had received only a curt note of acknowledgement in reply. James was tormented by the burgeoning conviction that his own disgrace had been visited upon his uncle, the man he had come to love as he had loved his own father.

James had sent a further letter informing his uncle when he

would be arriving at Birmingham, and now was uneasily wondering if anyone would be there to meet him.

Sean Fitzgerald was waiting at the Birmingham railway station and when he spotted James alighting from the carriage he hurried to greet him.

'Welcome home, Jamie. It's good to see you.'

James was both relieved and grateful for the warmth of his welcome.

Sean had brought the gig and mare, and when James's trunk had been loaded they set out for Tardebigge.

After the initial greetings, an awkward silence developed between the two men which lasted until they reached the outskirts of the city. It was the Irishman who broke that silence.

'Agghh, bollocks to this!' he swore robustly. 'You know that I'm your friend, Jamie, so why are we acting so bloody shy with each other. You've had a misfortune, but there's no call for you to come back here with your tail between your legs. Every surgeon worth his salt has had people dying under his blade, so don't be taking your man's death too hard.'

A sudden sense of release coursed through James. He was back with a true friend now, to whom he could unburden himself with complete candour.

'I can't help but take it hard, Sean. If it wasn't for me the man would still be alive and well. I killed him.'

'Not according to the inquest, you didn't.' Fitzgerald glanced at James's startled expression and chuckled. 'Me and your uncle were here at the Telegraph Office last night. Your uncle had arranged to have a man at the inquest, and he telegraphed us what the verdict was. Your uncle had to go back home then because of the practice, but he told me to stay on at a hotel so I could meet you today.'

For the first time since his arrival James was able to bring himself to ask about his uncle, and his heart was pounding fearfully as he did so.

'What does my uncle think about my disgrace?'

195

The Irishman's broad red features twisted in a grimace.

'Aggghhh, well now, I don't think he's best pleased with you.'

James's heart sank, and he sighed despondently. His thoughts turned to Lydia Landser, as they had done so many times these last days. But the vision of her bright red hair, and pretty freckled face brought only added despair. He had daydreamed about returning as a hero, dazzling her with his success, but instead he was coming back as a ridiculed fool. A failure.

James's spirits dropped to the lowest ebb he had ever experienced, and he sat silently immersed in his own misery for the remainder of the journey.

Darkness had long fallen by the time they arrived at Tardebigge. As the iron-rimmed wheels crunched loudly on the gravelled forecourt of the house, James felt the overwhelming urge to jump from the gig and run away from this reunion. It was not fear of his uncle's anger that powered this urge, but his own shame that he had brought such disgrace on his uncle's name and professional reputation.

Lamplight shone from the windows. The front door opened and the black silhouette of Septimus Nairn appeared in the doorway.

The gig halted, James drew a deep breath, and with thudding heart dismounted and went towards his uncle.

Septimus Nairn waited silent and motionless, grimly frowning.

James came to a halt on the top step, desperately uncertain.

Nairn took a single pace forwards, his arms opened wide and he hugged James with a fierce pressure.

'Welcome home, Nephew. Welcome home.'

Tears of heartfelt relief and joy brimmed in James's eyes, and he hugged his uncle's sturdy body with an equally fierce pressure, too choked with emotion to voice any words.

Later that night James related to his uncle and Sean Fitzpatrick all that had occurred in London. When he had finished the account he said, 'I bitterly regret what I've done. That poor man will be on my conscience for the rest of my days. I can't help but wonder if I'm fit to continue in the medical profession.'

Septimus Nairn's face darkened when he heard this, and he scolded furiously, 'Don't talk like a damned fool, boy! There wouldn't be a medical profession if doctors allowed their patients' deaths to stop them practising.'

'That's just what I told him,' Fitzpatrick put in. 'Jasus! I wish had a pound for every patient of mine that's died on me. I could buy a thoroughbred mare without needing to ask the price first!'

'I don't ever again want to hear you doubt your fitness to be a doctor, Nephew,' Nairn went on a little less heatedly. 'We all make mistakes, I've made many a one. But mistakes must be learned from. And I trust that you have learned from the one you've made.'

'I have, Uncle, believe me,' James acknowledged ruefully. 'I'll not be fooled again by any Yankee dodge.'

'Good!' Nairn was satisfied. 'And in future always remember the cardinal principle: the pain inflicted by the knife during an operation rouses and invigorates the vital forces of the human constitution. That is why God created it.'

'I'll remember, Uncle,' James assured fervently. 'I'll remember.'

Thirty-One

February 1844

E dward Harcourt was eating his midday meal with noisy
gusto. Across the table Liddy listlessly toyed with her own
meat and vegetables. He looked up and pointed his fork at her
swollen belly, admonishing her, 'Come now, Lydia, you must
eat it all up. My son needs ample nourishment.'

Liddy looked despairingly at her almost full plate and shook
her head. 'I've no appetite, Edward.'

'Appetite be damned! It's your duty to eat!' he hectored.
'You'll stay there until you've eaten every last morsel. I'll not
have you starving my son.'

She put food into her mouth and forced herself to chew and
swallow.

'That's the way,' he applauded.

Liddy continued mechanically chewing and swallowing until
her plate was empty.

During these last months she had learned many bitter lessons, and learned them well. Her husband's word was law, and
so long as she dutifully submitted then he treated her kindly
enough, but any show of rebellion on her part met with instant
brutal correction. Apart from the physical punishments she had
endured at his hands, there was also the constantly reiterated
threat that he would bring disaster down upon her father.
Harcourt had the power to commit George Landser to the
debtors prison at any time he chose, and Liddy knew that such
imprisonment would destroy her father.

In the early days of the marriage Harcourt had been insatiable and perverse in his sexual demands upon her, and the day that she had discovered that he had infected her venereally had been the worst day of her life. The self-degradation she had felt was driving her to the brink of madness and suicide.

Yet, paradoxically, as she had stood holding the phial of poison with which she intended to kill herself, in that same moment she had rediscovered her stubborn courage and had realised that if she took that poison then she was accepting defeat. She was surrendering her very existence because of a man that she had come to loathe. From that moment on in her secret thoughts she nourished a fierce rebellion and an equally fierce determination that one day she would free herself from his hateful bondage. She would take revenge for all the sufferings, humiliations, degradations he had inflicted upon her and her loved ones. But lacking his physical strength, and financial resources, she knew that she must employ cunning, stealth, and above all else, patience, if she was to achieve revenge. So, she had outwardly become the dutiful chattel that Harcourt wanted, and at the same time tried to discover all she could about his secretive business affairs, because these she was convinced would be his Achilles heel.

Liddy's emotions about the child she carried in her womb in this eighth month of pregnancy constantly fluctuated, sometimes love and wanting, sometimes hatred and rejection. Harcourt had convinced himself that she was carrying the son and heir he desired so passionately. Much to her relief he had stopped having any sexual relations with her as soon as her belly had begun to swell because he was afraid it might harm the child, a belief that Liddy had done her utmost to further. She assumed that he satisfied his brutal sexual appetites with paid whores during his weekly visits to Worcester or Birmingham, and could only feel a certain sympathy for those women he bought.

Now Harcourt rose from the table and told her, 'I have to go to Worcester. I shall return tomorrow afternoon.' He came to put his hand on her stomach. 'Take good care of my son.'

'I will, Edward,' she replied dutifully.

He left without another word and within minutes was driving his horse and gig down the long High Street.

Edward Harcourt's thoughts were eagerly anticipatory. There was a fresh young whore recently come to the Worcester brothel that he patronised and he intended to purchase her services for the entire night. The temporary loss of his wife's sexual services did not incommode him too much. His nature was far too promiscuous to find the pleasures of the marriage bed sufficient to content him, despite his previous belief that he had tired of whores. This belief had very quickly proven to be unfounded following his marriage. He was now beginning to regard his wife as he would regard a brood mare: her primary utility was to provide him with sons to inherit his wealth, properties and businesses.

A mile from the town he saw another horse and gig coming towards him. Recognising its two occupants he slowed his horse, and signalled with his whip for them to stop.

'What the devil does he want?' Septimus Nairn questioned irritably. 'I'll lay odds it'll be a complaint that our last bill to the workhouse was too high.'

James Kerr also felt reluctant to talk with Harcourt. Despite his efforts to put Liddy from his mind, the fact of her marriage to the banker still rankled. He had only seen her once at a distance since his return home, and had been shocked at how sharply the pangs of regret and yearning had struck through him.

The gigs halted side by side and Harcourt stared resentfully at Septimus Nairn's plastered right arm which was held in a sling.

'It's not healed then, Septimus,' he stated unnecessarily.

'Fractures do not mend quickly, Edward,' Nairn informed brusquely. 'It's healing as well as can be expected.'

'But not in time to assist at the delivery of my son, I fear.'

'No, I think not,' Nairn agreed.

'Then I'll have to bring Taylor in if there are any complications at the birth.'

'There shouldn't be any complications; your wife is young

200

and healthy. You've employed Betty Glover as midwife, have you not?'

'Yes.'

'She has more experience of birthing than any of we doctors hereabouts. I don't think you will have any cause for concern.'

'I hope not.' Harcourt lifted his whip in salute. 'Good day to you.'

As they drove on, Nairn stared quizzically at his nephew. 'Harcourt bears you no liking, I fear, Jamie. He tries even to avoid looking at you.'

'I've given him no cause to dislike me, Uncle.' James's expression was grim. 'But frankly I couldn't give a damn how he regards me, because as a man I don't think he's worth a damn! In fact I think he's scum.'

'Those are harsh words.'

'They're well merited words, as you know very well,' James snapped curtly. 'When a man infects his own wife with the gonorrhoea he can only be scum.'

Nairn frowned. 'Well, voice your opinions only between we two, Nephew. We are not judges of morality, we are doctors. And Harcourt is not the first and will not be the last man to infect his wife, not by many a thousand he won't. It's a simple fact of life that venereal diseases are rife in all classes of society. That is the way of the world, and always has been.'

James bit back the angry words of denunciation that rose to his tongue and drove on in silence, while in his heart he cursed the ill fortune that had prevented himself and Liddy Landser from coming together.

'Are you feeling perfectly well, Liddy? You look pale,' George Landser questioned anxiously.

'I'm perfectly well, Pa. And if I'm pale it's because I haven't taken the air for some time now. I've no wish to parade myself in the streets looking fat and bloated as I do.'

Shortly after her husband's departure Liddy had begun to feel a series of shooting pains in her lower belly, and now as a fresh one struck she shielded her face with her raised hand.

'Are you sure that you're all right?' her father demanded.

Liddy held her breath, and the pain lessened and disappeared. 'Yes, Pa. I'm all right.'

She smiled a little wearily as she looked at him. His religious conversion had not lasted very long and he was drinking again, but not as heavily as before. She readily acknowledged that Edward Harcourt had been true to his word and had ensured that her father was housed, fed and looked after by a manservant. Harcourt had also employed his man, Jenks, to trace her brother, Robert, and she knew now that he was in the army, stationed presently in Ireland. She had written several letters to him, but had only received one brief note in reply. Robert, it seemed, had found his niche in the cavalry, and had expressed no desire to be bought out of his service. But in his note he had asked her to send him some money, which she had at regular intervals.

'I've been to the Post Office, but there was nothing for either of us.' George Landser scowled petulantly. 'Your brother should write more often. He's abandoned us, you know, after all I've done for him, the ungrateful young hound.'

'No, he hasn't abandoned us, Pa. He's made a new life for himself, that's all.' Liddy sighed tiredly. Every time her father came to see her it seemed that they had the same conversation.

'And what have you been doing to find my daughter?' George Landser demanded.

'I can't do anything until I've had the baby, Pa,' Liddy replied somewhat defensively. She had still not steeled herself to tell Edward Harcourt that her father claimed the paternity of Katie Kennedy. And she was still not convinced of the truth of it herself. Then in self-justification, she added, 'I've had troubles enough of my own to deal with, Pa. But when the baby is born I promise I will try and find Katie for you.'

'It's very bad of you to treat me so,' Landser remonstrated heatedly. 'You know very well that I can't be easy in my mind until I've recovered the child. Really, Liddy, you are so selfish you make me angry.'

A burning shaft of pain lanced through Liddy's belly, and she cried out helplessly.

'What is it? What's the matter with you?' her father shouted in alarm.

She could only gasp out, 'Fetch the midwife, Pa. Fetch Betty Glover!'

Then the pain suddenly intensified, overwhelming her in agony until it tore long-drawn-out screams from the depths of her being.

Thirty-Two

I t was two o'clock in the afternoon and James Kerr and Septimus Nairn were sitting playing chess when the messenger came hammering on the house door.

As the thunderous onslaught continued, Septimus Nairn asked James, 'Will you answer it, Nephew? Mrs Biddle must be outside somewhere.'

James scowled with mock suspicion. 'You want me to go so that you can make a double move, don't you? It's the only way in which you can save this game.'

His uncle snorted indignantly. 'Then take the board with you, you arrogant young pup. I don't need to cheat to beat you.'

James rose smiling; he greatly enjoyed bantering with his uncle.

He recognised the young messenger as the apprentice to Dr Taylor, of Redditch, and he exclaimed in surprise, 'What brings you here, Mr Perkis?'

'I must speak with Dr Nairn, Mr Kerr. It's a matter of extreme urgency.'

'Then come in.'

In the drawing room the young man wasted no time in polite preliminaries.

'Dr Nairn, sir, Dr Taylor has sent me to ask you to come immediately to Mr Harcourt's house at Bromsgrove. Mrs Harcourt is in childbirth and her condition is grave. Dr Taylor has recommended to Mr Harcourt that you be brought in to consult on the case.'

'Go on ahead, Mr Perkis,' Nairn instructed. 'I'll follow on directly. James, will you have Tom bring round the gig.'

* * *

As James and Septimus Nairn travelled towards Bromsgrove, James's resentment at what he considered Liddy's rejection was submerged in his worry for her.

'Why should Taylor call you in for a childbirth, Uncle? If it was a surgical operation I could understand, but surely he's competent to deal with a birthing?'

Nairn's features creased in a grim smile. 'Hugh Taylor is protecting himself, Nephew, should Mrs Harcourt die. He obviously fears the case to be a hopeless one, but by calling me in he can then say that everything possible was done. After all, he has sent for the finest surgeon in the Midlands, has he not?'

James's worry became an acute fear.

They covered the few miles' distance at a fast clip, and when they reached the house were met by Edward Harcourt, his two servants hovering anxiously behind him.

'Thank you for coming, Septimus.' His face was grim. 'You'll save the child, won't you?'

'I shall do my best endeavours, Edward.' Nairn exuded a calm confidence. 'Now there is no time to waste, we'll talk afterwards.'

But as he went to move on Harcourt stopped him. Putting his head close to Nairn's ear, he whispered, 'You must save my son, Septimus, no matter what else might happen. You must save the child. The child's life comes before the mother's.'

Nairn glared at him, but said nothing, and Harcourt flushed guiltily and moved aside.

Dr Hugh Taylor greeted them at the bedroom door. He was a stoop-shouldered, middle-aged man, with a worried frown; the thick lenses of his spectacles caused his eyes to seem grotesquely enlarged.

'This is a most difficult case, Septimus.' He shook his sparse-haired head. 'Most difficult. Most difficult. I fear it's a neglected shoulder presentation with impaction.'

'How long has she been in labour?'

'More than forty-eight hours.'

'Then why in hell's name have you delayed so long before calling on me?' Nairn demanded angrily.

'I've only just been called in myself, Septimus. Betty Glover was the sole midwife.'

'Glover's had enough experience to accept her own limitations. Why didn't she fetch you sooner?'

'Because she claims that all appeared to be going well. Personally I'm of the opinion she wanted to keep the birth fees totally to herself, until she realised that she was going to lose the mother and child both if we were not brought in. I've given her a piece of my mind and sent her packing.'

'God save me from greedy midwives,' Nairn spat out disgustedly.

James was filled with a fearful dread as he looked at Liddy lying on the bloodied and saturated bed. She was only half-conscious, writhing and moaning, her night-shift drawn up over her hugely swollen belly, her face grey-hued.

'She looks to be in a very parlous condition, Uncle.' Then his eyes widened in shock. 'What's that? There, between her legs?'

'It's the baby's hand, Nephew.'

James stared uneasily at the tiny hand protruding from the woman's shaved vagina. He found the sight obscenely disturbing.

'Note how dusky and swollen it is, Nephew. What is the cause?' his uncle, quick to note James's reaction, questioned sharply.

'Interference with the venous return,' James answered automatically, and abruptly his unease was superseded by a professional objectivity. The small protruding hand lost any obscene connotation and became only a medical fact.

'What do you want me to do, Uncle?'

'Watch and listen,' his uncle replied curtly, and asked Taylor, 'Have you attempted version?'

'Good Lord, no! I daren't try it! After all this time the lower uterine segment must be stretched to near breaking point.'

'Just so,' Nairn concurred.

He carefully examined the moaning woman's swollen belly by touch, the fingers of his left hand kneading and moving constantly. Then he beckoned James.

206

'Try if you can to identify the foetal parts. Head, legs, et cetera.'

The flesh was cold and damp beneath James's hands as he palpated, and he deliberately closed his eyes, concentrating solely on his sense of touch. But he was finally forced to admit defeat.

'I'm unable to do it with any degree of certainty,' he admitted reluctantly.

'That's because the upper segment of the uterus has retracted so firmly on the child that it has become a hard barrier. The liquor amnii has drained away, and the head and shoulders are so firmly wedged into the pelvic brim that they are virtually immoveable.' Nairn spoke with an absolute authority. 'If I attempt an internal version of the foetus, then I shall rupture the lower uterine segment and the foetus could extrude into the abdominal cavity.'

'It's a hopeless case, Septimus. A hopeless case.' Hugh Taylor shook his sparse-haired head. 'I fear we've lost her.'

'We?' Nairn frowned quizzically, and Taylor hastened to amend that statement.

'Well, no, not we, Septimus. It's all that damned Betty Glover's fault.'

'Quite so,' Nairn agreed grimly. 'Do be sure to remember that, Hugh.'

'Is the foetus still living, Uncle?' James was completely absorbed. For him, for the time being, the mother and child had now lost any personalisation of identity. They had become purely anonymous entities on which the battle against Death would be fought out.

'Almost certainly it's dead.' Nairn took a wooden, trumpet-shaped stethoscope from his bag and handed it to James. 'Try to pick up the foetal heartbeat. Listen here, and here and here.' He indicated places on the swollen belly.

James bent low, head to one side, large trumpet-bell against his ear, the small bell pressed firmly into the belly. After a while he shook his head.

'I can detect nothing.'

207

Nairn studied Liddy's sweat-wet grey face, and checked her heartbeat. Her eyes had rolled up into her head and only the whites of the eyeballs glistened between the half-closed lids.

'We've lost her,' Taylor muttered. 'It's a hopeless case. A hopeless case.'

Nairn shook his head. 'No, Hugh, we haven't yet lost her. I believe there is still a chance to save her. A slight one, admittedly, but worth trying.'

'What are you going to do?' James questioned.

'Decapitate the foetus,' his uncle replied calmly.

'Cut its head off?' James couldn't believe he had heard correctly.

'It's the only way. Once the head is separated it can then be moved and so free the torso for extraction.'

'But that's a very dangerous procedure. One slip and you will kill her,' Taylor protested.

'It's her only chance of life,' Nairn asserted.

'And what will Harcourt say to decapitation, even if you should carry it out successfully?' Hugh Taylor looked very doubtful. 'Wouldn't it be better if we performed a Caesarian delivery?'

'Why so?' Nairn frowned challengingly. 'There's no chance of her surviving a Caesarian.'

'There's precious little chance she'll survive anyway.' Taylor's expression became petulantly stubborn. 'Look here, Septimus, you must think this through. I know just how desperate Harcourt is for an heir. He would want us to take any risks that might save the baby. If we present him with a decapitation he could well accuse us of deliberately killing the child in a vain attempt to save the mother who will die anyway. It could mean the ruination of us. He's a powerful man and wields much influence.'

Septimus Nairn's eyes were blazing but his voice was cold and calm.

'What do you suggest we should do then?'

Taylor appeared to choose his words with great care and his

tone was mollifying. 'She's dying, Septimus. I've no doubt on that score. She may last another hour or so, but I'm afraid that her death is inevitable. What I propose is that we wait, and when she has gone, then we perform a Caesarian and extract the foetus in a whole condition. We can then present it as an heroic operation performed to save the baby's life. Tragically, because of the incompetence of Betty Glover, it came too late. But we shall have no blame attached to us. We shall have done everything that mortal men could do to try to present Harcourt with a living heir.'

'And a dead wife,' Nairn gritted out.

'She is going to die anyway. You will not save her with this decapitation even if you perform it successfully. She will still die, and we shall then have a headless baby to present to Harcourt.' Taylor's querulous voice grew shrill with exasperation. 'Dammit to hell, Septimus! Are you being deliberately stupid? Can't you see what you will do to our reputations if you decapitate?'

For James the tension was almost unbearable. He found it difficult to breathe easily and his fists were clenched so tightly that his fingernails dug painfully deep into the palms of his hands. He stared intently at his uncle, mentally willing his medical hero not to agree with Taylor, willing him to at least attempt to save Liddy's life.

Nairn chuckled with a grim amusement, then jerked his head contemptuously. 'You'd best leave now, Hugh, and preserve your precious reputation. I've no more time to waste in arguing with you. I'm going to decapitate the foetus, and try to save the mother. If I fail, then feel free to lay the blame entirely at my door.'

James's tension dissolved instantly. He felt like cheering because his beloved uncle had refused to surrender to Death, even at the risk of damaging what he treasured above all else: his reputation as a doctor. Liddy was to have a chance of life.

Nairn now totally ignored Taylor and acted with decisive purpose.

'Come, Nephew, help me. We must place her in the lithotomy position, with her buttocks just hanging over the edge of the bed, so that you can have a clear field.'

'What?' For the second time James couldn't believe what he had heard.

'You will have to carry out the procedure, Nephew.' Nairn touched his own plastered arm. 'I can't do it with this useless arm, can I?'

'But I've never practised this,' James objected, and the thought that he might end in destroying Liddy's life almost unmanned him. 'I can't do this, Uncle. I could end by killing her.'

'You can and will do it.' Nairn was obdurate. 'Because you are the only one here who can even attempt it.'

'Dr Taylor can do it,' James argued desperately.

'Oh no I cannot, young man.' Taylor refused vehemently. 'And I want to make it plain that I am totally opposed to it being done.'

Nairn pointed at Liddy's grey face. 'She is dying, Jamie. You are her only chance of life. If you play the coward now, then you will never feel free of guilt, because you will have failed miserably when she most needed you.'

James stood motionless, dragging in long deep breaths, fighting to summon his resolution.

Then he nodded. 'I'll do it.'

'Goddamn you, Septimus, you're going to ruin us both.' Taylor groaned, and then came to help them to move the limp woman as gently as possible into position.

'You take her right thigh, Hugh, and I'll take the left. We must hold her thighs like this and try to ensure that she makes no movement. She must not move,' Nairn exhorted, and instructed James, 'Get the hook, and follow my instructions.'

James exerted all his strength of will to put all emotion from his mind, and to look upon Liddy purely as a medical problem. He took the eighteen-inch long decapitating hook from the medical chest. It was made of steel, with a wooden handle, the rounded inner edge of the sharp-pointed, flattened hook serrated like a saw.

Following his uncle's directions he knelt down before Liddy's spread thighs. He tied a length of cord to the protruding wrist of the foetus and carefully pulled on it until more of the arm appeared, then he trod on the end of the cord to keep the pressure on the arm.

'This will keep the foetus fixed,' Nairn explained to James. 'Now pass your left hand into the vagina and make palmar contact with the neck and shoulder of the foetus. The rear of your hand must be in contact with the anterior wall of the pelvis . . .'

James obeyed, and as his flesh penetrated Liddy's flesh he became totally focused on the mechanics of the procedure, feeling suddenly detached and calm, hearing only his uncle's voice.

'. . . Now that your hand is in position, pass the hook with its point held backwards along your left palm until it reaches the neck of the foetus, ensuring the back of the hook is facing the bladder, then rotate the instrument so that it passes over the neck. Next, move your fingers to the front of the neck to ensure that the hook point is not digging into the chest. To cut through the neck, pull the handle well back to maintain a firm pressure, and keeping your fingers on the point at all times move the hook in a gentle rocking motion.'

Nairn fell silent, and James concentrated entirely on the action, his right hand moving the handle up and down, up and down, up and down in a slow rhythm. His expression intent, his breathing audible in the silence of the room, praying fervently that Liddy would not move, knowing that even the slightest jar against his hand could bring disaster.

He felt the tool complete the decaptitation, and blood trickled from Liddy's vagina.

'It's done!' he exclaimed, and Nairn issued more instructions.

The blood flow thickened as James withdrew the hook, laid it down and used his right hand to pull carefully on the arm of the foetus.

It came free in a rush of blood, and then he extracted the severed head.

'Squeeze the uterus and expel the placenta,' Nairn told him, and James used both hands to manipulate internally and externally until the placenta came free.

'Now we must pray that the uterus retracts well and there is no further haemorrhage,' Nairn murmured.

James rose from his knees, grimacing as his stiff muscles stretched.

Liddy was still motionless, her breath sawing through her gaping mouth, the whites of her eyes glistening through half-closed lids.

Towels and bowls of water had been placed in the corner of the room, together with a pile of fresh clean bedding.

When he was satisfied that there would be no further haemorrhaging, Nairn instructed, 'We'll lift her on to the floor while James changes the bedding. Then clean her before we allow anyone into the room. Harcourt has bad news enough to bear without letting his wife been seen like this.'

'This was wonderfully done, Septimus, and you, James,' Hugh Taylor congratulated admiringly. 'I don't believe that there's another two men in this country who could have performed it better.'

'There isn't,' Nairn said with a hint of smugness.

'What do you want me to do?' Taylor asked.

Nairn sighed regretfully as he looked down at the small head and torso.

'He would have been a fine boy. Sew the head back in position as best you can, Hugh. Then wash the poor little mite and wrap him up so that only his face is visible. Stitch the winding sheet securely. We shall tell Harcourt that he had been dead in the womb. He'll be able to bear that better than knowing a fool of a midwife didn't call us in time to save his son.'

When all the tasks had been completed, the three men stood for some moments staring at the still comatose Liddy lying in the freshly changed bed, her pallor grey against the white pillows.

James was silently praying that she would live. He felt utterly drained both mentally and physically, and very close to tears.

'Will she live, Uncle?' he asked quietly.

Nairn shrugged his broad shoulders. 'I've no idea, Nephew. But whatever happens we have the satisfaction of knowing that we've done our best endeavours to give her at least a chance of life. Now it is up to God.'

James could not resist patting his uncle's shoulder and telling him with fervent admiration, 'If she lives she owes her thanks to you, Uncle, not to God. For it's you that will have saved her life, not Him.'

'No, James, we saved her life. You and I together. You're no longer a surgeon's apprentice, my boy. You're a surgeon now.'

'And destined to become a great one, I'll take my oath on it.' Taylor added his plaudit and clapped James on the back. 'Well done, James. Well done indeed.'

But James could feel no glow of pride. He could only stare anxiously at Liddy and struggle to hold back his tears.

'I want you to stay here and watch over her, my boy. Keep a close watch for any haemorrhage,' Nairn instructed. 'Not that I fear there will be. But it's best to be sure. I shall now go and tell Edward Harcourt what has happened.'

When he returned to the bedroom half an hour later, Nairn was seething with anger.

'What's the matter, Uncle?' James questioned anxiously.

'That man disgusts me.' Nairn said between clenched teeth. 'He thinks only of himself. When I told him what had happened here, he could only speak of his own grievious hurt at losing his son.' Nairn came to stand looking down at Lydia. 'He showed not the slightest concern for this poor girl, and when I asked him if he would like to come and see her, he merely told me that it would serve no useful purpose. I confess, I was near to knocking him down at that point.'

James's own anger fired. 'I've a good mind to go downstairs and do exactly that.'

Nairn frowned. 'And how will that help this poor girl, Nephew? Your only duty is to bring her back to health. Not to give Edward Harcourt the thrashing he so richly deserves. So let me hear no more of such talk coming from you.'

He turned to Hugh Taylor, who had by now finished his sad task and had laid the dead baby in the cradle already prepared for its birth.

'Do you have any objection to myself and my nephew continuing to care for her?'

'Indeed not. I would welcome you doing so,' Taylor assured gratefully. 'This is a case that I fear has found me somewhat lacking, and the sooner I distance myself from it, the happier I shall be.'

Long hours passed during which James kept a constant vigil. He sat at the side of the bed, gazing at Liddy's pale face, mentally reliving the talk and laughter they had shared. He accepted the realisation that what he felt for her was love, and also sadly accepted that as another man's wife, she was lost to him.

At last she stirred and her eyes opened. He bent towards her, telling her softly, 'It's all right, Liddy. I'm here with you. Everything is going to be all right.'

She smiled and murmured his name, and he took her hand between his own, warming her chill fingers, as slowly she returned to full awareness.

'My baby?' She sensed that something bad had happened as she recognised the sadness in his eyes.

He could only shake his head, and she began to weep.

He moved beside her and, as if she were a small child, gently cradled her in his arms, murmuring soothingly to her.

At last her tears ceased to fall, and she nestled close to him, drawing comfort from his tender embrace.

'Stay near to me, Jamie. Please stay near to me,' she pleaded brokenly.

'I will,' he promised. 'I'll stay near for as long as you need me.'

214

Her bodily exhaustion overcame her and she drifted into sleep.

James remained cradling her in his arms, and tenderly kissed her forehead, whispering to her, 'No matter that you belong to Edward Harcourt, I'll always be near when you need me, sweetheart. Always . . .'